VAMPIRE'S PROMISE

Mafia Monsters Series Book Three

ATLAS ROSE

They promised to keep me alive.
They promised to keep me safe.
But what happens when death is payment for a debt I never knew?
Death or an eternity in servitude?
The Costello's are steeped in betrayal.
Lies and corruption taint my family's bloodline, owing debts to monsters more dangerous than the Vampires I love.
Now the Inner Circle has come to collect.
Only I won't go easy. To protect those I love I'll fight for them a thousand times over...*if need be I'll die as well.*
In a dark alley I face down my corrupt past. I have one small chance to keep us alive. As my thoughts turn to those I love; Elithen, Hurrow, Justice, Rule and my savage Unseelie bodyguard, Russell, I pray we make it...*hearts and lives intact.*

BE THE FIRST TO KNOW OF A NEW RELEASE!

Click here to signup for my newsletter.
Like my Facebook Page
Join my Facebook Group

Chapter One

ELITHIEN

"WHAT THE FUCK DID YOU JUST SAY?" JUSTICE GROWLED, and took a step closer.

But the piece of shit just smiled, his blue eyes sparkling even as he sat strapped to a chair in the middle of a warehouse with three Vampires and an Unseelie desperate for his blood in front of him.

"You heard me, *Vampire*," the mortal answered. "You think Caedes doesn't know about *everything*? How the fuck do you think I found the men to kill the Prince?"

The words were like a shotgun blast to my chest.

"Who the fuck do you think paid for me to leave the country?" *After I murdered her bodyguard and threw Ruth into the river to drown.*

Vicious was beside me in an instant, his silver eyes glinting with rage. He held a gun in his hand...muzzle pointed at the lawyer's chest, the grip toward me. But I didn't need a bullet. I didn't need steel. Fangs carved through the tender flesh inside my mouth as cold, steely rage washed through me.

"I'll fucking kill you…" the bodyguard growled. *"I'LL FUCKING KILL YOU!"*

Movement was a blur in the darkness. The hard *thump* of bodies colliding rang out as Justice stepped in front of the bodyguard. *Give the order…*the desperate howl raged in my head. *GIVE THE GODDAMN ORDER!*

None of them wanted his death more than I did.

None of them *craved* the taste of his blood like I did.

Alexander was more than corrupt.

More than a murderer.

He was a fucking nightmare…one she could *never* escape. Not while he still breathed.

"E?" my enforcer called my name…but I was already stepping backwards…already turning away from them. "E, what the fuck is he saying?"

Laughter echoed through the warehouse.

Laughter…and control.

The sickening sound rang out in the darkness.

*Ruth…*I turned at the last minute…the sound of my boots ringing in the darkened warehouse.

"The Inner Circle are coming!" Alexander howled with delight. *"THEY'RE COMING FOR YOU, VAMPIRE…AND I'M COMING FOR HER!"*

I fumbled for my phone in my pocket, my fingers trembling as I stabbed the button and listened to the phone ringing. Caedes was here...Caedes was here...and he was hunting the only one I've ever loved. In that second, I knew...it'd been their plan all along. Caedes wanted to take from me all over again.

RUTH! I raged inside my head. *RUN!*

Chapter Two

"This is becoming a regular thing, huh?" Heels clicked against the floor as I slowly made my way across the sitting room. We were alone...*again*. Only, tonight was different. Tonight, I wasn't overcome with exhaustion...tonight, I was high on power and purpose.

Tonight, I wanted more of what we'd had last time.

The memory of that rose to the surface of my mind. The stone countertop in the kitchen cold against my ass...the trail of his lips leaving fire on my skin...warm chocolate, spread thighs, and sharp fangs. Biting, sucking.

I lifted my gaze to my own reflection in the window catching red against the black of night. The panties and bra my favorites...too bad they weren't going to last long. My Vampires had a habit of tearing through my underwear with wicked fangs, desperate to get to...*me*. My hair was swept up and secured with a clip. I was more than ready for a replay. *Even the memory made me wet.*

But Rule didn't answer. He just stood at the window and stared out into the night...his thoughts a thousand miles away. The gleam of guns strapped across his chest glinted in the reflection.

He'd been like this for hours, pacing, staring, packed to the fangs with weapons. They all had. Elithien, Hurrow, Justice, and Russell. My Vampires and bodyguard had been tight, tense...*jumpy*. But this one...this one dressed in midnight blue was quiet and aloof...and nonresponsive to me.

"You don't like what I'm wearing?" I teased, reaching around and unclasping my bra. "I can always take it off."

One shrug, and the straps fell down my shoulders. The Vampire turned then...and for a second, I had his undivided attention. His dark eyes shone as they slipped to my bare breasts, and his fingers swept over my ribs, capturing the swells, the tips of my own fingers dancing across the peaks as I hardened.

"Fuck me," he whispered. "Ruth, what are you..."

"I'm a little cold here," I murmured, my other hand dipping to the barely there lace panties. "But not here."

RUTH, RUN!

My hand froze, fingers skirting the top of my panties, as Elithien's scream tore through my mind.

I stumbled backwards, and one heel slipped, my ankle buckling. Rule was there in an instant, gripping me by my arms before he pulled me into his chest. I lifted my gaze to his as panic found me, and his phone rang.

The screen glowed, shining through the pocket of his crisp white shirt. There was a flash of annoyance. He lifted a finger in a *wait one second* gesture.

"E?" He answered it in an instant, his dark eyes shifting from desire to rage in an instant. *"The fuck? Yeah...yeah, I'm on it... I'll wait for your call."*

He pressed the button, ending the call...those unmerciful eyes glinting with cold, hard rage. "We're leaving...*now.*"

I fought for balance as he pulled me upright, his long, powerful thighs driving us as I stumbled and ran, bare breasts jiggling. "I can't go out like this!"

He grabbed Justice's long black trench coat draped over the back of a dining room chair and pushed it toward me. "Put this on."

"What's going on?" I shoved my arms into the sleeves and pulled the coat tight around me.

I knew better than to fight, better than to not *move* when I was told to move. I knew better than to do a lot of things...one of the perks of being raised by the fucking Mafia.

But it wasn't my safety that drove me now—I glanced over my shoulder as Rule pushed me forward, one forceful hand on my shoulder—I was terrified for them. "Elithien." His name rang inside my soul.

"He's safe...but *we* need to get out of here."

We? My pulse thundered with the word as I fumbled with the lock on the back door.

"Here." Rule reached around me, yanked the bolt backwards with a *snap,* pressed the combination of the lock, and the door opened.

We were outside in a heartbeat, my heels sinking into the ground as I ran. I lifted one foot and yanked my heel free before taking another step and tearing the other off. But Rule was already pulling a gun from the holster strapped across his chest and scanning the darkness.

Stones were cold against my feet as I hurried, but pain was nothing. Not when my Vampire's desperation still rang inside my mind.

A car door opened and closed, and the roar of V8 power filled the air as the Audi Arrant pulled out of the long bay behind the house. He braked hard, reached across the seat, and shoved open the door. "Hurry, Ruth."

It was seconds...mere seconds from the scream in my head to me climbing into the car and yanking the door closed. We shot forward, stones flying up to pepper the undercarriage of the car. Headlights carved through the night as Rule tore the car around the house and out of the driveway.

We were headed toward the city before I knew it, gears working hard and throwing me back against the seat as we shot forward. I snapped my seatbelt across me and held on for dear life. There were no questions at times like these. No demands...no tears.

There was just...*survival.*

City lights sparkled in the distance as the engine of the Audi howled, tires skidding as we took a corner hard. I shifted my gaze, catching sight of the turn, my body preempting the battle.

The warehouse...that's where we were headed. But instead of the jerk of the wheel, Rule shifted up a gear and charged ahead.

"Rule," I cried as the sparkling black water rose in front of me.

The wheels hit hard on the entrance of the bridge, driving us upwards. Momentum took us airborne before we came back down with a *thud*. Panic filled my veins with ice as Rule gripped the wheel and glanced into the rear-view mirror.

The bridge was bad...all kinds of bad.

No way out...no way that didn't involve water.

Black, shimmering water. The moment that thought hit me, I was back there, sinking down into the darkness...that cold grasp of fate dragging me under. *No. Please, no.* My hand found the armrest, and my nails punctured the stitching as I closed my eyes.

"I won't ever let that happen," my Vampire growled beside me. "Not ever again, you hear me? Not. Ever. Again."

Desperation made me open my eyes. My fragile mortal soul hung in the balance. But he wouldn't let that happen...not now...not ever. Headlights shone through the windshield, blinding me as we tore across the bridge and exited onto the on-ramp for the freeway.

Rule handled the Audi like a NASCAR driver, shifting down, only to pump the brakes then punch us into oblivion. As the white lines blurred and we hurtled toward our destination, that cold, lethal part of me kicked in.

"Gun," I demanded.

Rule jerked his gaze to me, brow lines furrowed deep. "What did you say?"

"Give me a gun." My hand shook as it rose. "I won't let them hurt you."

The sneer was arrogant and proud as he reached up, tore the second Sig from its holster, and handed it to me. "That's my Mafia Princess."

Steel hit my palm, stilling the shaking in an instant. I curled my hand around the grip, forefinger pressed along the side. Someone was coming...someone they were afraid of—someone who wanted to hurt us. They'd come for my Vampires...then they'd have to go through me.

Rule downshifted, swerved around a minivan, and charged down the off-ramp to the outskirts of the city center. This wasn't a place for residential houses. This was a place filled with corporate buildings and government offices. We shot past the drab concrete FBI command center and kept going. Was that who we were hiding from? The goddamn FBI? Carina Chase filled my head. Fucking bitch had haunted me for far too long.

"Not the FBI." Rule glanced at me and kept driving, past the Homeland and Foreign Affairs, before turning into the dark city streets. Buildings hemmed us in from either side, but the streets were empty as Rule scanned the rear-view mirror and slowed the car. One smooth turn of the wheel and he nosed us into a driveway, then reached overhead, tugging down the visor for a second while he grabbed a card.

Green lights flashed on the sensor before the boom gate rose. I leaned forward, scanning the office building before we slowly drove in and down, driving around one level, then another. Overhead security lights did little to combat the darkness, leaving the headlights our only decent source of light...until he switched them off and kept going.

Darkness plunged into the car. I pressed the Sig against my thigh as weak pale light splashed against the dashboard and was gone. Rule turned the wheel with as much precision as he would during the day, going around and around. "Yay for enhanced eyesight."

"That's not all we use our strength for." He turned that ravenous gaze toward me as he drove past the weak overhead light and parked in the darkness. "*You* of all people should know that."

One brush of his finger against the tied trench coat, and the cool air slipped in. The Audi's throaty growl vibrated through the seat as he pushed the part wider.

"I thought someone was coming after us?"

"You think I can't watch our six and appreciate what a stunning fucking woman you are?"

I pressed the gun against the seat as the back of his finger moved over my nipple. He turned his head, staring out into the night, sliding his finger around and around, making my body clench and my breath catch before he turned back to me.

"You look so fucking fierce right now," he whispered, leaning toward me.

"Rule...what the hell are you—" I started as he stabbed my seatbelt release and parted the opening of Justice's coat.

"Did you think I didn't see you when I stared out the window? Female...I see you in my fucking sleep." He pushed against my thigh, parting my legs. "Now...where were we before this interruption?"

His finger slipped under the elastic of my panties and pushed inside.

"Oh, Jesus." My hand went to the armrest as I clawed for a hold of *anything*.

Only this time, for a *very different reason.*

He slid his finger upwards, curling to dance around my clit. I couldn't stop the heat, and parted my legs wider.

"Fuck me, you're wet." He slipped in once more, working my slit with slow, agonizing strokes until he was fucking me with his fingers.

"Turn to face me," he commanded, his dark eyes glinting, fueled by adrenaline and desire.

Unable to resist and desperate to connect, I lifted my knee and slid against the seat, driving his fingers deeper. A moan rumbled in the back of my throat as I shifted again, rocking my ass forward, thrusting as fear turned to desire...and hunger.

"If I wasn't watching every goddamn inch of this garage right now, I'd have your ass in the air and my mouth buried right here."

I gripped the seat and the armrest, bucking my hips as that heat rose inside me, desperate and urgent.

"That's it, come for me, Princess."

I clamped my eyes closed, lifting my hips to meet his fingers. "Fuck me."

"There's nothing I'd rather do," he growled, his fingers slipping from my pussy as I drove my hips into the air. "Jesus fucking Christ."

I needed more, needed it harder, thicker...

With a savage growl, he leaned across, grabbed my ass, pulled me toward him, and leaned down. The second his mouth met my slit, I cried out. One hand gripped my headrest, the other pressed against the roof. His tongue slipped inside me, the sensation devastating my control. I clenched my ass, bucking against his mouth as his fangs pressed against me...and tipped me over the edge.

I cried out as those warm waves surged through me. He took every shudder as he growled possessively and swallowed.

"You were saying?" he murmured, easing my hips back down. I slid against the seat, holding on with what little strength I had left.

"What the fuck was that?" I panted.

"Princess, you wear things like this." He dragged his finger along the underside of the elastic, brushing against my trembling core as he moved my panties back in place. "And I'm gonna make it my life's goddamn purpose to fuck you senseless every opportunity I get."

I sucked in hard breaths, waiting for my soul to find my body as the darkness lit up with the glow of his cell phone.

Rule answered it in a heartbeat. "We're safe. Eastside. Yeah, I can be there...yeah, here she is." He handed me the phone, concern flaring. "He wants to talk to you."

My hands shook as reality crashed back down. I grabbed the phone and pressed it to my ear. "You okay?"

"Yes, just wanted to hear your voice is all. You're safe with Rule. He's going to bring you to me, okay?"

"Okay, but Elithien?"

"Yes?"

"When I get there." I took a long breath and tried to steady my voice to sound normal. "I want a damn good explanation as to what the hell is going on."

"Stay with Rule. I'll see you soon."

The call ended without a good bye, or an *I love you.* That wasn't Elithien's style. He was the Alpha, always thinking... always in charge, driving our existence forward one savage step at a time.

"Seatbelt, Princess. Safety first," he murmured.

I fumbled with the damn thing, straightening the coat and clenching my thighs. My body was humming. Heat lingered between my thighs as Rule drove us back around the garage, climbing higher and higher, but instead of taking Madison Street, the way we'd come in, he headed for Sommerset Avenue.

I tried not to look at him as we drove under the overhead lights, tried not to find those perfect lips and remember that guttural growl, the sound of him swallowing my release.

It wasn't working.

I forced myself to turn and focus out the window as I grasped the gun beside me on the seat. He was in predator mode in an instant, scanning driveways and parked cars before he eased the Audi forward and hit the headlights.

We drove fast, stealing out of the wide-open streets to shoot down a back alley and come out somewhere near Hungerford. I had no idea where we were going, but after so many different alleys and streets, we slowed at a construction site and nosed in. Rule reached for the visor again, but this time, he didn't need it.

The massive steel gate across the front slowly slid back, leaving us to drive along the half-finished five-story building. "Is this it? This the place we're meeting them?"

He didn't have time to answer as the headlights splashed against Elithien and Justice's Explorers parked at the rear of the site.

They were here...

Now I wanted to know what the hell was going on...and I wasn't taking silence or lies for an answer...

Not anymore.

Chapter Three

The cold wind tore through me as I stepped out of the Audi. I grabbed the trench coat and clutched it closed. Gravel bit into my feet, making me stop long enough to put my heels back on. They weren't exactly work attire as I lifted my gaze to the plastic-wrapped building site. But damned if I was going to walk on a nail.

"You okay?" Rule murmured, holding out his hand for me.

I stepped around a puddle, took his hand, and followed. "I didn't realize you had holdings this side of the river."

"We have places everywhere...diversify is the motto."

"Right" I murmured, ducking a little as we stepped over the framework of a window and stepped inside. The place was a skeleton in the front. But the more we walked, the more structural it became.

Steel walls. Doors with locks—*how big was this place, anyway?* Brickwork towered on all sides as we stepped through a door and Rule locked it behind us.

I shivered with the cold, turning my focus to the light spilling from a doorway at the end of a long hall. Deep snarls and panicky male voices spilled out, growing quieter as I started walking. I left Rule behind, heels clacking loudly as I hurried toward them.

Something was happening, something terrifying. I needed to understand. The long leather ties of the coat slapped against my thighs as I clutched it around me and stepped into the doorway. Weak light shone from dangling construction lights fastened to the walls. The place was little more than a shell. A table sat in the corner, a sink on a steel frame, but it didn't matter how bare the room was...it was filled *with them.*

"Ruth," Elithien called my name and stepped away from them.

His dark eyes glinted silver as he reached out, cupped my face, and kissed me. Tension lingered in the air, the sensation so sharp it felt like the tip of a knife pressed to my skin. I reached up, sliding my hand along his cheek, then pulled away.

Fangs shone in the murky light as he stared into my eyes. "I love you," he murmured.

The words themselves weren't a surprise...but it was the way he looked at me...the way *they all looked at me* that made my panicked pulse boom in my ears. "You want to tell me what the hell is going on?" I scanned every gaze.

Hurrow swallowed hard and met my gaze. Justice was on edge, fists clenched at his sides...his pallor had a tinge of gray. But it was Russell my gaze stilled at. The guy was wired, with a wide, shell-shocked gaze, and hard, heavy breaths. He turned away when I sought his eyes. He couldn't even look at me.

Instead, he paced the hollowed-out shell of a room, wearing a path through concrete dust, throwing off the kind of vibes that'd make a fucking SWAT team nervous.

"It's nothing," Elithien lied. "Just issues with a disgruntled customer."

"You seem to forget who you're talking to here," I growled, meeting my Vampire's gaze. "I'm not someone you can placate with half-truths and watered-down explanations. This," I lifted my hand toward Hurrow, then Justice, then Russell as he stopped, facing away from me and staring at the wall like he wanted to do some renovating of his own. "Doesn't feel like a fucking misunderstanding. Now...how about we try this again. What the fuck is going on, Elithien?"

"Ruth," he started.

I clenched my jaw so hard it creaked. "Careful, Vampire." I forced the words, fear and anger sparking a fire inside me.

He froze, licked his lips, and couldn't seem to speak.

"Rule." I reached out my hand. "The keys, please."

But the Vampire at my side didn't move. He knew who gave the orders around here...and it wasn't me. I gave a slow nod, understanding now where I stood. On my own...just like I had been before. I turned away as agony tore through my chest.

"Don't leave," Elithien protested.

I stopped in the doorway, my voice stone cold. "Then give me a fucking reason to stay."

Silence. Empty, cutting silence.

I took a step as he spoke. "We found him."

Found him...found him...found him.

I spun so hard the room blurred. "You did what?"

Elithien didn't move, only held my gaze. "We found him, Ruth."

I was stepping back in to the room before I realized I'd moved. "You found...*him.*" I couldn't even say his fucking name.

Darkness rose inside me, the fetid taste of the cold river water filling my mouth. I shifted my gaze to Russell...pale as a fucking ghost. "Did you kill him?"

Yes. That's the word I waited for. I didn't even know how to feel about that.

"I want to," Elithien answered.

I flinched, drawing my focus back to him. "What?" *I heard wrong...*

He moved toward me, reaching out to grasp my hand. "There's nothing I want more than to end that piece of shit."

"I don't get it." I searched his gaze. Taking a life was wrong. Taking a life was *criminal.* But this...this was *personal.* Of all the men I trusted to protect me...to *avenge me*...I placed my trust most in this one.

"We can't," Russell answered. "We can't, okay."

"The fuck you can't," I forced through clenched teeth, and lifted the gun. "Where is he? I'll do the fucking job myself."

There was nothing in this world I wanted more. As Alexander's face filled my mind, I knew if I did this, my life as I knew it would be over. I'd become someone else...someone I wouldn't recognize.

I'd be more than a survivor...

I'd be a murderer, as well...

I lifted my gaze to Russell. I was okay with that.

"No." My bodyguard shook his head. "There's more at play here."

"Then, *feel free to explain it to me.*" I shot Elithien a glare.

"He's backed by some very powerful allies." My Vampire moved closer. "And before we make a move, we need to understand the players involved. I don't...*make this decision lightly.*" He lifted his hand, hooking strands of my hair behind my ear. "Believe me."

Pain and rage collided inside me. I hated in this moment, hated more than I'd ever hated in my life. More than I hated my cousins, who'd always made me feel like the outsider in my own family. Hated the fact I was forever alone. Alex took something from me, something I'd *never* get back. He tore it apart with his lies and his schemes...and shot it all to hell.

Now I had an opportunity. I had a way to make the demons go away. I lifted my gaze and held my Vampire's stare—I did believe him. *I just didn't care.*

"Take me," I demanded. "Take me to see him."

Elithien shook his head. "I can't...even if I wanted to. The sun will be up soon...and it's not safe to return home."

I glanced at the others. "Where are you going?"

"We have other places." My Vampire lifted his hand. "Will you come?"

"Of course I'll come with you." The words left me in a rush. My head was spinning, emotions colliding. I tried to gather the strands, weave them together...hold onto them tight, *along with the anger.*

"And Ruth." Elithien stepped closer, his gaze falling to the neckline of the coat. One slide of his hand, and he unraveled the leather tie, parting the coat. His hand moved to my hip, baring my breast.

"Jesus," Russell groaned, and looked away.

But it was my Vampire I focused on...my Vampire who, underneath all the hate and rage, fought his own fucking nature to keep me safe. My Vampire I yearned to feel. "Yes?" I answered.

"This can stay on," he finished. "For a little while at least."

There was a twitch at my lips. I was quickly understanding fear meant something different to these Immortals. Fear made them burn hotter...fear made them want me more.

Fear made my Vampires insatiable.

I took his hand and clutched the coat closed as I followed him back along the hall and out into the hollowed shell of the building once more. Lightning tore across the sky, heavy drops of rain splattered as we ran for the Explorer and climbed into the back seat. Hurrow was a heartbeat behind us, sliding behind the wheel as the deluge descended with a thunderous roar.

I sucked in hard breaths, brushing sodden strands of hair from my face as Elithien leaned over, grabbed my leg, and pulled it onto his lap. "You okay?" he enquired.

Hurrow pressed a button on the console and a blast of warm air hit me, dancing across my skin, tickling the wisps of my hair at my temples. We were moving almost before I knew it, slowly rolling out of the construction driveway under the cover of darkness.

"Yes," I answered as he ran his hand along my leg and slid my heel free.

"You scared me back there," he murmured with a bite of cold anger. "Don't ever do that again."

Silver glinted from his eyes as we passed under the streetlights. Anyone else might've been terrified by the tone...but I wasn't anyone else. I held his gaze as heated air warmed me and answered, "Then don't give me a reason."

His fingers grazed my shin, working their way downwards, rubbing my foot as Hurrow handled the car. There was a hunger between us. A cutting, cruel urgency. He was hurting tonight, raw and exposed, like a wounded animal backed into a corner, and even as the hairs on the back of my neck rose, I knew he'd never hurt me—not intentionally.

Still, we were beasts here. Beasts sitting in the back of a speeding car heading to God knows where, staring at each other from across the seat. I moved first, pushing upwards, spreading my knees as I straddled him.

His hands wound around me, drawing me against his hard body. My wet hair smacked his cheek as I kissed him, and that cruel hunger rose inside me. He'd found Alex, hunted him down like the piece of shit he was. Elithien wanted his death, *craved* his death. I could see the desperation in his eyes, hear it in his strained words, feel it in the tremor of his body.

He wanted blood...and he wanted it *for me*.

To protect me.

To *avenge me*.

This had nothing to do with saving face. Nothing to do with money or power, nothing to do with feeding one monster to kill another. Nothing to do with a deal, like it'd always been with my family. But it was *everything* to do with me.

I kissed him, holding his face in my hands, my lips taking his over and over, soft at first, testing him, *finding him*. The leather sash of my coat was gone, his hands roaming my bare skin.

This was primal. This was danger.

Like a spark igniting...in this moment we were alone. His hand dove between us, the back of his fingers stroking my slit as I unbuckled his belt and unzipped his pants. He was already hard for me, already desperate to be inside me.

"Don't tear them," I whispered, breathless and urgent. "Or I'm going to run out of underwear by the end of the week."

"Then I'll buy you more..." he promised, sliding my panties aside.

His hand cupped the back of my neck as he plunged inside me, hilt deep, driving his hips until I was stretched and trembling. Until I felt nothing but the girth of him...and the invasion. I threw my head back, crying out as he pressed against the small of my back, driving my hips down harder, until that brutal *thud* turned predatory.

Fuck me.

I stared into the eyes of a beast...one who was consumed with single-minded fury.

"E," Hurrow called from the driver's seat as the hairs rose on my arms.

My thighs stretched wider. I was lost in that attack, vulnerable and mortal, as Elithien's fangs grew longer and he stared at me with ravenous hunger.

"Do you want me to pull over?" Hurrow growled.

Fear tainted his words as that dark, *merciless* hunger consumed the space. He could feel his Alpha shifting, tilting past the point of pulling away. But I never hesitated, even as he slammed my hips on his, driving his cock savagely inside me. I stared into that abyss...and into the eyes of the monster he truly was—the monster he hid from me.

"I...see y-you," I whispered over the savage slams of our bodies. "I l-love you."

A snarl vibrated in the Alpha's chest. The warning sound like nothing I'd ever heard before, formidable, unforgiving. Violent, filled with danger. He shifted sideways, lowering me until my spine hit the leather seat.

"E?" Hurrow growled, louder.

"Just drive," the Alpha commanded, that unfathomable gaze boring into mine as the punishing thrusts eased. "I'd never hurt you," he growled, his tone as cold as stone. "But, female...I might just lose my fucking mind if you ever try to leave me again."

I lifted my hands and cupped his cheeks as those slow thrusts worked that fire inside me, stoking, claiming, making me come alive. This was no fragile love with Elithien, no ploy to claim a mortal's soul. If I was honest, all those things and more had filled my head at some point since we'd met.

But here and now...with his power driving into me, making me slide my hands from his face to grip his shoulders, yanking him harder against me as I shuddered, I saw his love—*and it was fucking blinding*.

The car swerved hard and slowed down. I'd forgotten where we were for a minute, lost in the shine of Elithien's eyes, and as the car stopped and Hurrow climbed out, I knew this wasn't done...*we weren't done—not even close*.

He didn't pull out. Instead, he pulled me from the back seat as Hurrow opened the door. My arms went around his neck, my legs wrapped around his waist. He kissed me, staring into my eyes as he walked. It didn't matter where we were. It didn't matter what we faced. I was safe with him.

Even in his darkest moments...I was always safe.

My heart thundered, my breath came hard and fast as the hiss of electric doors echoed and the sharp slap of his footsteps rang out. Then we were climbing, timber stairs edged with black steel, and overhead lights as we made our way through an expansive space to the end of a hall.

Buttons were pressed, the same locks as the house west of the river opened with a *click,* and we were inside, falling onto the bed as dimmed lights came on with the movement.

"I'm all wet," I protested as the black trench coat fanned out against the clean sheets.

He lifted me, worked the coat from my body, and slid from between my thighs. His hands went to the thin string at my hips, the fabric rolling as he peeled my panties free. "I can smell Rule all over you," he murmured, and shifted that brooding gaze to mine. "If anything happens to me..."

"No." I lifted my hand, my finger pressed to his lips.

He captured my hand and kissed my palm. "If anything happens to me, they will take care of you."

Tears shimmered in my eyes, like a dam burst inside me.

A car crash finally igniting.

He was the flames.

They were all the flames. Burning inside me like a damn inferno.

He stretched my arm over my head. I lifted the other in instinct, feeling his fingers grip my wrist. He was inside me with one hard thrust, slamming the bed against the wall, pinning me down. I'd never been so turned on...so agonizingly desperate for a man to consume me.

"You are *ours*," he declared, riding my body, making me whimper and groan. "Say it...*say who you belong to.*"

"You." My heart blazed as I whispered. "I belong to all of you."

With a guttural sound, he thrust upwards, driving to that moment of insanity, and as I toppled into his desire, I knew I'd belonged there all along.

I cried out, slamming my eyes closed, savoring that ignition as I quaked and clenched. Elithien lowered his head, driving his cock inside me over and over until with a growl he stilled, spine arched, hands driving my wrists against the mattress, and released.

Hard breaths punctured the space. His grip eased as he rolled, hands sliding down around my waist to drag me with him. In that space, I lingered. In that space, *I breathed.*

"It'll be daylight soon," he warned, eyes closed, lips parted. "Don't go anywhere without the bodyguard, and whatever you do...don't go home."

I turned my head, brow furrowing. "Which home? What the hell am I supposed to wear all day?"

But there was no answer, just emptiness as my Vampire exhaled and his body stilled.

"Great," I grumbled, and rolled onto my back to stare at the unfamiliar ceiling. "Just fucking great."

Chapter Four

I ROLLED OUT OF BED, STRETCHED, AND SEARCHED THE floor for the rolled-up, ruined panties before I finally gave up. "Another pair gone," I muttered, and lifted my gaze, finding the door to a bathroom, and a closet next to it.

Cold still lingered, dancing deep in my bones, making me shiver as I went to the bathroom and flipped the light switch. Lights flickered, dancing before they came on. "Holy shit, this place is massive."

White, gray, and black filled my view. Cold tiles, crystal-clear glass, double side-by-side shower heads. Definitely masculine. Definitely sexual. Had I just stumbled upon my Vampire's bachelor pad?

Don't tell me, this was where they brought all the pretty, mortal women for a good time.

The memory of that first time in their mansion came back to me. That soft woman's sigh ringing out as they took turns between her legs and at her neck. The flare of jealousy was so savage it burned the cold right out of me. I turned my head to where Elithien lay, the white Egyptian cotton sheet half draped across him.

I could almost picture him here. That cold, predatory silence making him even more attractive. They all wanted the hunter. All wanted to be fucked by the apex predator, and there was no more apex than him, than my monster...my mafia monster. "Except maybe for me."

The whisper rang out as I crossed to the closet and turned on the light. The soft white glow warmed quickly, brightening as it went. The place was sparse, a few suits, shirts, three pairs of slacks, socks, shoes, and boxers.

"Figures," I muttered, and turned, my breath catching. My thoughts stilled.

There was something else there. A section of the closet which had been empty...but it wasn't empty now.

A pair of panties hung perfectly on a hanger. Midnight black, the fabric so sheer they were barely there. My heart thundered as I stepped closer. *A remnant from a love affair?* My stomach clenched tight, that fire burning inside as I caught the note hanging from the steel hanger, and twisted the corner to read what it said.

Don't plan for these to stay on for long either, Ruth.

E.

A smile crept onto my lips. I lifted the hanger free and turned toward him. The bastard. The cheeky bastard. There were no other clothes...not for me. I reached up, snatched a crisp white shirt from his side of the closet, and headed for the bathroom again.

It might've once been a bachelor's pad. Its purpose made solely for catch and release. But that was before...before me. I placed the clothes down on the counter and made my way to the shower. The spray was hard and hot. The needle-fine spray stung as I closed my eyes and stepped under the heat. But soon the burn melted away. I tilted my head, letting the water cascade through my hair, then grabbed the bodywash and started to clean.

My thoughts returned to that hollowed-out room, the exposed bricks, basically an empty shell. But it was that look in Elithien's eyes, that truly terrified stare that gripped me. Terror like I'd never seen before...terror...*not rage.*

My hand slowed and slid down my arm, leaving a smear of bodywash in its wake. Elithien was a Vampire...an Alpha in his own right. He wasn't scared of Alex. He wanted him dead as much as anyone. So why had he reacted the way he had? Why did that shimmering steel in his gaze feel too much like a blade against my neck...*unless there was something he wasn't telling me?*

Some secret.

Some part of this he didn't want me to know.

I glanced at the open bedroom door. Something that had made him react the way he had. Something...that made him think he wasn't going to survive this. *If anything happens to me, they will take care of you.*

The words chilled me to the bone. I focused on that doorway and the still body of the Vampire I loved and murmured, "What the fuck is going on here?"

My heart thundered...my pulse raced. I stood underneath the steaming spray of the water and yet, I couldn't feel a thing... only terror...*only fear*. I reached up, pressed my fingers against my chest, and with a shiver, hit the handle, turning off the spray.

I stepped out, made my way to the counter, and grabbed a towel from the rack. My hands slid down my hair, then over my body. But I didn't feel the soft skin, *or feel anything at all*. There was a disconnect growing inside me, a lost, uncontrollable feeling of fear.

One I knew only too well.

My thoughts turned to the red rope in my home, my real home. The home where I'd found myself once again and in that moment, I wanted to feel that once more. To feel the hard slap of the leather against my skin. *To feel him*...inside me. That look of hunger came back to me from last night in the back of the Explorer.

I'd never seen Elithien so fragile before, so *unlike him*. I flipped my hair over, wrapped the towel around my head, then stepped into the panties and pulled on the shirt. It smelled faintly of him, that dark spice he threw off...the one I couldn't seem to get out of my head.

My belly rumbled, gnawing and gurgling. Somehow in the panic of the night, I'd forgotten to eat...and now...now it was— *hell, I didn't know what day it was, let alone what time.*

I worked the buttons of the shirt, leaving the top two open, and stepped up to the keypad on the door. Jesus, don't tell me I was fucking stuck in here all damn day. My heart skipped as I punched in the combination I used at the house. Red light blinked green and the locks disengaged, opening the door wide enough for me to step into darkness.

The moment I stepped out, the door closed behind me again. I blinked into the dim light before the sound of movement came from somewhere deeper in the house, and an overhead light came on.

I was drawn to that sound...knowing exactly who it was. Bare feet slapped against the polished concrete floor as I made my way along the hallway and through the dark expanse toward the overhead light in the kitchen.

"You hungry?" Movement came from the shadows as Russell stepped forward. "You're probably hungry...after all the..." he stilled, brows furrowing as he searched for the right word. *"Exhaustion."*

The way he said it made me uncomfortable. Still, he worked without looking at me, opening the stainless steel door of a refrigerator that seemed to blend in with the walls.

This place was empty. Cold, lifeless walls and sparse furnishings, a thick faux-sable throw tossed over the end of the black leather sofa, like a half-hearted attempt at a little warmth for the place.

I guess when they were the undead, they'd care little for comfort. One glance around this steel coffin and it showed.

"Looks like there's bread, cheese, butter, and tomato," Russell announced, staring into the belly of the refrigerator. "How about a grilled cheese sandwich? That's pretty well at the top of my culinary skills."

"That sounds perfect, actually," I answered, and slid onto one of the bar stools to watch him work.

"Coffee? There's no milk." He pulled out three tomatoes and a hunk of cheese, balancing the butter on top as he curled his finger around the tail end of the bread and yanked it free.

"I'll take it any way I can get it. Do you want some help?"

"No..." he snapped, then winced and softened his tone. "Thank you."

He piled the ingredients onto the counter in front of me, took a deep breath, and turned to the coffee machine, pressed a button, then stabbed it, all the while muttering under his breath before his shoulders sank and he finally gave in. "Actually, I could use a hand with the coffee...if you don't mind."

"Of course." I slipped off the stool and rounded the end of the counter before doing my best with the sleek contraption. The truth was, I could barely manage my own machine...let alone anyone else's.

But somehow, I pressed the right buttons and was greeted with a whir and a gurgle. I searched the cupboards, bumping into my bodyguard as I moved.

He jumped out of the way as though I'd scalded him, cutting me a glare that softened. I pulled open a cabinet, found four coffee cups, and grabbed two for us to use, placing one under the spout of the machine before I finally turned to face him. "Okay, enough. Talk to me. Tell me what's eating you."

"Nothing," he forced the word, his laser-focused fucking gaze fixed on the slice of bread as he ran the butter all the way to the edges with military precision.

"I call bullshit." I crossed my arms. "Either I did something last night that pissed you off, or there's something else going on here. Either way, I don't deserve the cold shoulder or the snarly gazes. We're all adults here, you have a problem, then I want to know about it."

"Why?" He turned, his dark eyes glinting with cruelty...*or was it pain?* "So you can go running to your Vampire? You seem to do that a lot...spend all night with them too, as far as I can see."

I flinched at the words and searched his eyes. Hard eyes. *Cruel eyes...*

If anything happens to me, they will take care of you.

Those words echoed in my head and stabbed through my chest. All I could see was Russell's anger...and all I felt was pain. This wasn't meant to happen...none of it was. Not the Vampire, not Alex...not falling in love with five fucking Immortals who battled each other for a piece of me.

My throat tightened, that hard lump aching. Tears threatened, but I clenched my jaw instead, swallowing that cutting agony and turned it into rage. "Fuck you."

I took a step closer, leaving that hissing machine behind. "Fuck you with your judging stare and your jealous tone. You think I planned for any of this to happen? You think I *want* to hurt you?"

"No," he murmured. "But you seem to be doing a damn fine job of it."

I crossed the space between us faster than I could track. My hand was rising, as though someone else had control of me in that moment, someone made of fire and born from pain, someone who lashed out, striking him across the cheek with a sharp *slap.*

He barely flinched. Just stood there, eyes shining, lips pursed, barely a strand of sandy blond hair out of place. His cheek was reddening as he slowly placed the butter knife on the counter and lifted his gaze to mine.

One hard breath and he grabbed me. Hands on my shoulders driving me backwards until I hit the wall with a thud. Pain slammed into the back of my head. But I didn't whimper...I didn't moan. I just held his stare as those blue eyes darkened and slowly turned black.

Rage and desire flared in his eyes as he leaned close. "I'm riding the edge here, Ruth," he growled, pressing his body against mine, and lowered his face to the side of my neck. "Trying to stay controlled. Trying to respect the boundaries. So don't...*push me. You may not like what you find.*"

He turned his head and inhaled, drawing my scent in deep before he straightened, dropped his hands, and slowly stepped away. He didn't look at me once as he returned to the counter and the slow, methodical buttering of the bread.

But he was wired, with jumpy muscles and a deadpan stare. And there was a hunger in the air, a chill I hadn't felt before. One that pressed against me, savage and dangerous. I couldn't move, not even when he layered slices of tomato on top of the perfectly sliced cheese. He wasn't here...not really. He looked like Russell, moved like Russell...but the man underneath the skin was changed...*and he scared me.*

He carried the buttered sandwiches over to the pan heating on the stove, picked one up and placed it in the center. I watched as he pressed it firmly with a spatula, then lifted the edges, making sure it was browned all over before he flipped it. When it was perfect, he slid the sandwich onto a plate, and neatly cut through the middle.

Only then did he meet my gaze. Only then did he walk toward me. Still, I was riveted by those unfathomable midnight eyes. "I'd never hurt you," he murmured. "But seeing you...with them, it's tearing me apart."

"Russell—" I started.

But he shook his head and handed me the perfectly toasted sandwich with a sad smile. "They're better when they're hot," he reminded me, trying to be the person I knew, trying to maintain his own sense of self. He was trying to be a man...*and not a monster.*

So I did the only thing I could do. I picked up the sandwich he'd made for me and I ate...

We spent the day dancing around each other, with careful glances each other's way and soft sounds, loud enough to comfort each other with our presence, but not directly—*never* directly. I couldn't meet his gaze again, not without seeing that hunger...and hearing the strained desperation in his voice. *I'd never hurt you. But seeing you...with them, it's tearing me apart.*

We were changing. Right before my eyes.

Pulling...pushing. Taking a knife to my heart.

I wanted to touch him, to kiss him. I wanted to tell him that it'd be okay, that *we'd* be okay.

But I did none of those things. Instead, I slowly made my way through the empty rooms, finding a worn book of Lord Byron poems. So I stretched out on the sofa, dragged that faux-sable throw across me, and opened a page to his words...

When we two parted

In silence and tears,

Half broken-hearted

To sever for years,

Pale grew thy cheek and cold,

Colder thy kiss;

Truly that hour foretold

Sorrow to this ...

Tears came then, slow, silent, slipping down my cheek as I turned my head and stared at the wall before I closed my eyes. Pain clutched me close, dragging me into the darkness with a hand clasped across my mouth. And in that quiet, sleep came. Cruel sleep. A battleground of darkness. I tossed and turned, until a brush came at my cheek.

The touch so gentle it was a whisper.

I rose to the surface as the sofa sank and groaned with a weight.

...that weight gave me comfort. That weight gave me ease. I sank swiftly, tumbling and falling.

"Sleep, Ruth. I'm right here."

Chapter Five

I woke with the whirr of electric shutters, then blinked and scowled as the steel slats on the windows opened and displayed the nighttime city landscape...*on the wrong side of the river.*

A deep breath and the smell of freshly brewed coffee, and it all came back in a rush.

The car...the panic. Rule, Elithien...*and Russell.*

I lifted my head from a pillow neatly tucked underneath me to find my bodyguard moving around in the kitchen. *Oh...that's right. We weren't talking. We were pretending that everything was okay and we were safe together, when the truth was that being together was killing us.*

I slipped my feet from the sofa as footsteps headed my way drew my gaze. He walked toward me with two steaming cups in his hands and that hardness in his gaze. But at least he wasn't pushing me against the wall and unleashing the rage and the desperation in his eyes.

"Still no milk, sorry," he muttered.

I reached up and took the cup. "Thank you. Did you sleep?"

"Some." He glanced out the window at the city lights.

He'd been beside me as I fell asleep. I was sure of that. The brush of his fingers...and the comforting deep sound of his voice were fragile in my mind, slipping away like sand through my fingers, making me wonder if I'd dreamed it all.

Doors opened, and steps echoed through the house. Justice came out first, fresh from the shower, hair still slick and wet, cutting a glare toward us before he opened the refrigerator and grabbed a bottle of water.

I sipped the coffee and rose as Elithien opened his bedroom door and walked out, buttoning his shirt, looking devastatingly handsome. Which made me become achingly aware of what little I wore. I needed clothes...my own, preferably.

But we had other matters to discuss...matters more important than my wardrobe—or lack thereof. Hurrow and Rule stepped out of their bedrooms.

"Elithien," I called his name.

He stilled and lifted his gaze, glancing at the coffee in my hands and Russell staring out the window.

"I haven't forgotten." His brow furrowed as though he could feel the tension in the room between us. "I'll hold up my end of the agreement."

"I need to stop by my house."

There was a shake of his head. "Absolutely not."

"I need clothes, Elithien. I need...*things.*"

"Rule will go." He glanced toward the Vampire and motioned him forward.

"No," I growled, taking a stance. "I want to go."

His dark eyes glinted, and his perfect lips parted. I waited for more lies, lies that told me how little they trusted me.

"Is there a reason you don't want me out there?" I took a step toward him. "Is there something you're not telling me here?"

"No," he forced, and held my gaze. "Of course not."

"Then it shouldn't be a problem, *should it?*" I pushed, and took a sip of my coffee.

One steely look from Elithien, and Rule was heading toward me. "Looks like it's you and me, Princess."

"We'll meet you there," Elithien growled. "Russell—"

But my bodyguard was already moving, reaching out to take my cup and heading for the kitchen. There was that look from my Alpha again, concerned...*cautious*, as he followed the sullen male with the steely eyes that missed nothing.

"Let's go," Rule said, grabbing my hand and yanking me closer. "We can stop at a drive-through on the way. This place never has enough to eat."

I didn't particularly like it here. Not the coldness, or the emptiness, or even us when we were in here, reminding me a little too much of their life before me...and their life after.

"Ready?" Rule captured my chin and tilted my head back.

My pulse sped as I looked into the Vampire's stare. The tiny curl of his lips and that savagely erotic gaze settled on me until the rush of water from the kitchen ended and the cups hit the sink with a *bang,* loud enough to draw every gaze in the room. Elithien jerked his gaze to the bodyguard, then shifted that critical stare to me.

"I'm so fucking ready," I murmured, and stepped out of Rule's arms, heat rushing to my cheeks.

Five males, and each of them looked at me like they were drowning...and I was their only hope. Their need was choking, and I couldn't take it...not a second longer. I left them all standing there and headed for the front door. But one shove of the handle and it only gave a *clunk.*

"Let me out." I slammed the handle once more as panic rose like a rag down my throat. *"I said, let me out."*

"Easy, princess." Rule reached around me and flicked the lock.

I shoved the door wide and stumbled out into the cold sting of the night. The Vampire was behind me, striding down the stairs as I hugged the thin cotton shirt close and hurried to the midnight blue Audi.

Doors closed with a *thud,* and we were inside with the new-car smell and the faint memory of sex.

"Okay," he murmured, not yet starting the car and glancing my way. "You wanna tell me what's going on with you?"

I stared straight ahead as the Explorer started with a growl behind us. Headlights flooded our interior for an instant. I could feel him back there, watching us with that infernal Unseelie gaze.

"Nothing." I denied, turning my head to look out the window.

But Rule wasn't having it, thrusting out his hand to grasp the back of my neck, gently forcing my gaze to his once more. "Let's try that again, shall we?"

There was something about Rule, something that crumbled my control, brick by brick. "I don't know how to do this. I don't know how to love without breaking hearts."

There was a tiny flinch behind his eyes as he searched mine. "I take it this isn't about the coven?"

I didn't answer. I didn't need to.

"Did he hurt you?" That cold edge of rage seeped into his words.

"No...*God, no.* He wouldn't do that. This is about *me* hurting *him.*" I clenched my jaw and looked away.

"The male is in love with you." Rule's hand slipped from the back of my neck as he eased back against the seat. "That's easy to see."

"And I think I'm falling for him." The words were quiet. "I think I'm falling for all of you, and how fucking ridiculous is that? I couldn't satisfy one man, let alone five of you."

"You couldn't satisfy *him?*" the Vampire questioned, and that old hurt came flooding back.

The pain. The loneliness...the degradation of what he'd done. "No, I couldn't...not enough to stop him from fucking other women behind my back, at least."

"Sonofabitch."

I cringed.

"You aren't the one who wasn't enough, Ruth. Not then, and not now." He turned toward me. "I need you to hear me on this. *You* are fucking incredible. *Too fucking incredible.* If there's any fault here, it's not with you. It's *never* with you." He lifted his gaze to the rear-view mirror and the blinding lights bouncing back. "That male has a lot going on, and you are only one part of it, just remember that, okay?"

"Give him a little slack," I muttered.

"More importantly, give *yourself* a little slack. We're all stumbling around in the dark here, trying not to step on each other's toes."

If that wasn't the most accurate image of what my world had become, I didn't know what was. Darkness. Hunger. *Need.* Rule leaned forward and stabbed the button on the Audi, and the engine came to life with a purr.

He pulled out of the underground parking garage, driving slowly along the narrow drive, then signaled and pulled out onto the city street. I pushed back against my seat and shifted closer, until we were skin against skin. "We're going to need to stay at that place, aren't we?"

He glanced my way, then back to the road. "Not necessarily."

The way he said it made me inquisitive. I pushed up. "Exactly how many places do you have?"

He just gave a shrug and didn't answer, evading me...*like the filthy rich usually do.*

How much money do you need, Ruth? A thousand...five thousand...five million...fifty million...it's yours.

I'd thought Elithien was joking. Apparently not.

We turned into familiar streets. I looked back, catching the headlights of the Explorer behind us. My house was in darkness, alone, *empty*. We pulled up against the curb outside and waited for Russell to nose the Explorer into the drive.

He was out of the four-wheel drive in an instant, scanning the grounds before he went to the door. He moved like a soldier, gun drawn, held at his side. Gone was the fresh-faced man I knew. This new version was harder, colder...and downright savage.

He stepped up to the door and was inside in an instant. Lights flicked on, his shadow visible across the front windows before he disappeared and returned barely a minute later, stepping out to wave us inside.

"Wait," Rule ordered, climbing out his door and rounding the front of the car in a heartbeat. "Stay close," he said, scanning the night as he opened the door and held out his hand.

I took it, heart hammering, and climbed out, my bare feet hardly meeting the asphalt before I was lifted and carried toward the open front door as he climbed the stairs.

The door closed behind me, and we were alone. It wasn't my home, not anymore. It had no warmth, no feeling. Not that it ever really had. Betrayal tainted the air.

"We don't have much time," Rule urged, making me flinch.

"Of course," I answered, heading up the stairs to my bedroom. Still, I couldn't help but glance over my shoulder at the closed door of my office.

No doubt my uncle had gone through all my plans and documents...my damn life's work to change Costello Corporation to a new direction. My heart pounded as my thoughts sharpened. I hurried into the bedroom and hit the lights, yanking the shirt over my head and pulled open my dresser drawers. Some of my things were already at our home across the river, but there was enough here to last me for a few days at least, until I could get more. I grabbed a black bra, one that matched the sheer panties Elithien had selected, and slipped it on. I gathered what I could, dumping my underwear onto the bed before I hurried to the closet. Jeans, a t-shirt, and a hoodie later, and I hurried to grab an old duffel bag, packing in as many clothes as I could.

I took all my comfort clothes, leaving the designer labels behind, yanked on socks and laced up boots before I hurried to my bathroom. Essentials and a quick brush of my teeth, then I was heaving the bag over my shoulder and out the door.

I rushed to my office, hit the lights, and scanned the bare walls. They'd taken everything...all my plans, names and details of my contacts. The sight was a punch to my gut, freezing me motionless for a heartbeat.

"Ruth," Rule called from downstairs.

"*Coming,*" I responded, and forced myself to move.

I didn't have time for heartbreak...not tonight, and as I rounded my desk and crouched in front of my safe, my thoughts turned to Alex.

My fingers trembled as I punched in the combination and yanked open the door. One scan and I breathed a sigh of relief. Everything was there. The money, my passports—my gun. I shoved the Sig in the waistband of my jeans and tugged the oversized hoodie over it before I stashed the money and documents away in my bag and rose.

But as I rose, something glinted at the corner of my desk, drawing my gaze. Gold gleamed, half hidden under a stack of papers. I pushed the corner of the pages aside, and froze.

"No," I whispered, feeling the warmth rush from me. My hands trembled as I looked at the thick, ornate, gold ring with a blood red ruby shining under the office lights.

I closed my eyes and breathed deep, trying to steady the racing of my heart as I opened them again. But the heavy, very expensive man's ring was still there, glinting and glaring, urging me to pick it up, to feel its weight, then maybe I'd know it was real.

The ring that belonged to my father...*the same one I'd buried him with.* I jerked my gaze to the room as a chill swept through the open door. The light overhead didn't seem as bright anymore. It didn't pulse and glow, not as clearly as it had seconds before, leaving shadows to hug the corners of the room...*and me.*

The thud of footsteps below made my pulse stutter. I reached out, fingers trailing the thick ornate design on the band, then the smooth face of the five-carat ruby on the top. My heart was in the driver's seat, making me reach out, grab the ring, and slide it into my pocket. I couldn't leave it behind, not something so precious.

And as I rounded my desk dark, seething anger rose. What possible reason could my uncle have had for taking it from my father's, cold, dead hand? *None...he had no fucking reason at all!*

I was done here...done in every sense of the word. Only memories lingered in this place, and most of them weren't worth remembering. I threw my duffel bag over my shoulder, gave one last look behind me, and charged down the stairs. "Ready."

Rule turned and lifted his gaze, the corners of his lips curling. But it was Russell I looked to. Russell that met my gaze with a hard stare of his own. "Now we've finished primping we can finally get down to business."

Primping? When the fuck was packing my clothes *primping?* I stepped forward, turning to give him a cutting stare, and growled. "You know, you can be a real prick sometimes."

He gave a cruel sneer. One that both hurt and pissed me off. Furious, I walked past him and out the door even as he barked, *"For fuck's sake, I go first!"*

"You know...go fuck yourself," I snarled, knowing damn well he heard me as I stormed to the Audi.

"You sure told him," Rule snickered, following me to the rear of the car and opening the trunk.

I jerked my gaze to his, rage burning through. "I do *not* need your grief as well right now."

He lifted his hands in surrender as the trunk lid rose and I stowed my bag away. Steel bit into the small of my back as I moved, the pain strangely comforting as I shoved the lid down and went to the passenger door.

The Explorer was already backing out as I slid into the passenger's seat. Rule climbed in, pulled the door closed behind him, and started the engine. We drove in silence, making our way back to the freeway and over the bridge once more.

The more we drove, the angrier I became. I'd been assaulted, thrown into the water, and almost drowned. I'd had people...*good people* murdered in front of me by the one man I'd thought I could trust. *No.* The one man I'd been *conditioned* to trust.

Conditioned by all the other men around me...my entire fucking life. *Don't ask questions, don't stand out. Don't take control. Don't be too strong...certainly not stronger than the men around you.*

I jerked my gaze to that shimmering midnight vein that cut through my city. I'd been a woman living in a male world. A world that just wasn't meant for me, and now I was hunted once more, driven from the only place that felt even remotely like home, to what?

To run?

I shook my head and ground my teeth. "I don't think so."

"What don't you think?" Rule asked. Damn Vampires, they heard everything.

"Nothing. *Not a thing,*" I answered, and stared at the water as we passed.

He turned after the bridge, just like I knew he would. I shifted in my seat as we passed the Wolve's clubs, and that racing feeling came flooding back.

"You're okay. No one's going to let anything happen to you." Rule glanced my way as that warehouse loomed on the horizon.

"There...you're keeping him there?" I whispered.

"Breathe, Ruth. Just breathe."

The other Explorer was already waiting for us. Dark shadows moved around the front of the four-wheel drive before Justice stepped out into the light. He'd been waiting for us. He lifted his head, gave a wave to the camera at the corner of the building, and the gate to the compound slowly opened.

"You sure you want to do this?" Rule followed Russell, nosing the Audi up to the building. "No one will think any less of you if you don't want to go through with this."

I pressed my spine into the seat as the terror moved in. "I'm doing this once and for all."

But my answer wasn't to his question. My answer was to myself.

I opened the door and climbed out into the night. All eyes were on me, waiting for me to crumple and fall. I closed my door, the feel of my fingers against the car numb and strange.

"Ruth, you okay?" Elithien asked as he stepped toward me. I hadn't seen where he came from.

I nodded, unable to trust myself to speak, and met that steel glint in his eyes as my lovers swarmed around me.

"He's ready." A growl came from the doorway as I rounded the corner of the warehouse and stepped toward the side door.

He was a massive male. Powerful. An animalistic gaze that settled on me as I passed. But he was different than the Vampires, making me want to scurry backwards and run like hell, until it hit me. "I know you."

He started to shake his head as the memory came back to me. "You were there," I explained. "That night at the Jewel. I sat at your table."

"The redhead with fire in her eyes." His gaze narrowed. "Now I remember."

A snarl ripped through the air behind me. A warning. One that made the towering male chuckle. "Easy, Vampire. I'm not making a move."

"Just remember that, *Wolf*," Justice warned as he grasped my arm and steered me inside.

The thud of my boots echoed in the huge, nearly empty space. I hadn't seen the inside...not where they'd kept Russell...or those they called *the Fae*.

A spotlight shone in the middle of the space. But I hardly saw the glare, *all I saw was him.*

I knew it was him, knew even with the hood over his head... knew even as he sat on the chair, his hands handcuffed behind him. *I knew...even wearing the khaki trousers he once hated... and the light checkered shirt he wore to golf on Sundays.*

I knew when he breathed.

When he turned his head at the sound of my steps.

And when he stilled, knowing it was me.

My boots caught, throwing me forward. Someone caught me. A strong arm wrapped around my waist, pulling me close to him as I stopped in front of the man I'd once loved and tried to remember how to breathe.

"Ruth?" the husky croak came from under the hood. *"Is that you?"*

Breaths hard and sharp, sawing in my chest.

Pulse racing...*thudthudthudthud. Like thunder.*

"I know it's you," that gravelly voice insisted. "I'd know your scent anywhere."

"Shut the fuck up," Justice snapped in front of me. "You don't get to speak."

But the *murderer* under the hood stilled... then slowly chuckled.

That sickening sound rumbled through the space, burrowing into my mind.

I was going to take you with me, the words echoed from the pit of darkness. *But when I saw what they did to you, I knew that was no longer part of my plan.*

He'd tried to kill me...*would've killed me*...if it hadn't been for *them.* I lifted my gaze, finding Elithien. "Take it off...I want him to see me."

He didn't move, just stood there, that silver shine fixed on me until he gave the command. "Do it."

Justice moved, stepping in front of me...protecting me from the *murderer's* view.

Darkness crawled around us. Shadows that moved. Shadows that breathed as my bodyguard flanked my side. My fingers danced, trembling against my thigh as Justice dragged the cloth from his head.

"Move, Vampire. Let me see the whore."

My protector moved fast, his fist flying through the air before a sickening *crunch.* The chair rocked to the side, two legs lifted and hovered for a second before they crashed back down. There was a moan, low and pathetic, as Justice leaned his massive frame forward and growled, "Talk about her like that again and I'll tear out your fucking throat."

It wasn't a threat. *It was a promise.*

I'd seen Justice in action, seen him shatter a man's fist into a hundred pieces. Seen him snap a light pole in two...all to get to the one man who sat before us now. The man who'd tried his best to kill me.

"Justice," I murmured.

My protector became aware of me again and slowly stepped to the side, leaving me to stare at this *stranger.*

His swollen eye was almost closed. A bruise on his cheek was angry and purple, distorting the whole side of his face. He blinked and lifted his gaze, trying to smile, but winced instead as his busted bottom lip split wider and oozed.

His tongue snaked out, swiping the fluid that leaked from the split.

"What happened to you?" I enquired.

The question had nothing to do with his injuries

"Your fucking *Vampire...*" he started.

"No," I gently cut him off. "*What...happened to you?*"

He flinched at the question, shallow breaths consuming him, like he fought his own beast for space inside his body. He had no answer. None he wanted to acknowledge, at least.

Call it whatever you want; greed, power, *control.* A corruption of the soul.

He tried to sneer, tried to laugh. Tried to murmur things that'd hurt me. They might've...*once.*

But I was beyond listening. Beyond feeling anything other than the desperation to end it all. To put to rest the monster in my nightmares...*and avenge the man I cared for.*

"Goodbye, Alex," I murmured, and lifted my hand to the small of my back.

The steel was in my hand in an instant. There wasn't a shake as I lifted the muzzle. I was so far removed from my existence, nothing could touch me now, and as I curled my finger around the trigger, I knew it was over...*finally.*

And in the space between one breath and the next...*I pulled the trigger.*

Chapter Six

"NO!" ELITHIEN ROARED. HE MOVED FAST, LUNGING through the air.

The chair scraped.

The bullet clipped Alex's ear as he ducked to the side and howled.

I was stunned for a second. My heart smashed against my ribs as the sharp, putrid stench of burning flesh wafted through the warehouse and filled my nose.

My throat tightened, and my stomach followed, punching acid into the back of my throat, making me stumble forward, the gun still in my hand. Screams erupted, terrified piercing screams that made no sense.

"You can't fucking kill me!" Alex roared as bright red blood slipped from the edge of his ear. *"You kill me, and you're all fucking dead. DEAD, YOU HEAR ME?"*

"What the *fuck, Ruth!*" Elithien barked, and turned that blistering stare to my companions. "She had a fucking gun? You *didn't think to tell me?*"

Rule and Russell just stood there, lips parted, dumbfounded expressions on their faces.

"I didn't know," Rule finally answered, and turned those dark, glinting eyes to me. "I had no idea."

"Well...*then have a fucking idea next time!*" Elithien roared. The sound of his fury raged inside my head, making me wince as I swallowed the bitter tang.

Alexander just sat there, hazel eyes glinting with adrenaline and fear. "You can't fucking kill me, you stupid *bitch.* You can't fucking kill me at all."

I lifted a shaking hand and swiped the bitterness from my lips. "What is he talking about, Elithien?" I looked at my lover then. My strong, violent *Alpha* as he just stood there looking at me like I was a complete and utter stranger. "What the fuck is he saying?"

Sickening laughter slowly rumbled from Alexander as he looked from my Vampire to me. "Well...well...well, looks like I'm not the only one lying to her."

"Shut the fuck up," Elithien growled, and held my gaze.

Lying...he was lying to me. I flinched at the sting as somewhere in the back of my mind, that cruel knowing surfaced. I'd known he was hiding something, known he was avoiding my questions. But I hadn't known this...*was this the real reason he'd wanted to find Alex? Not to avenge me at all...but for his own cruel purposes?*

A crack of laughter tore from my lips as I held the Vampire's gaze. But it didn't sound funny. *It sounded like anguish. "That's why you wanted him."* I took a step backwards and slowly nodded, aware of the gun in my hand. "I should've known. I should've fucking *known.*"

My world narrowed, right down to the tiny cracks that shattered my heart.

"Ruth, *no,*" Elithien denied, his brow furrowing with his own private hell. "This isn't that."

Hope made me still. Blinding hope. *Pathetic* fucking hope. I was too far gone, ruined by his touch...and his love—no matter how false that truly was. "No?" I answered, my voice carrying that strange brittle tone. "Want to fill me in, then?"

My eyes warned him...*careful now, Vampire.* My hand was still clenched around the gun's grip.

"Ruth." Justice lowered his gaze to my hand and took a step closer. "Want to give me that gun?"

"No. I don't," I answered, cutting him a glare, stopping him where he stood.

It wasn't about the gun or the bullet anymore. I wasn't delusional enough to think it was the threat of a bullet to the chest that stopped them from coming for me. But it was every second we'd spent together from that first time I drove over the bridge with a rat in a bag to confront them.

"I'm waiting." I turned that stare back to Elithien, daring him with my gaze. "You'd better make it good."

"Just kill him," Russell growled behind me, that deep rumble like an echo from a bottomless well. "We'll take our chances with whatever comes."

"*We* won't be fucking taking a thing," Elithien snapped, the shine of those silver eyes wild. "You think they'll come after us?" He lifted his hand and pointed at Alex. "You think I wouldn't spill this *piece of fucking shit's* blood right here and now *if it was just about us?*"

Silence filled the warehouse. The kind of silence that made the hairs on my arms rise.

"Elithien's right." Hurrow stepped forward, cutting in between us. "They'll come for Ruth."

"And *that* I won't allow," Elithien growled, meeting my gaze.

The energy in the warehouse was electric, burning all the way down as I breathed deep. I saw him then...*really saw him.* He didn't care about Alex. He barely looked at him. *He looked at me.*

"It's not about Alex, Ruth," my Vampire murmured as he stepped closer. "Not anymore. That USB you found, the one that contained files of the Inner Circle. It was proof that someone in Costello Corporation betrayed Alliard. They had him killed, and along with that, a change of our world."

I couldn't think. Couldn't understand...*that's why the files were on there?* My cousins. "Judah and Blane."

"I'm pretty sure they didn't have a clue what was in those files." He crossed the space slowly, stopping in front of me. "But someone in your organization did...and that someone...*I intend to find.*"

I flinched at his words, my mouth going dry while faces raced through my mind.

"But right now," Elithien murmured, lifting his hand to brush his fingers down my arm until he closed his hand around mine and slipped the gun from my grasp. "Right now, we need to keep him alive."

Something sparkled in his eyes when he said that as his voice echoed in my mind. *But it won't be forever. Trust me on that.*

Trust. It always came down to that. Such small things, really, faith...hope. Love. I gave a slow nod and released my hold, not resisting him taking the gun from my hand.

"It makes sense anyway," Alex muttered, his voice devoid of anything remotely kind. "Makes sense she'd spread her legs for you...must be fucked-up genetics, just like her whore of a mother."

The words were a bucket of icy water, tearing me from this moment to slam into that savage part of my nature once more. I lunged, driving myself through the air toward him. My nails clawed the air an inch from his face as Hurrow caught me around the waist. *"I'LL FUCKING KILL YOU ANYWAY!"* I screamed.

He just laughed, the disgusting sound punctuated by the glint in his eyes.

I drove myself forward, thrashing in Hurrow's arms like a wildcat. I was one in that moment, carving my nails through the air until I snagged his shirt. Not a fucking Immortal alive could stop me in that moment as I yanked Alexander forward.

Chair legs lifted, his hands still cuffed behind him to the chair. "I'll fucking kill you if you talk about her again."

The cocksucking scum just smiled, knowing he'd hurt me once again.

"Ruth," Hurrow growled.

"Vampire wh—" Alex started before a sickening *crack* cut off his words.

Hurrow had moved dizzyingly fast. One moment, he stood in front of me...the next, he was where Alex had been a second before he flew backwards, chair and all, landing with a crash on the floor, and stayed there...silent.

"Fuck's sake." Elithien took a step toward the piece of shit.

"I won't have him talk about Ruth like that." Hurrow straightened, his fist unfurling at his side. "He doesn't speak, not about her...or he doesn't speak at all."

"And how the fuck is he supposed to talk to Caedes like that?" Elithien strode toward the silent body of the man who'd tried to murder me and stared down at him like Alex was nothing more than dog shit on the bottom of his shoe.

He was...dog shit.

Actually, he was worse.

My hands shook and my knees trembled as everything hit me all at once. I closed my eyes and stumbled away.

"Ruth." Russell was there, forcing me to open my eyes once more, to see the man who'd died trying to protect me. We were the same in that moment, broken the same...the scars so deep they were mutilations, changing us for the rest of our lives. He lifted a hand to me.

I tried to see him as he'd been before...perfect blue eyes that smiled even as his lips pursed. That warm, almost southern-boy charm. But that image didn't linger, no matter how much I tried to breathe it into existence. Instead, I was left with those deep, bottomless dark eyes, the ones that said, *look at what you've done to me...*

I stumbled away from him, whirling on Elithien as he came up behind me. "It has to be this way, Ruth. I wish to fuck it didn't... but it has to be this way."

I tried to catch my breath, but the thought was so fast, tearing through my chest with razor-sharp claws. *My mom...my mom...* No one spoke about her, not that way...not *any* way. Pain lashed deep, making me press my hand to my breast as a low moan echoed from the still form.

Elithien just stared at him as Alex opened his eyes and blinked, then he turned and walked away. But my mind was reeling, trying to find some chord of truth to what Alex had said. That time in my life was dark, made darker by the fact I'd woken up one day to the news my mother had been killed in a car accident.

Dad had been devastated, locking himself away in his study night after night...pulling away from the one person who needed him, me. Until one day, he changed in an instant. He made an effort, forcing himself to smile and laugh and continue with life, carrying on with meetings that sometimes went well into the night, hatching a plan with the Vampires behind my back to put one of their own into mortal government. That plan resulted in a party at the exclusive bar called the Jewel.

A bar where I'd almost died fighting for my life in the dark, filthy alley it backed onto. I would've died that night, if it hadn't been for Elithien. I lifted my gaze to his. He'd saved me, in more ways than one. Now he stood here, desperate for me to understand, and yet...

A moan tore through the warehouse, low and painful, cutting short with a barking cough that sounded raw. *Good.* I met Elithien's gaze once more. "Okay, I want you to explain it to me...and Elithien, do not lie to me again, or we're through."

Darkness shone in his eyes with my demand. There was a tiny twitch at the corner of his mouth as though he was both proud and turned on by the bite in my words. I swallowed hard, pushed my chin in the air, and added, "And while we're at it, I want to go home...*our* home and not that fuck pad you have in the city."

"Fuck pad?" he repeated, one brow rising as he stepped closer.

"You know what I mean." I lowered my gaze, my cheeks growing warm.

"He's waiting for my call..." Alexander's wheeze snaked through the air.

I jerked my gaze to him lying there on his side, hands clasped through the metal slats of the chair, two steel legs of the seat in the air. "He's waiting to tell me the next part of his plan."

"Plan?" I winced at the word and looked at Elithien.

He stood there motionless, his stony expression giving nothing away. That sickening laughter spilled through the warehouse once more.

"You can't fucking kill me," Alex muttered. "You have no idea what hell is coming for you all. But I do...*I do...*"

Panic gripped me as I turned to Elithien once more. I was starting to understand now, starting to see the poisoned veins reaching far beyond me. I was starting to see how that poison was infecting and destroying everything Elithien possessed.

"Take her," my Vampire commanded. "Make sure she's safe."

"There's nowhere you can run, Vampire. Nowhere *he* cannot reach her."

A growl echoed in the warehouse, and that one deep, guttural vibration was met by another... then another...*and another,* until every Vampire and one very pissed-off Unseelie bodyguard looked at the small, pathetic mortal like they were starving and he was one very easy buffet. They'd tear him apart...limb from limb.

Alex stopped laughing then...and that silence spoke volumes.

"Wolves?" Rule murmured.

Elithien shook his head. "We can't go back there, Ruth, and we can't depend on the Wolves." My Vampire glanced at Alex. I could see the fear building. I didn't know this *Inner Circle.* But whoever they were, they made him on edge and that spoke volumes to me.

Elithien wasn't a man who was rattled easily, but right now as he turned to me once more, I saw he was a lot more than rattled...*he was terrified.* "No home, Ruth. Not yours or ours."

"I have a place," Russell volunteered, and glared at Alexander. "Somewhere they won't find her. She'll be safe there...but only *her.*"

"No," Elithien started.

"Nonnegotiable, Vampire," my bodyguard growled, and took a step toward me. "You want her safe, or under your control?"

That stopped my Vampire cold. Something passed between them, an unspoken battle of the wills where neither backed down. Justice took a slow step toward his leader's side.

"Fine." Elithien gave in.

"E?" Justice jerked his gaze to me... then my bodyguard. "No," he shook his head, the leather eye patch catching the light. *"No fucking way.* I'm not—"

"She goes, Justice," Elithien commanded, turning to face the towering male. "Unless *you* have somewhere you are one-hundred-percent sure she'd be safe?"

My big, beautiful protector was silenced...and tortured, as he lifted his gaze to me. I moved without thinking, striding away from Russell to slam myself against him.

His body took the impact, a heavy, muscled arm going around me in an instant as he wrenched his gaze from Elithien to me. That savage glint softened, leaving only need behind. "You have to go, sexy. But I need you to stay alert. I need you to stay..." *alive.*

My throat thickened as Alex chuckled. "Isn't that fucking sweet. Hey, at least you found love finally...if only with a walking corpse."

The sadistic growl that rumbled in Justice's chest was chilling.

"How does that work, exactly?" Alex jabbed. "Is his cock—"

"Hurrow," Elithien growled.

"My fucking pleasure," his second-in-command answered.

I didn't look when the *crunch* came again, only winced and held onto Justice as he flicked his gaze behind me, then leveled me with pure, driven love. "Go with him. I'll come for you. I'll always come."

That lump in my throat grew thicker. Tears shimmered in my eyes as I turned and glanced at the still pathetic mess on the floor. At least he was silent now, as though that made a lick of difference. I could still see him in my head, still hear his words. My own private nightmare.

"Wait," Justice growled as I strode to Russell.

I stopped, and *waited*. For a second, my heart hammered. For a second, I thought my protector had a plan to get us all out of this mess.

"Rule, walk her out," Justice commanded. "I want to have a chat with the Unseelie."

My stomach tightened as my gaze connected with Russell's. My bodyguard just gave a nod. "Go with Rule, Ruth. I'll be out there in a second."

"Princess." Rule held out his hand for me. "Let's step outside and let the big boys discuss what they need to discuss."

I didn't want to leave them, knowing things were going to be said that couldn't be unsaid. It was like both sides of my heart battled each other...only it was me who felt the pain. It was me who felt the terror...and there wasn't a damn thing I could do about it.

I nodded, grabbed his hand, and let him guide me back out of the warehouse and into the night.

Chapter Seven

I wrapped my arms around my middle and waited... for what felt like forever, until a massive shadow strode out from the corner of the warehouse and went to the gray Explorer.

"Be safe, Princess," Rule murmured, and moved closer.

I tilted my head, meeting his kiss. Rule was the only thing that'd kept me sane after I walked from the warehouse, waiting for my bodyguard, while inside...inside sounded like the detonation of a bomb. The walls of the warehouse shook, even the ground under my feet quaked.

Rule kept busy, transferring my bags into the Explorer, trying not to notice the warehouse walls shuddering and shaking. I was leaving...*for how long?* The answer was an empty silence inside me as the driver's door opened and closed with a *slam*.

"We'll come for you as soon as it's safe," Rule murmured, his arm tightening, then sliding from around me.

I swallowed hard, watching him leave before going to the passenger's side. I climbed inside, leaving the door open for a heartbeat as I turned to Russell. "You okay?"

He moved fast, reaching over me to grasp the handle and yank the door closed with a *bang*.

"Fine," he forced through clenched teeth, but he didn't pull away. He just stayed there, his hand on the armrest beside me as a chill danced across my skin. The scent of something dangerous and feral filled my nose. If I had been anyone else, I'd be cowering in fear. But this was Russell...*this was my bodyguard.* The man who'd returned from death to protect me and was now a half-breed Unseelie creature of the night.

"Russell?" I questioned softly.

He turned his head, nostrils flaring as those pitch-black eyes closed before he moved forward, just a little, enough to press his cheek to mine. But he didn't kiss me. He didn't press his chest to mine. He didn't take...*anything*. A hard draw of breath was followed by another, *and another,* and that menacing cold seemed to warm, like the beast was slinking away from the man. Until slowly, he slid back to his side of the four-wheel drive.

I glanced at the warehouse, my heart thundering in my ears, wondering what the hell Justice had said to him.

"I'm sorry," I murmured, and reached for the seatbelt. "Sorry that they're so possessive."

He leaned forward, clenching his fist and working his fingers before punching the button and starting the engine. He was trying his best to come to his senses, trying to quench that savage hunger inside. "They care, that's all," he answered.

As he turned his head, I caught the smear of blood on the side of his face. "What the fuck?" I lifted a hand, grabbed his chin, and forced his head to turn toward me.

There was a scrape on his cheek, one that ran all the way up to his temple. One that was healing even as I watched...*still, it was there*. "Motherfucker," I growled, stabbing my seatbelt release and yanking the door handle.

"Ruth, no," Russell protested, and chuckled. He leaned across me and pulled the door closed again. "I'm fine. I can give just as good as I get, believe me."

"I don't *want* to believe you." I stared at the door, clenching my jaw until the muscles in the back of my neck bulged. "I don't want to see you hurt, *any of you hurt*. And I *sure as hell* don't want you hurt over me."

"Just boys setting the ground rules."

"And what rules are those?" I turned toward him and held his stare, refusing to let him look away.

"Let's just say we're going to be sleeping in different rooms."

"Greedy, controlling Vampire," I growled as anger burned.

"Insufferable, in-fucking-love, Vampire," he mused, and shoved the four-wheel drive into reverse.

"I'm sorry."

"Don't be. You think I didn't fight to get my point across?" He gave me a look as he reached one hand behind me, gripped the headrest, and backed out of the parking area.

The look was all I needed. He'd fought alright. If he looked like this, I was sure my Vampire looked worse. I lifted my gaze to the warehouse as a chill found me. "Is Justice okay?"

A chuckle spilled from my bodyguard's lips. "He will be, let's put it that way."

I could see those two going head to head, neither giving or taking an inch. I winced and reached out, placing my hand over his on the gear shift. "Even when you're the one hurting, you put my feelings first."

He gave a macho shrug as he stopped the car, put it into drive, and punched the accelerator, tearing us through the west side of Crown City, past the dark, seedy Wolves' clubs and God knows whatever they hid out back. We were heading back over the bridge before I knew it. Sparkling lights and glistening, dark murky waters. I tried to piece it all together. The night...*the pain.*

Alex had been right in front of me. Smiling. *Alive.*

Makes sense she'd spread her legs for you...must be fucked-up genetics, just like her whore of a mother.

Just like her whore of a mother...

Her whore of a mother.

Her whore of a mother.

A low, tortured sound escaped from that hollow pit in the middle of my chest.

"You hanging in there?" Russell asked.

I couldn't look at him, couldn't speak. I gave a slow nod and kept on staring out the window.

I wanted Alex dead and *I wanted this over*. I pushed my spine against the seat and stared out the window even harder. I wanted some kind of peace. Whatever that looked like with four broody Vampires and a...*craving* Unseelie. I turned my head, finding him in the glow of the dashboard lights. There was so much I wanted to say to him. Most of it started and ended with, *I'm sorry*.

I *was* sorry. Sorry for forcing this life on him. Sorry for being such a desperate, pathetic mortal. I tried to remember how I'd felt before they came into my life. Powerful wasn't really a word that came to mind. Desperate, *hungry*. Constantly fighting to fit in. Always desperate to prove myself.

Those thoughts gripped me until I looked up and realized we were plunging headlong into the mortal side of the city. *The mortal side*. How fast my world had changed. "Where are we headed, exactly?"

"Jamesborough Point. My uncle left me a property there a few years ago when he passed. I never really knew what to do with it, so it's kinda just sitting there."

"Oh, I'm so sorry."

He gave a small smile. "It's okay, we were never really close, but being a recluse kinda meant he didn't have someone to take care of what he left behind, so lucky me."

Loss. We shared that along with everything else.

"This is it," he announced, leaning forward and staring through the windshield at an older two-story house. "It might be a little dusty inside. The cleaning lady is kinda crappy...*that's me*, if you're not sure...I'm the cleaning lady."

I smiled, letting a small chuckle slip free as he pulled into the cracked driveway and stopped the car. "Just stay here for a second. Honk if you need me." He shoved the car into gear, the headlights shining on the worn white garage door as he climbed out, closed the door behind him, and raced into the darkness along the side of the house.

The rickety old garage door was rising before I knew it. The headlights glared on Russell as he lifted the wooden door, sliding it all the way open before he strode to the Explorer. A gust of cold wind pushed in as he opened the door and slid behind the wheel once more, then eased the Explorer inside. There was a motorcycle on one side. Chrome shone against the glare, peeking out from under the cover of a blue tarpaulin.

"Your uncle's bike?" I asked as the engine died.

"Mine, actually. It was my dad's." He climbed out, leaving me to follow.

I moved to the rear door, pulled it open, and grabbed my duffel bag as he yanked the garage door back down and locked it in place. I took one look at the thick layer of dust over the bike and I was moving, leaving the parking lights to blink off as I reached the open doorway leading to the rest of the house.

Russell went first, flicking on lights, revealing the way. "There's some food, mostly canned I keep here for emergencies. But there's coffee and long-life milk if you're not too fussy."

"I'm not." I scanned the darkened rooms as I left the hallway behind and stared out into the endless black.

"The river," he murmured, stepping closer. "You okay with that? I can close the curtains..."

I swallowed hard. "No. It's fine."

"Here, let me grab that and find you a room. The shower is good, plenty of hot water. If you want, you can freshen up while I rustle up some food."

"Food sounds incredible." I couldn't tear myself away from that inky darkness.

It called to me...not the glinting lights on the surface, but that undercurrent...that dark, endless depth where I'd sunk *down... down...down...*

"Ruth, you okay?"

I flinched at the words and jerked my gazed to him, forcing a smile. "Sure."

Concern flared, furrowing deep lines in the middle of his brow. "It's not always going to be like this. It won't always be us in hiding...won't always be the bad guy staying safe." Hate glinted in his midnight eyes.

"I know." I turned away, desperate to change the subject. "Now, about that shower?"

His smile was fast, almost as fast as he was as he grabbed the bag from my hand. "Yes, ma'am."

He led me along a hallway to the bedrooms that opened out on the front of the house. Still, it was too dark, out there and in here. Weak yellow lights left the corners of the room in a murky gloom. The sight reminded me of the detached office at the pier where I'd seen the Unseelie beast called Kapre.

"You can have this room. It's the cleanest one, bed's already made and fresh sheets from when I stayed here a few weeks ago, before...before the accident."

The accident. I smiled as he set my bag on the end of a neatly made bed and met my gaze. "Shower's just through there. The hot water takes a bit to come through and some of these old pipes howl a little. But they'll get the job done."

"I appreciate it," I assured him, stepping to the side as he headed for the door, stopping him cold.

He looked down at me, his massive six-foot-three frame yielding to all five-foot-six of mine. I lifted my hand, just needing to touch his face. But there was that agony there, that deep-cutting pain that made me stop, my fingers inches from his cheek.

"Enjoy your shower, Ruth," he said before he stepped to the side, leaving me standing there as he left the room.

I stood there for a moment, listening to the heavy thud of his boots before I went to my bag and unzipped it, grabbing a shirt and comfy shorts, then headed for the bathroom.

He was right, it was old and the pipes howled and banged against the inside of the walls as I twisted the handle and waited for the spray. But the place was warm...homey, making me ache for my own childhood home.

Makes sense she'd spread her legs for you...must be fucked-up genetics, just like her whore of a mother.

I stilled, the bar of soap midway across my belly, as the hot water beat down on my shoulders. He was a liar. A disgusting, sick, perverted liar. But the way he'd said it...the way he'd looked me in the eyes and smiled, as though he *just knew...*

*Makes sense she'd spread her legs for you...*a chill broke out across my skin. I leaned backwards under the heat and washed the rest of my body before I switched off the spray. The shower door grated as it closed with a bang. I grabbed a folded towel from the shelf and hurried to dry. *Makes sense...makes sense...*

My jeans toppled from the edge of the bath as I grabbed my clothes. My father's ring fell from the pocket, hitting the tiled floor with a *clink*. Red glinted under the weak bathroom light, the shine almost turning the jewel black. I reached down, grabbed it, and shoved my arms through the cotton t-shirt before I stepped into the soft boxers.

Why? The word raged as I grabbed my clothes and towel and stepped out of the bathroom. Why take his ring...and why leave it for me on my desk? What possible motive could my uncle have to do that?

Revenge?

Payback for all the nights he stood at the pier watching as they dragged the bottom of the river for my body? Any other family might've felt relief...or maybe happiness, knowing I was alive. But I'd learned a long time ago the Costellos were not like anyone else.

We were crueler. Harder. *Unforgiving.*

The delicious smell of food hit me as I opened the bathroom door. My belly howled, snarling and savage as I hurried to the bedroom, dumped my clothes, and hustled to the kitchen.

Russell was pouring soup from a saucepan into two separate bowls, and in the middle of the counter was a plate with fluffy, golden brown naan bread.

"Canned soup and bread," he revealed. "That's the best that's on offer."

I'd had one grilled sandwich in over twenty-four hours. I could've wept with gratitude. "Smells amazing. I'm starved."

He slid a spoon across the counter, grabbed his bowl, and carried the plate to a small table in front of the wide sliding glass doors. I picked up my bowl and followed, took a seat opposite, and dove in. The grilled bread was delicious and chunks of garlic made the hearty tomato soup that much tastier. I ate quickly, shoveling spoonfuls of soup into my mouth and sopped the remnants with the last pieces of bread.

"You weren't joking when you said you were starving," Russell commented, a spoonful frozen halfway to his mouth.

"I..." I breathed deep and let out a low moan, pushing the waistband of my boxers lower. "Have never eaten so damn fast in my life."

There was a wry smile before he pushed his bowl toward me. "You want more? I can always heat up another."

I smiled, shook my head, and lifted a hand in surrender. "I can't possibly fit another bite in."

He waited, eyes carefully searching mine for the truth, before he commenced finishing his own meal. He would've given me his food. He would've emptied the cupboard and unpacked the freezer if I needed it, of that I had no doubt.

It was nice knowing that. Kind. *Warm.* Different than the Vampires. I watched him as he scraped the last of his soup and broke off a piece of bread, slowly placing it into his mouth, his jaw muscles working. I swallowed hard and looked away. *God, he was breathtaking.*

I rose, grabbed my bowl, and took it into the kitchen.

"I can wash," he called after me.

"I got this," I replied, flashing him a smile. "It's the least I can do."

I hit the tap, then scrounged for the plug and the detergent.

"You just gotta..." The chair scraped against the floor as he rose.

"What? Don't think a rich girl can do dishes?" I teased, shoving aside scourers and bottles. "Where is the damn plug?"

"Here," he answered, right behind me. I straightened as he reached past me, acutely aware of how his chest brushed against my shoulder and his thighs skimmed my ass. "You just press it down, see?"

That deep throaty voice did things to me, things it had no right doing. I just stared as he pushed the middle of the strainer and it closed over, turning into a plug, and dragged Elithien's face into my mind. "Thank you," I muttered. "Not so smart after all, am I?"

He chuckled, and moved away, *thank God*. He busied himself clearing the table. I ran the water, half-filling the sink, and added enough detergent to make bubbles. I washed while he moved around the room. It was nice here, apart from the looming midnight water. "Your father, has he passed, too?"

"*Dad?* God, no," he answered, opening a drawer and grabbing a dishtowel. "Only the good die young, remember?"

"Like that, huh?"

"Let's just say having a mob boss for a father would be a walk in the park compared to him."

I winced at the term and stopped washing.

"Shit. Sorry, Ruth." Footsteps thudded as he came toward me. "That was a fucking insensitive thing to say."

I gave him a weak smile and resumed washing. "Yes, but it was true."

"Doesn't mean I get to shit on your circumstances. You didn't ask to be born a Costello. I'm sorry."

I didn't ask to be me, but that's what I'd been handed. There were many people far worse than I was. "I have a role to play," I answered, turning the bowls over and placing them on the edge of the sink. "That's all. A face, a persona. But that's not really me. That's not the me deep down inside. That's the fire I was born with. The pledge of my bloodline and my father's legacy. I can't fail him." I lowered my head. "I just can't."

He reached around me with one massive arm across my chest and pulled me back against him. "You won't...you couldn't fail even if you tried. You are one of the most incredible people I've ever known. I knew it the moment you woke in that hospital bed, bruised and broken. Still, you helped those children. You used everything in your power to ease their pain and pushed your own aside. That's the definition of a hero."

I laughed, and pulled the middle of the plug, watching as the water drained from the sink. He gently grabbed my shoulder and turned me to face him. "You are a hero to me. You saved me that day, Ruth. You fucking saved me, and we both know it."

I tried to swallow the lump in my throat, and held his gaze. "No, not a hero, selfish and petty. I needed you to live, Russell. I need it to ease my own fucking guilt."

"Guilt?" he growled, and stepped closer, those infernal eyes gleaming with heat. "And here I was thinking you wanted me to ease more than just your guilt."

A hard bark of laughter tore free. "You're beginning to be as bad as the damn Vampires."

"Beginning is fine, I'll be better than they are soon. I'm hungrier for you and *more dangerous than they are.* You just don't see it yet."

I stilled with those words, staring into the endless abyss of his gaze. *Kapre,* the name floated in the back of my mind. *Formidable...and as vast as the night.*

He lifted his arms, his perfect lips curling with a smile. "You could've put yourself first. Hell, Ruth. You almost died." *Not almost.* The words surfaced. *There was nothing almost in that midnight world.*

"Anyway, I'm glad you're here." I pulled the dishtowel from his hands. "And I'm glad you're with me."

"Just stops me from being anywhere else," he responded, that savage Unseelie glint sparkling in his eyes as he lifted a hand and brushed a strand of hair from my face before he continued. "Even if it's fucking torture."

I thought he was going to kiss me then...*I wanted him to kiss me.* Instead, he seemed to come back to his senses, dropped his hand, and grabbed the towel back from me once more. "You must be exhausted. That sofa at the...what did you call it? *Fuck pad,* wasn't the most comfortable. But if you're too wired to sleep, there's some old books and magazines around here somewhere."

Dismissed, just like that. I smiled and stepped to the side, leaving him to dry the dishes. "It's okay. I think I might just take a walk. Hey, you don't happen to have the internet still connected, do you?"

"The internet? Sure, it's still wired. There's also my old laptop over there on the cupboard if you want, as well."

I followed his pointing finger and spied an old PC sitting on a small bookcase. "Thanks, yeah, that'd be good."

I left him there, made my way to the computer, and lifted the screen before I unplugged the charger.

"The battery's old, so you might want to take that with you," Russell called before I switched off the lead and unplugged it from the wall. I was back inside the bedroom a moment later, sitting on the bed, the power cord connected to the wall and staring at the brightening screen as the computer came to life.

My fingers hovered over the keypad. I turned my head, finding Dad's ring beside me on the bed, and the thought that there was part of him with me in that moment was somewhat strangely comforting.

I'd never looked at a picture of her death, never entered her name and seen her face splashed across the screen, and as I pressed my fingers to the worn keys, I tried to find the strength to do just that.

Makes sense she'd spread her legs for you...must be fucked-up genetics, just like her whore of a mother.

I clenched my jaw, staring at that ruby ring, then with Alex's words ringing in my ears, I typed in her name, *Cassandra Costello, death.*

Her face was a punch to my chest, perfect honey brown eyes and gorgeous lips. She was a classic beauty, all the way down to her flawless figure. I couldn't remember her, not really. I was barely six years old when she died. *Car crash on a lonely bend in the road,* Dad always told me, and for a while there I was too scared to ask about her.

He'd had a look when he spoke about her, his cold blue eyes devoid of any flicker of life. So I stopped asking, and after a while, it became easy not to mention her name. But now I wanted to know...

I picked up Dad's ring as I scrolled through links about her, my fingers running blindly over the intricate gold pattern. Over and over...sliding across the stone, and down...until I heard a *click* and pain sliced through my finger. *"Ow!* What the fuck..."

I stared down at his ring, and the tiny gold barb that stuck out from the swirling design. My finger was bleeding, welling in the hollows of the swirls. Cold slipped across my skin, a bitter cold, like somewhere there was a door left open, although I felt no breath of air.

Darkness moved in the corner of the room where the weak yellow light didn't reach, and at the edge of that darkness stood a hooded figure.

I dropped the ring, and the laptop slid from my lap to fall onto the bed. For a second, I was frozen...as that figure lifted his head.

A scream tore free, bloodless and burning, tearing from my chest to shred the air.

"RUTH!" Russell roared, footstep thundering as the hooded man took a step forward, blocking the yellow light as he came for me.

Chapter Eight

ELITHIEN

"Feel better now?" I asked, staring at the piece of shit lying in the middle of the warehouse floor.

Alex just lay there, hands cuffed behind his back, eyes wide, watching us. But it wasn't the mortal I spoke to...*it was Justice.*

The Vampire who'd just had his ass handed to him by a fucking half-bred Unseelie.

"Yeah," the Vampire snarled, wrenching his six-foot-four frame from the crumbled brick wall. A wall that now had a hole the size of a Vampire in it. Bits of debris broke free, falling to the floor as he shook the mess off. "I kinda do."

I shifted my gaze, checking his busted lip. There was blood, bright red drops shining bright under the overhead lights. But there was fire in his gaze as he met my stare. His voice had an edge to it. A cutting edge...*a hostile edge.* He turned that edge to the mortal. "I *still* want to kill something."

A whimper came from the mortal, low and whining, as Rule stepped inside and closed the door.

"She's gone." He stared at the blood on Justice's lip, then at the six-foot-four hole in the wall. "What'd I miss?"

"Nothing," Justice snapped.

Brute strength had met brute strength. That's what he'd missed. A pissing contest of epic proportions. Vampire against Unseelie, an avalanche meeting a tsunami. All because they were in love with the same women...*because we were all in love with the same woman.*

But none of that mattered now. What was love if she wasn't alive? A slow fucking torture, that's what. "Get him up," I commanded.

Hurrow did the honors, grasping the filthy scumbag by the collar of his shirt and lifting him until the chair righted. The smell of his panic rose swiftly, cutting through the stench of testosterone that filled my nose as I slowly made my way toward him. "Now, you're going to tell me exactly what Caedes knows *and* what he plans to do about it."

"Bathroom," the insignificant mortal croaked, and lifted his head, those blue eyes piercing. "I want to go to the bathroom and I want something to drink."

No, the word drifted. *Let him sit in his own filth. Let him die there, as well.*

Death was the answer...the answer to her nightmares, the answer to her fear. I winced as that helplessness came rushing back. I'd kill him a thousand times over if it meant a minute of peace for her. We all would. One command was all it'd take... one simple fucking nod and his mortal life would be over.

Still, Caedes would come, and with him, the others of the Inner Circle. That I couldn't allow. "Take him."

I watched as Hurrow gave a snarl and bent to stare into the mortal's eyes. "Make one fucking move."

"I won't," Alex whimpered, and lowered his gaze, beaten.

The cuffs were gone in an instant, his arms slowly dragging lifelessly through the backrest of the chair until his hands flopped into his lap. He rubbed them, wincing as he tried his best to get his blood flowing. "Bathroom," he muttered again.

Hurrow glanced my way, waiting until I gave a nod before he grabbed the lawyer by the back of the neck and lifted.

"Ow! Wait! *You're hurting!"* he screeched, stumbling to keep up as my second hauled him across the warehouse toward a small hallway at the end of the expanse. A moan bloomed from the small patch of darkness as they slipped from view.

I turned away, leaving the Vampire to do what he did best...*threaten and intimidate.* Instead, I pulled my phone from my pocket. Darkness was rising, crawling out of the cracks, slipping into my world. I felt that wall at my back, felt the hunger rising inside me, born from desperation...and tainted with bad blood.

Alliard had envisioned a better future, one where mortals and Immortals could coexist. His vision, although blinding, was fatally flawed. The Inner Circle would never allow it. He'd wanted to battle anyway. He'd wanted a fighting fucking chance...*and look where that had gotten him.*

But this was not the deal I'd made.

This was not what I wanted.

Now came the fallout.

I needed information. I lifted my gaze to the shadow off the hallway. I needed to know what Caedes intended to do about the betrayal, and how many of the Inner Circle I'd have to kill to keep her alive. I lifted my gaze to the internal stairs that ran all the way to the rooms overlooking the warehouse...and the millions we had stored away in the vaults. Millions that belonged to the Vampire coming for me. With a snarl, I headed for the stairs at the back of the open floor and climbed.

The Wolves and Fae were the closest thing I had to allies. If allies meant they had as much invested in keeping the Inner Circle at bay as we did. We all had our dirty little secrets here in Crown City, we all had a reason to meet this threat with everything we had.

I lifted my head as I climbed. Now to convince Phantom and Shrike of that. I turned the handle and pushed open the door. The dark shock of Unseelie power raced through me, making me wince even after all these years.

The front room was empty as I walked through. Movement came from the shadows at the end of the hallway as I moved deeper into the office space. This place was a mask for Mojin, a place on this side of the veil to use as a base. His real world... was in the world-in-between-worlds, where all his dark secrets were hidden from view.

I glanced at the closed doors along the hallway, sensing that menacing taint in the air. I stopped, lifted my hand, and twisted the handle before pushing the door wide.

"It's not there."

I didn't need to turn my head to know who it was. Shrike stepped out of the shadows at the end of the hall. The Unseelie stared straight at me, judging me. The room was in ruins, steel plates welded to the walls were buckled and bowed, inch-thick bolts sheared straight through. The strength it must've taken to do that!

"Should've let me kill it when we had the chance, Vampire."

I winced and inhaled the fetid stench of the room. The hate and loneliness...the utter desperation and fear. Foulness had seeped into the walls and bled into the floor. It had ruined this room, ruined it In more ways than one. "Is it too late to change my mind?"

"Yes," Shrike answered softly, and stepped closer. "Far too fucking late."

I tried to laugh it off. Tried to pretend it was nothing more than lighthearted banter. A joke between friends. Only we weren't friends...and this was no laughing matter. My thoughts turned to the bodyguard...and my mortal. He was out there *alone with her.*

Panic pressed against me, that wide, vast midnight river rising to the surface of my mind. "Mojin," I spoke the Alpha's name.

"He's busy."

"Too busy to know about the arrival of the Inner Circle?" I held that unfathomable stare. There was nothing, no reaction. Just that stony, unflinching stare, like he hadn't heard me at all. But he had, and I was willing to bet he was scrambling.

"You don't want to disturb him right now." Shrike warned.

Oh yeah, he was scared alright.

"Then you'd better tell him to hurry the fuck up."

With a snarl, the Unseelie stepped forward, top lip curled. But I couldn't care about his precious little ego now...not when so much was at stake.

He turned, heavy footfalls echoing on the stairs, and in a heartbeat, the hallway brightened as a deep, sultry green glow filled the space. The light grew brighter, pulling with it the hunger of the Unseelie world. He was gone before I knew it, leaving only that hunger behind, hunger that reeked of magic, stained with greed and sex.

Need slammed into me. My fangs grew and my senses sharpened. My cock twitched and grew hard, and as I closed my eyes, I thought of her. Her warmth...her soul, her body beneath mine. Her body I claimed as mine. *She was mine...ours*, and had been long before I met her in that alley. An image filled my mind, a picture of her, with worn edges and the smudge of fingerprints on the surface. It was Ruth smiling, eyes alight, standing in the middle of her family's shipping yard and looking every bit the lioness I knew her to be.

I opened my eyes and that desperation mounted. *Save her...love her...protect her.*

The green glow of the Unseelie world still lingered in the hallway as I yanked out my phone and swiped the screen. Phantom answered on the second ring, heavy footsteps thundering in the background as his snarl echoed through the phone. "What is it?"

"We have a problem."

"Don't we fucking always."

"An Inner Circle problem."

The heavy thud of steps suddenly stopped. There was a harsh breath, a deep breath as though the Alpha had been running for quite some time. "Explain."

"Caedes is coming."

Silence. Nothing but savage silence, then, *"I'm on my fucking way."*

The call was ended in an instant. Allies first...my mind raced, tearing through names and faces, finding those I could trust... *there weren't many.* But it didn't matter. Bridges would burn over this. Whole cities would be razed to the ground. If the governor of our Vampire laws was coming, that meant the Wolves and the Fae were close behind.

A cry echoed through the bulletproof glass of the offices. I turned, leaving that fading Unseelie glow and the stench of the half-breed behind. But the moment I took a step, fear bloomed inside me. She was still in danger out there, and not just from those who sought to harm me.

The bodyguard...

He wanted her, wanted her more than a man should, and far more than I liked. He knew the rules...he knew where he stood. But push a man too hard, and his heart just might crack. He'd leave...leave her stranded, leave her vulnerable. The thought of that made my damn soul shake.

I could go to war with Caedes...as long as I knew she was safe.

I swallowed hard, fighting the demons of my past. We needed the lawyer, as much as I fucking hated the fact...we needed him. I forced myself to move as that sultry green glow behind me brightened and, as I hit the door to the warehouse, an inhuman howl filled with pain tore from behind the veil of the Unseelie world.

My boots barely rang on the stairs as I made my way down to them. Our prisoner was tied to the chair once more. His cheeks glistened with water and the grimy front of his shirt was sodden to the skin. All three of my coven stood in front of him. If that wasn't enough to intimidate the toughest of mortals, I didn't know what was.

"Speak," I commanded, cutting him a glare. "Like your life depends on it."

The mortal lifted his gaze. There was fresh blood at the corner of his eye, and his cheek was even more swollen.

"Tripped," Hurrow muttered. "Mortals are clumsy like that."

"What does Caedes know?" I took a step closer, into the mortal's space. "What does he plan on doing?"

The pathetic fucking ant just smiled. His swollen lips stretched taut, revealing blood-smeared teeth, until Justice started to pace along the floor in front of him. The movement made the mortal nervous...*he should be*. The sound of an engine caught my focus. Hurrow was already turning, his brows furrowing, until they smoothed once more. The deep, midnight purr of Phantom's bike filled the air, growing louder until the sounded stopped. I tracked the Wolf as he strode around the edge of the warehouse, until the door opened.

A millennia at war had made us aware of each other. Legends were told of the Vampire and Lycan war. A war of bloodshed. A war of death. But the past was just that. We were a new breed now. A more *evolved* beast. One that tamed that savageness inside ourselves in each other's presence.

Hungry eyes scanned the open floor and settled on the mortal. There was a twitch of Phantom's lips, a curl of distaste. The male secretly despised mortals, thought them spineless and weak. *Maybe he just hasn't met the right one?* That one...perfect specimen to bring him to his knees.

"E, he growled, his dark eyes fixed on the trembling piece of shit. "Not only do you bring me a mortal...you bring me a lawyer, as well...and we *all* know how much I hate lawyers."

"Y-you k-know m...me?" Alexander stuttered, blinking.

One eye was swollen shut, but the other saw just fine. He flinched as it settled on the Wolf. *Yeah,* they knew each other.

"This is the piece of shit in bed with the IC?" Phantom straightened and looked at me.

"Tell him," I ordered, and my voice had an edge to it...a chilling cold. Above us, the upper door opened and Shrike strode out.

"Yes," the Dark Fae growled as he approached us. "Tell us all about our friend Caedes."

Six Immortals practically swallowed the space. There didn't seem like there was enough room for us, nor our power...and the mortal paled, his good eye sweeping from one to the other as Shrike crossed the space and stopped.

"H-He's waiting f-for my call. He'll k-know...he'll know. He won't tell me a d-damn thing. I want to make the call..." Alexander barked, his blue eye sparkling with fear.

Rage filled me, malignant and chilling, driving my steps closer, until I loomed over the piece of shit. "You make demands like you're in control here, like we're *civilized.* But you forget who you're dealing with...you forget that underneath this mask is a monster just *dying to get out*."

He turned ashen then, and those smiling lips no longer smiled. They just trembled.

"Retaliation?" Phantom muttered.

I hated this feeling of being backed into a corner. It made me want to lash out...made me want to *strike first...and make it a killing blow*. I nodded, knowing I severed every fucking thread of loyalty I had.

"Fuck me," Phantom growled.

"I guess *I told you so* is a little like salt in your wounds?" Shrike snarled coldly as he turned his hostile stare to me. "I sure hope it is."

"We need to find out exactly what Caedes knows," I clarified.

"And if the others are willing to take out their biggest earners because *some of us* don't play by the fucking rules," the Fae added.

That's what it came down to...a nice simple reprimand...*Vampire style*.

Chapter Nine

"RUTH!" RUSSELL ROARED. HEAVY STEPS THUNDERED AS the bedroom light flickered.

In the space between one flare of darkness and the next, the shrouded figure was gone.

Russell tore through the doorway, filling the room with that infernal midnight cold. *"What?"* He scanned the window. "What is it?"

I lifted my hand, another drop of blood welling before it fell to the pale blue comforter as I pointed to the space behind the door. "There was a man, right there, in the room."

Concern flared as he jerked his gaze to the space behind the door. He pulled the handle and double checked, but there was nothing. "You sure?" my bodyguard snarled, and pressed his hands to the wall, prowling...*feeling.*

"I'm f-fucking positive," I said, hating the tremble in my voice. "He was right there...coming toward me."

He cast the words over his shoulder. "What did he look like?"

I tried to answer, tried to put into words what that chilling cold had looked like as the shrouded figure reached for me, and spoke. "Tall, menacing, covered with a hood so I couldn't see his face."

He flinched at the words, his jaw muscles bulging as that feral Unseelie rage tainted the air. "Stay right here, *don't move,*" he commanded. "I'll be back as soon as I can."

He was gone in a heartbeat. The heavy thud of his steps sounded, moving from room to room, searching for anything, until there was the slide of the glass door. I wanted to crawl from the bed and follow, feeling like a ten-year-old all over again, one who was terrified of the monsters in the dark.

Only now, it was a monster of the dark who protected me...

He believed me...just like that, he believed me.

He never made fun of me, never ridiculed me.

Never made me feel *worthless.*

He just left, tearing through the house, searching for the terror in the dark.

For me...

My heart hammered as I clutched Dad's ring to my chest, my finger tracing the sharp barb sticking from the band as the silence stretched out like that endless river, threatening to pull me under. Footsteps mingled with the pounding of my heart. I swallowed hard and tried to slow the speed until Russell stepped into the doorway and met my gaze. "Whoever it was, he's gone now."

I shoved off the bed, launching like a wildcat through the air. He caught me like I was nothing, pulling me against his chest. His muscled arm slid across my shoulders, pinning me against him. His fingers curled around the back of my neck, safe...*I was safe here.*

"You're okay now," he soothed, and the vibration spilled into my chest. "You're okay."

I held on for a second longer, then pulled away. "I know how I must sound. But I promise you, he was there."

"I believe you." He didn't meet my eyes. But he didn't need to. I heard the conviction in his tone...I felt the comfort of his arms. "You're okay now."

With a slow exhale, I untangled myself from his arms. "I don't feel okay. I don't feel like any of this is okay."

"What were you looking at?" He glanced at the open screen on the laptop.

"My mom. Her death, mostly."

"That piece of fucking shit. He got to you, didn't he?" He dragged his fingers through his sandy blond hair. "He got into your fucking head."

"I don't know," I whispered.

"He did, and don't say otherwise."

"The way he spoke," I wrapped my arms around my waist. "The things he said about her." The moment I said the words, I knew what I needed to do. "I want to go home."

Russell was shaking his head before I even finished. "The Vampire would kill me."

"Not *that* home," I corrected. "*My* home, the one where my father lived."

He froze, those remorseless eyes narrowing on me. "Why?"

I turned from him, crossed to the bed, and picked up my father's ring. "This was on my desk in my office when I grabbed my clothes."

"And the gun," he added.

"Yes," I snapped. "And my damn gun. But this is the ring he was buried in, Russell. *This* is the ring that should still be on his finger."

His brow furrowed, gaze narrowing as he closed the space between us and grasped my wrist. "You're bleeding." He scanned the bed, his nostrils flaring as he found the small drop of blood on the comforter.

"It must be a flaw." I turned the ring, pointed the intricate design up, and shifted it to the light.

The gold thorn glimmered, the tip tainted red with my blood.

"What the fuck?" he muttered, and took the ring, turning it end over end before he lifted his gaze to mine. "Who would take this from your father's body?"

"I don't know," I lied. There was only one person who *could* have, my uncle.

"And you think going there now is going to help you?" he asked, handing the heavy ring back to me.

"It beats sitting here too terrified to fall asleep."

He searched my gaze for a moment, then slowly nodded. "You want to go, we can go. But you need to stay close to me, Ruth. I'm not kidding here."

"I'll be so close," I promised, stepping toward him, "you'll feel me like a second skin."

Hunger flared in his eyes as his jaw muscles bunched. I needed this...needed to be out of here, needed to be prowling the damn night, unable to stay still. I didn't want to be still. I wanted to be fighting, or fucking. I wanted to feel more than fear. I stepped closer, drawn by that feel of his body against mine. "What did you do to Justice in that warehouse?"

The question took him by surprise. His eyes widened for a second. "Nothing he didn't have coming."

"And what do *you* have coming?" I lifted a hand and traced my finger down the hard planes of his cheek.

I wanted him, wanted that warm powerful body against mine, wanted his fingers on my bare skin, and those lips...*Jesus, those lips.* A surge of desire collided with the fear, the effect...*devastating my control.* "I want you," I whispered, and stared into his eyes. "You can do anything you want to me. Take me...anyway you need."

A sound reverberated in the back of his throat, low...*dangerous.* "When I *take you,* Ruth, it's going to be forever. Just think about that. Think about what that means to you...and to your...*other lovers.* They have rules, and I'm trying my damnedest to abide by those rules. But when you say things like that..." he reached up and grasped my wrist, lowering it between us until I cupped his thick, hard erection. "You make it *almost impossible to be the good guy.*"

My fingers curled, following that wide girth all the way to the head of his cock. Christ, he was huge.

"Now," he growled as he curled his massive frame over me. "About that goddamn ring."

I slipped my hand away and he let me go, that brooding, erotic gaze tracking my every movement. We were ready in minutes, grabbing my bag, and this time taking the laptop as we piled back into the Explorer and backed out of the garage. It felt good to be moving again, making our way back through the city under the cover of darkness. But nighttime wouldn't last forever.

"You sure you're ready to go back there?" My bodyguard glanced at me as the headlights splashed over ornate driveway entrances.

"No, but then again, when will I be?" I answered, forcing myself to remember the times I was happy there, and not the emptiness at the end when he was slipping from me. "There was only ever him and me. I found that strange after a while. Why he never brought home another companion after mom died. But then, as I grew older and came to love him for who he was, I realized that just wasn't his style. He loved her... endlessly." I met his gaze. "A love like that rarely comes around once in a lifetime."

My words hung in the air as he swung the Explorer into the Costello driveway and crept the car along the drive. The place looked dark, *lifeless*. Not like my house at all.

"I'll be back in a second," Russell mumbled, and pulled the fourwheel drive up to the garage before climbing out. I tried to fight the nervousness inside me, but the trembles broke through as the garage door gave a shudder and slowly rose.

He ducked under the rising door and hurried, slipping inside the Explorer, pulling the door closed, then rolled the car into the empty four-car garage. I glanced at the place where Dad's Bentley had sat, the car now secure in my garage at home. It felt like a lifetime ago that the Bentley had become mine.

I lifted my gaze to the entrance of the house now shrouded in darkness. Maybe it *was* a lifetime ago...so much had changed for me.

"Let me go in first," Russell warned, then killed the engine and climbed out. He moved swiftly, closing the door and striding through the garage to disappear inside the house.

I followed this time, stepping out of the car to follow him into the house. *My house,* that thought reared as lights flicked on along the hallway. I made my way to the massive kitchen and hit the light switch, straining to listen to my bodyguard as he moved through the house. I couldn't hear him, not a thud of his boots or the groan of a door.

The place was silent. Like a morgue.

I stared at the sheen on the marble counter, struck by a memory of when I was almost beaten to death outside the Jewel. Dad hadn't wanted me to go out there, didn't think it was safe for me...did he somehow sense what would happen in the days after his death? I wondered about that, trapped by the cruel twist of fate as the groan of a door hinge came from behind me.

I spun, heart hammering, staring at the empty doorway. In my mind, the shadows shifted at the end of the hall, but one strained breath, and there was nothing. Nothing but the howling wind outside. Nothing but the ghosts of my past.

"You okay?" Russell checked as he strode into the kitchen, his gaze following my line of sight until it ended at the doorway.

"Fine," I answered, and lifted my gaze to his. "Just skittish."

He crossed the floor and opened his arms, letting me step close and wrap my arms around him. "You've every reason to be. But you're safe here. You're safe with me."

I clung to him, dropping my head to press against his chest, breathing deep until the shudders eased and I stepped away. That hunger sparked between us, low and feral, a primal need to bond. I inhaled deep, drawing in the scent of his body and his strength. He smelled familiar. He smelled raw and dangerous. He smelled *powerful,* and I clung to that as my nerves felt less rubbed raw and that darkness in my mind lingered. "There's food in the pantry, and the storeroom's fully stocked, as well as the freezer. There's also a safe in the back study, embedded in the wall. The combination is 16-11-73, my mother's date of birth. Take what you need."

I knew what he'd find. Guns and ammunition, lots of both, enough to weaponize a small army...or one of the most powerful families in the city. It'd keep him busy, which was all I needed.

"Coffee?" he queried.

"God, yes," I answered with a smile. "The best money can buy. In the butler's pantry." I jerked my gaze to the left.

I didn't know what I'd find here, what demons I might uncover. Desperation drove me, making me lengthen my stride as I stepped out of the kitchen and turned left. I wanted to prove Alex a liar. I wanted to shove the truth so far down his throat he'd fucking choke. I wanted an excuse to end this, once and for all, and if there were other Vampires coming for Elithien, then I needed to be prepared to help him...the way a Costello should.

I was far from helpless, far from being the weakest of the pack, and as I grasped the door handle of my father's main study and pushed, I knew this was where I belonged. Lights flickered, brightening the space until I winced. Black and white Italian marble flooring. Rich red cedar desk, hand carved and ornate. Glass shimmered and steel shone. This place reeked of testosterone. I turned my head, glancing at the seating area and the fireplace kept for only the select few guests.

This place had been my father's sanctuary, and for a while, his expensively furnished cell. He'd hidden here, locked himself away when I was so very young. I was told he was *grieving*. Told his broken heart had to heal. I was told to *run along now, and leave your father be,* even as my heart broke, as well.

Memories. They were cruel and inviting, urging me to step inside and cross the space to the pictures of her sitting above the fireplace. Private pictures of her of when they first met, when she was shy and awkward, hiding her face as someone else captured the moment. I reached for a golden frame and pulled it down, finding an image of her was when she was older...how old, I wasn't sure. The young, gangly woman had turned into a stunning version of herself, with the kind of old-world elegance you only see in old black and white movies.

Makes sense she'd spread her legs for you...must be fucked-up genetics, just like her whore of a mother.

This woman...was no whore. This woman was the wife of Denzel Costello. This woman looked *fierce.* I placed the photo back and turned, sweeping the tops of my fingers across the high-backed leather lounge, a twin to the one opposite. I was never allowed in here. This room was strictly *for the men,* as though a cock and balls had anything to do with how this family operated.

This family was built on lies...corruption...and money.

And anyone could command that.

I once had a future for my family business, and now I had an empty shell. There was no more Costello Corporation. No more *'men's club'* anymore. There was a locked office building in the heart of the city...and memories of what was lost.

I made my way toward the desk, pulled out the oversized leather chair, and sat, before opening the first drawer and rifling through my father's things. I just wanted something personal. A marriage certificate, a journal she might've kept, something...*anything.*

But there was nothing hidden amongst the Montblanc pens and Dad's favorite Ruger. There was nothing tucked away in the bookcase full of first edition books. There was nothing anywhere. I dropped to the floor on my knees, listening to the faint thud of Russell's steps a second before he stepped into the study.

"You do realize the arsenal your father has stashed away back there, right?"

The smell of coffee wafted in with him. I glanced over my shoulder as he walked in carrying two steaming cups. "You mean, what *I* stashed away back there."

"Really?" One brow rose.

"There'd been threats, a few of them actually, a couple of years back. We couldn't track the source." I grabbed the coffee when it was offered. "You know us Costellos, we weren't about to wait for the cops to step in and protect us."

"Or the FBI, if I remember correctly."

I blew on the coffee, my mind turning to the pain-in-the-ass, Carina Chase. I bet she was thrilled when they told her I was dead...I bet she was just fucking ecstatic when my building closed...revelling in her pathetic pissing contest. Old blood now avenged. Yeah, well...fuck her.

I turned back to the open door of the cupboard and stared at the safe.

"You forget the combination?"

"No," I answered, and sipped my coffee. "I remember it just fine."

It'd been given to me along with the deeds and titles to all his holdings. The truth was, even without the business...I'd be very comfortable for the rest of my life. Not Elithien comfortable... but taken care of, just the same.

Dad had made sure of it. Just as he'd made sure of a great many things in his life. "The Great Denzel Costello."

I took another sip and placed the cup on the plush carpted floor next to me before I took a deep breath, leaned forward, and pressed in the numbers embedded into my memory. I knew those numbers...I'd seen them every year, engraved into the headstone as we laid flowers on her grave.

It was the date of my mother's birth....

The buttons on the safe beeped as I pressed the combination, until there was a *click* and the door sprang open. I could feel Russell move closer, even though he never made a sound. I guess everyone wanted to know what the head of the Costello family kept in his safe. Money, diamonds...

But there was nothing more than a yellow manila envelope.

"Disappointing," my bodyguard complained.

I reached for the envelope and pulled it out.

"Unless it's the deed to an island in the Caribbean. Or shares in Microsoft? That'd be cool."

I smiled at the hopefulness, and shook my head. "That's wasn't Dad's style..." There was a piece of paper inside, just one.

I pulled it out, listening to Russell list all the things he'd love a Mafia father to leave him as the typed font at the top of the paper caught my eye.

DNA TEST REPORT
Case 3334897
Child 3334897-20 Ruth Costello
Alleged: FATHER
3334897-30 Denzel Costello

THE PAPER SHOOK, blurring the numbers on the sheet.

"Ruth?"

I slammed my eyes closed, my chest was tight...so fucking tight. That water waited...that dark endless water that pushed into my nostrils and spilled down the back of my throat.

"Ruth?"

Hands...I felt his hands, grabbing my arm, pulling me from the floor. There was a *clank* as the coffee cup was knocked over, and the bitter tang became the putrid smell of the river as I reached out. "I can't breathe...*I can't breathe.*"

As he pulled me against him, the paper slipped from my hand to fall to the floor...the numbers engraved into my mind...

Probability
19.9999994%

IN MY HEAD, all I could hear was Alexander's cruel laughter as the words surfaced. *My dad wasn't my real dad...*

Chapter Ten

ELITHIEN

"He's waiting for me to call," Alex insisted, slowly lifting his head to meet my gaze.

I just stared down at the sonofabitch, until he swallowed hard and looked away.

"He's waiting for me, and you know it." Defiance flashed in the lawyer's blue eyes. I wanted to rip them out, puncture that smug glint with my fangs, and suck the ooze until I felt those optic nerves twitch on the tip of my tongue.

"I'll call who I can," Phantom growled, and lifted his hand to point at the sniveling mortal. "But this, E, this is on you. *This is all fucking on you.* And get that piece of shit out of here before he brings the fucking vermin."

The Wolf left then, his heavy steps thudding as he strode to the door. I swallowed the wince, my gaze boring a hole into the lawyer until he cowered.

He was bait...and soon enough, the rats would be heading for us, desperate to find out any bite of information to feed back to Caedes. Because if Caedes knew the lawyer was missing, then the only logical explanation was that we had him.

Only, the Vampire wouldn't come to me...not directly. No, he'd send out feelers, men that'd kill before they questioned, and we were already out of goddamn time.

Shrike just turned. There was no snarl from him, no jab of the blade in my fucking back as he went. Just silence. Utter fucking silence. I'd rather the steel of his fucking blade.

"If you don't let me call, he'll know something has happened. If he even suspects..." the mortal started.

"Justice," I snapped. "Shut him the hell up."

"My *fucking pleasure,*" the mountain of a Vampire snarled.

Alexander's eyes flew wide as he shook his head. "No... *nonono,*" he squealed as nearly five hundred pounds of Immortal rage lunged, grasped him by the throat, and lifted *him and* the damn chair into the air.

There was a choking sound. A gurgle. The rest I didn't care to see. I turned away then, reached into my pocket, and pulled out my cell.

*This is all on you...*those words haunted me as I pressed the icon and waited.

"E," Vicious answered with a growl. In the background the *whup...whup...whup* of chopper blades was deafening.

I waited for a second, trying to find the words to say. This was no job I was giving the Breed, no amount of money could justify the means. "I have a problem," I murmured. "For your ears only."

"Wait a second," he growled. A click came across the line, other channels were disconnected as the call turned private. "I'm listening."

"I need information on the IC."

There was a heartbeat of silence. One I felt like a blow.

"What kind of information?" He was careful now, his tone deep...controlled. *Watch your step here,* it whispered.

"Is there somewhere we can meet?" I closed my eyes, hating that I needed more than I could give.

"Midnight tomorrow. Old Cutters Quarters," Vicious agreed. "And Elithien...*this better not be what I think it is.*"

The call was disconnected, and for a second, I stood there listening to the silence.

It was Elithien now...no longer E. He was distancing himself— they all were.

"He's waiting for me!" The slimy slug roared from across the warehouse. *"He'll know where I am!"*

The dried husk of my soul shifted under my skin, feeling the itch of a new fucking dawn barreling down on me, and the choice I now had to make.

The door above me opened, and out of the doorway came Mojin. The Fae glared at the mortal, then turned to me. The message couldn't have been clearer, *don't bring trouble to our business. Get him the fuck out.* I turned and strode toward the others. We were running out of options...and fast.

Except for the slaughterhouse. The thought rose. I glanced at the fucking mortal and entertained the idea of just tearing out his damn throat and dumping the body. But he could still be useful, the only problem was, I was running out of day-walkers I trusted...trusted enough to not be bought by Caedes. I winced, hating the obvious fucking solution.

I'd bring her back into this once more. Taint her with my own fucking treason. *Hadn't she suffered enough?* "Fuck." I lifted my phone and pressed the number for the bodyguard. Him, I didn't care about. Him, I'd use and discard. Him, I wanted as far away from Ruth as he could possibly be...*six feet under should do just fine.*

"Vampire," Russell answered carefully.

"We have a situation," I snarled. "You will be required to...*babysit.*"

There was silence. Strained silence, as though I'd interrupted something important. Thoughts crashed down on me. In my head, all I saw was her...naked, his greedy fucking mouth all over her breast and his cock sheathed halfway between her thighs, inching higher...tighter...*cramming all the way inside,* while he looked at her with utter devotion in his eyes.

Hate rose swiftly, cold and bitter, like an arctic fucking wind. I made no attempt to hide the hate from my tone. "Am I interrupting something?"

"Yes," he replied, his voice stone cold. "You are. You tend to do that a lot. I take it you need to move our...*problem.*"

Sonofafuckingbitch. My fangs punched through my gums, distorting my words. "There's an old piggery. Huntington and First."

"I know it."

"Then we'll meet there, and, Unseelie...*I smell you on her, and we're going to have a fucking problem.*"

There was a deep, throaty chuckle. One that hinted of rage more than humor. "Vampire...you have far worse problems than me." Then he hung up the phone.

I seethed, rage burning in my veins as the whimpers and moans of that pathetic ant echoed all around me. I jerked my gaze to Hurrow, and even he fucking flinched. "Get him in the car."

I turned away from them and strode toward the inch-thick steel doors of one of the safes. A pickup was looming, the rooms were almost full. Sixty million dollars, all neatly stacked on pallets inside. One of our biggest hauls yet. And yet in that moment...*I couldn't have cared less.*

I clenched my fist and lashed out, driving my knuckles into the steel, feeling it give way under my rage. A roar erupted, blistering along my throat as I unleashed it against the buckled steel. The walls trembled, the door shuddered...and all I saw was her.

My mortal.

My Ruth.

My one fucking good thing in the unforgiving darkness that'd become my world. I needed her...needed her like I needed blood. Needed her like I needed control. That's how I felt without her, powerless, *uncontrollable.*

I exhaled, knuckles braced against the buckled steel, and pushed away slowly, staring at all there was to see, the warped version of my own face, creased...*scarred.* Damaged. Would she want that when it was all over? When I'd either survived the battle and lost the war, or when I lost both and left her to cry, a pile of fucking ashes at her feet.

I thought of that as the eerie stillness of the warehouse slowly crept into my mind. Silence all around me. I felt their fucking gazes. Did they see me as cracking under the pressure...or as a lion pacing in a cage?

I turned, facing the cold stares of my coven.

Lion...at least they remembered what I was.

"Let's go," I commanded, and turned toward the warehouse door.

Footsteps scuffed, the chair was dragged until steel howled and the thing was kicked clear across the room. It seemed my frustration was spilling into all of us. Mojin watched me, standing on the stairs as we left the warehouse, taking the trash with us.

Justice and Hurrow bundled the lawyer into the black Explorer. The mortal was still handcuffed, and the black hood was back over his head. "Wait," I called.

They froze with the door opened. Hurrow turned as I scanned the scum's filthy clothes. "Make sure he's not wearing a device."

I was sure that the Breeds would've searched him and disposed of anything they found. I turned my head and glanced at the warehouse, but right now, with the Wolves and the Fae distancing themselves, I didn't trust anyone that wasn't us.

Justice stepped closer, his big hands making short work of the flinching mortal, patting him down and lifting his feet one by one.

"Here." Rule leaned onto the Audi, pulled back with a hand-held device, and cast it through the air.

The thing flipped end over end until Justice caught it in one swift move and thumbed the switch. Green lights flashed and a low droning sound echoed as the Vampire swept it over the mortal's collar, waist, and down to the ground, even taking his time at his boots before Justice straightened once more. "He's clean."

Alex was bundled into the four-wheel drive as I rounded the front of the midnight beast and climbed into the passenger seat. Doors slammed and grunts and whimpers from the lawyer followed, but they were fewer now, low and heavy with exhaustion.

He was tiring.

Thank fuck for that.

Hurrow slipped behind the wheel and Justice folded his frame into the back seat with the lawyer on the other side, leaving Rule to follow behind as we drove away from the warehouse and headed for the mortal side of the city.

The engine roared, speedometer climbing as we raced through the night. The slaughterhouse was a recent purchase, dark, gritty, not yet altered for the kind of protection we needed. One steel trapdoor separated the killing pens from the purpose-built room underneath. But it was clean, even if it did reek of death... and right now, that suited me just fine.

I was steeped in death. Choking on it and backed into a corner with blood on my hands, and before this was through, I'd be standing in a river of it. Caedes was coming with one agenda... and only one. He wanted me to suffer for a betrayal that hadn't been mine, and he'd destroy anyone I cared about to do it.

Desperation coiled inside me, rising like a serpent ready to strike.

"When we get across the bridge, I want you to pull over," I directed. "He makes the call, and he makes it tonight."

Silence greeted my command. Anyone else might've wondered if they'd heard me. But I knew they had...they just didn't like it. *One little bit.*

City lights sparkled in front of us as we hurtled toward the other side. We were across the city before I knew it, pulling onto the off-ramp and spearing through the darker streets of Crown City.

Once you were away from the throbbing veins of traffic, the city seemed to be forgotten, just darkened office buildings and empty streets. We turned onto one of those streets and pulled up hard on the shoulder.

"Burner phone," Hurrow muttered, reaching across and stabbing the button for the glove compartment.

I pulled out the phone and handed it to Justice.

"Number, and if you give me the wrong one, I'm gonna leave you in your own fucking filth for the rest of your fucking stay."

The threat was real, since even now the mortal reeked of piss and sweat. I wrinkled my nose and looked out into the city, hating that this piece of shit had ever touched her.

The lawyer stuttered a sequence of numbers, ones he'd obviously memorized. I winced. "Put it on speaker...I want to hear every fucking word he says."

The inside of the four-wheel drive lit up as the dial tone filled the space. It rang...and rang...*and rang.* Just as I was about to snap, it was answered by silence on the other end of the line.

"Caedes," Alex spoke...harsh breaths followed.

"You're in Crown City. Why?"

I ground my teeth at the sound of the Vampire's voice.

"C-couldn't stay away," the lawyer stammered, and my rage inched higher. Caedes would hear the lie in his tone...*I could hear the fucking lie.*

"The bitch is that good, is she?"

I reached for the armrest, fingers clenching until there was a *crunch.*

"Unfinished business," Alex explained. "She shouldn't have survived."

"Take care of your *business* then, and leave." *While you still can.*

Unspoken words lingered until the bitter stench of panic filled the air.

"Wait!" Alex barked. "Is there somewhere we can meet? Somehow I can reach you?"

"Why?"

Goosebumps raced across my skin as the lawyer hurried to answer. "You wanted to know about my...*unfinished business* once. I can show you."

I clenched my jaw as Hurrow jerked a gaze my way. Rage flashed in the Vampire's eyes, cold, savage fury filled the vehicle. He'd spoken about Ruth? Told that sadistic fucking barbarian about *our Ruth?*

I shook my head at the Vampire, but that hunger for blood lingered.

"Tomorrow," Caedes snarled. "At the place called the Jewel."

"*Wait—*" the lawyer called.

But there was already silence on the other end...the call was disconnected. Harsh gasps of breaths followed as the lawyer slumped against the seat. "There...*I did what you wanted.*"

The Vampire had been guarded, maybe a little too guarded. Hurrow jerked his gaze toward the city and pulled back out onto the street. Justice made short work of the cell's SIM card, snapping it in two before he rolled down the window and threw it out onto the street.

"A shower," the lawyer demanded, finding a thread of steel in his spine. "And remove these fucking cuffs."

"Fine," Justice snarled next to him. "But if you even *think* about discussing Ruth with *anyone* ever again, you're not going to need a goddamn shower. You won't have any *skin* to wash."

Caedes knew about Ruth...

Caedes knew about Ruth.

"*Hurry,*" I growled, and pulled out my phone, hitting the number for the bodyguard once more. I waited for the pain-in-my-ass Unseelie to answer before I spoke. "We may have a problem."

Chapter Eleven

"Problem?" I shook my head as tears blurred the page in front of me. "What kind of problem?"

I tried to focus on them, tried to tear myself away from that cold, sinking feeling in my chest as I stared at the percentage and tried to understand. My words were flat, *lifeless*...that's how I felt, devoid of a spark...empty and void and...*nothing*.

I was nothing.

"The problem," I repeated, lifting my gaze. "My Vampires."

Russell didn't want to answer, shifting his gaze to the desk behind me. There was a wince...then another. "I don't think you should—"

"No," I forced the words through clenched teeth. "No, you don't get to do that." I took a step backwards as the first lash of pain cut across my chest.

Desperation followed. *Cruel.* Suffocating.

"Don't shut me out." There was a tremble in my tone. A weakness I hated. "I can't be alone...*please don't leave me alone. Not right now.*"

The muscles in his jaw bunched. His lips curled, baring his teeth, revealing a tiny flicker of the dangerous male he was. "They need us to watch *him.*" He jerked his gaze to mine. "While they sleep. You're gonna have to sit there hour after fucking hour and look at the man who tried to kill you. You ready for that?" His dark eyes blazed with rage. "'Cause *I don't want that for you.*"

I froze with that flare of rage. Locked down, thoughts frozen. All I could see was those shining blue eyes in my mind as he laughed at me. Hour after hour...looking at him...*listening to him.* "Yes, yes *I will fucking look at him.*"

My breaths came harder now, shallow...racing...racing...*racing.*

"Hey!" Hard hands grabbed my shoulders, making me flinch as he met my gaze. "It's fine for you not to be okay with this. I'll tell them no. I'll tell them to find someone else to fucking babysit the piece of shit. Leaving you alone was *never* an option, okay? You're stuck with me, remember? Gruesome fucking Unseelie powers and all."

I tried to smile, forcing the corners of my lips to curl, and stared into those midnight pools, and for a second...for one heart-pounding second, *a monster stared back.*

"Ruth?" Russell asked. "You okay?"

I swallowed hard and nodded, wrenching myself back to the moment. "Yeah. Yeah, I'm okay. I can do this. I can do this because they need us."

Trust was a commodity. One we were in short supply of...

"There's no shame in bowing out, Ruth. You don't need to be strong all the time. Not with me." He lifted his hand, his curled fingers brushing along the length of my jaw.

"They need us. That's all there is to it," I answered, my voice finding that edge. "I'd do the same for you...and so would they."

"I dunno about that," he chuckled, and dropped his hand. "You want to take what you need here and we can go?"

I gave a nod and knelt, slipping the page back into the envelope before I leaned forward, shoved it back into the safe, twisted the lock, and rose. There were pictures on his desk. Images of me...Dad once told me 'look at the pictures, look at every one of them, they show you when they're smiling and proud, thinking they have you in their grasp. The pictures wrinkled and worn from all the years hiding in their wallet, those are the ones you focus on...those ones...*they're special.*

'Ones they'll do almost anything to keep.

'Those are the ones you go after...when blood needs to be spilled.'

I stared at the images of us now, the ones he'd drawn closer at the end. The ones of me and him, but too many questions surfaced. Too much hurt...and too much pain. I turned away and strode from the study, hitting the light and plunging the room into darkness as I went.

I forced myself to move, forced myself to stride back to the kitchen. Weapons and ammo were spread neatly across the shining marble counter, semi-autos and pistols. I grabbed a sparkling Sig Sauer and slipped it under my hoodie at the small of my back.

"You're not going to make me regret that, are you?"

I busied myself, striding into the pantry and grabbing the calico shopping bags from under the counter. "I've got control over myself. Don't worry."

"Ruth, worry is my natural state when I'm around you."

I smiled, shook my head, and tossed him two of the bags for the weapons and ammo, while I filled up two more with as many snack bars, UHT milk, coffee, and canned foods as I could to last a few days.

We made two trips, loading the Explorer with what we needed, which included a heavy jacket for me, and plenty of thick blankets to sleep on. The term 'slaughterhouse' didn't exactly fill me with the warm and fuzzies.

We'd loaded the Explorer and climbed in, backed out of the driveway, and were heading to the city once more.

"Shit," Russell muttered, glancing at the rear-view mirror.

I turned, checking over my shoulder at the faint glimmer of a brightening sky. Dawn was coming...and it was coming fast. My bodyguard punched the accelerator, spearing us north to the industrial section on this side of the city. Still, that brightening of the pitch black gripped me, my heart was pounding, fear racing, sweat breaking out all over my body.

"Russell," I urged.

"I got it," he reassured, glanced into the side mirror, and wielded the wheel like he was a warrior and the car a honed blade.

I held on, listening to the weapons clatter as they slid, and prayed we got there in time. Pain greeted me when I reached out to them. That sharp sting of agony that came with the rising sun. I closed my eyes and clenched my jaw. They needed us. Needed me...guilt pushed in. I held on while Russell sped us toward the slaughterhouse, until the flash of red and blue came behind us.

"Shit. Hold on, Ruth," Russell ordered, taking us hard into a turn.

But the flashing lights stayed with us. Red and blue. *Red and blue.* My pulse raced as reality clicked in. "What if they recognize me?"

There was a snarl, then a sharp jerk of his head. Midnight eyes glinted, seizing mine before they softened. "Pull your hood over your face. I'll do all the talking."

The last thing we needed right now was a media frenzy. I gritted my teeth as the Explorer slowed. I could see it now *Mobster boss's daughter back from the dead!* I eased my hand up and tugged the navy blue hoodie low.

"I'll do all the talking," Russell repeated as he braked hard, coming to a stop on the side of the road.

*Ruth...*Elithien's plea carved through my mind.

He was desperate, pinned down by the growing daylight and torn apart by agony. Russell pulled to a stop, shoved the four-wheel drive into park, and splayed his hands on the wheel as the patrol car pulled up behind us. The strobing lights made me nauseous. I swallowed, and swallowed, fighting the clenching of my belly as the officer neared the driver's door and tapped on the window.

My breaths raced with the whir of the glass lowering. Torchlight flicked on, blinding me. I winced and turned my head, shielding my face.

"Have any idea how fast you were going?" the officer asked, the light boring into my face.

"Fast," Russell answered, keeping a tight rein on his rage. "Want to lower that beam from her face?"

But the glare never wavered. "License...and registration."

My heart lunged, slamming against the inside of my chest as Russell moved, shifting his gaze toward me. Those dark eyes glinted like endless pools of hate as they met mine. *"Ruth,"* he pleaded, and the beam of the officer's light moved...flooding the rear of the car.

"What the fu—" the cop started. "Get the fuck out of the car! *Get the FUCK OUT OF THE CAR RIGHT NOW!"*

Guns were sprawled across the leather seat. They shone in the savage glare of the beam. I knew why Russell was desperate now...why he looked at me with hopelessness in his eyes. It wasn't finding the guns he was scared about. *It was me.*

"You!" the cop roared as the light blinded me. "Get out of the *fucking car NOW!"*

I shook my head and blinked, finding bright white spots where Russell's face had been. It was the same look he'd had before, the same desperate look of rage.

"I can't stop," the beast rumbled beside me.

Fear rose swiftly, standing the hairs on the back of my neck. Glassy midnight eyes met mine, wide, *terrified.*

"He shouldn't pull a gun on you," I caught the frantic whisper as black veins spidered along his cheek. "Shouldn't threaten." The words were desperate.

I could feel that hunger, feel that *Unseelie need*. His muscles bulged, his hands seemed to growl larger. I jerked my gaze to the glare of the torchlight and lifted my hands. "Okay...I'm getting out now. I'm getting out."

The cop's two-way crackled and the screech of feedback savaged the air. I winced at the noise, shoved my hand out, and clawed for the handle.

But Russell was moving as well, this time turning toward the officer and shoving open the door.

"Stay where you are!" the cop ordered.

I flung myself backwards, falling out as the door opened. The *crack* of a gunshot boomed as Russell threw open the driver's door and lunged. I lost sight of him. Lost him to the sickening sounds of rage...*sounds I'd heard before.*

Cold crept along my arms as that chilling *bite* grew bolder. I hit the pavement and drove my boot against the asphalt, scurrying sideways and took cover, my spine pressed against the side of the car. Terror filled me, stealing me away from the moment and plunging me back into that unshakable fear.

Screams came. Mortal screams...*pleading screams.*

The sound was a fist around my throat, choking the life from me. Tears blurred as my whole body shook. If only he'd let us go...if only he'd *let...us...go...*

Movement came from the shadows still clinging to the darkened alley. Darkness where the strobing red and blue didn't quite reach, and as that shift of darkness moved again, I felt myself rising on shaking legs.

The street was quiet now. There were no pleas, or screams, not even the crack of the two-way to shatter the early morning air. There were just those strobing lights. Lights that bled blue and red, washing over the man who stepped out of the darkness...

And came into the light.

A sound slipped from my lips. Tortured. *Weak.* The man who'd found me in that small bedroom in Russell's house had found me now. The groan of a car door came and a heartbeat later, those jarring, flashing lights ended, leaving me staring at the hooded man before he lunged.

"No!" I screamed and threw my hand up to cover my face.

"Ruth?" The heavy thud of footsteps invaded a second later I was lifted and pulled against a mammoth chest as thick, muscled arms wrapped around me. His chest buffeted me with hard, heavy breaths as he lowered his head, drawing my scent in deeper. "You okay?" His hands slipped along my body, splayed fingers covering as much ground as they could.

"I thought he was going to pull the trigger." His dee, growl was gravel in my ears as he carried me back to the passenger seat. "But you're okay now. You're safe...*safe with me.*"

Hard breaths.

Sawing from my chest.

Safe with me.

I lowered my hand as the car door slammed, my gaze riveted on the darkness...a darkness that was empty. As my heart boomed and that uncontrollable feeling of dread washed over me, my bodyguard climbed into the driver's seat.

"Ruth," he sighed, his tone tainted with remorse. "Ruth, look at me."

I turned my head, but it wasn't me doing it, it was that numbness. That cold, detached part of me that floated in the depths of the river...a river I'd never escape.

"I had no choice. You get that, right?"

There was blood on his face. Just a smear...one small smear that looked inky black in the dim morning light. I swallowed hard and nodded, trying hard to focus on that stain and not that unfathomable hunger that lingered in the dark pools of his eyes.

"Say you get it," he pleaded, desperation and rage like oil and water in his tone.

"I get it," I answered. "Now can we just get out of here?"

He yanked the Explorer into drive and peeled away from the curb, gunning the engine as we tore through the outskirts of the city and raced to the old industrial area. Pale sunlight seeped into the cabin of the four-wheel drive as we pulled into the driveway of what was known as the Slaughterhouse. I stared at the looming gray building with its four concrete levels and the stench of death.

Russell braked us to a hard stop as we rolled through the open gate and into the old parking bay. "Stay there for a second." He shoved out of the driver's door and raced to the open gate of the tall solid fence.

My damn hands were shaking, fingers trapped in fists, still it didn't stop the shudders. If anything, it made them worse. The stench of death pushed into my nostrils, and clawed its way into my lungs. I was scrambling, shoving the door open to stumble and fall to the cracked concrete at the front of the Explorer.

Acid spilled, burning all the way along my throat, making my eyes water as I coughed and spluttered as the howl of hinges savaged the early morning air. Footsteps closed in, and the rear door opened as I wiped my mouth with the back of my hand and straightened.

"You okay?"

I didn't have time to be anything else. "Yeah. I'm good." I turned toward the foreboding building, then forced myself to move.

I couldn't feel my Vampires anymore, not their pain or their desperation. I'd failed them...when they needed me the most. I shoved the weapons and ammo back into the bags and hauled them from the car.

"Ruth?" Russell questioned behind me.

I pushed off, shoved the door closed, and hauled the bags with me. He already thought I was hallucinating back in his house. The words weren't there, but the careful glances were. If I told him about seeing the shadowed man again, he'd think I was breaking. Fuck, maybe I was. Maybe after everything, this was what it came down to...me, finally snapping under the pressure.

I followed him into the stench of death and fear. The Slaughterhouse may not've been in use for the last ten years, but the air was still tainted here, even more so as we strode toward a boarded-up glass door left ajar and pushed our way inside.

I winced at the stench of old blood. My heart raced and my knees trembled as that fetid stain of death cloyed in the back of my throat.

"Swallow, don't breathe," Russell suggested. "It'll help."

I followed him deeper into the shadows and past what had once been a reception area to the bank of offices at the back. Plastic sheeting covered the doorway. We pushed through to what was a demolition site...and a far cry from the *fuck pad*. I winced at the words and shifted my gazed to an inch-thick steel barrier that sectioned the entire floor.

My breath caught with a sudden wash of fear. For a second, I couldn't move, pinned by an uncontrollable urge to flee. A snarl sliced from Russell's lips, low, guttural, standing the hairs on my arms. I tried to breathe, tried to think as that touch danced along my arms and lingered.

"Magic," Russell growled. "Same as the warehouse, same as the Fae."

That *magic* hovered, then slowly moved in like a beast, scenting me in those seconds before it struck. I closed my eyes as terror claimed me, making me shake and whimper until, in an instant...*it was gone.*

Gone, leaving nothing but the stench of death, then finally, with shaking knees, I could move.

It's okay. Just wards to protect us. Same code as the house. Elithien's faint voice drifted to me. *Couldn't wait...sorry.*

"I got it," I gasped, and stumbled forward, trying to push my heart back into my chest.

The keypad sat beside the door in the newly built walls. I punched in the same number I used at our home across the river, and heard the hiss as the door slid open.

Bright lights greeted me. I winced at the glare and pushed through into what looked like some kind of bunker.

"*Fuck you!*" Alex roared. "Get me the fuck *off this thing right now!*"

Chains rattled, jolting and gnashing with metal teeth. Movement came from deeper in the space as we hauled the bags inside, listening for the hiss and then the *click* as we were locked inside.

"*Get me down!*"

My stomach rolled at the sound of his voice and the hard steel bite of the gun at the small of my back wore at me.

"Don't look at him," Russell urged, and pushed ahead, striding to where the piece of shit howled and thrashed. "Let him suffer."

But I wanted to look at him. I wanted to see how much he hated being...*a prisoner.*

To see how he felt to be so fucking helpless...and in pain.

I dropped the bags to the floor and stepped away, moving deeper, to where the blinding lights didn't quite reach, and high in the air, Alex hung from a meat hook.

"*I fucking hate you!*" he roared, blue eyes blazing. "*Fucking bitch!*"

But instead of panic and terror...I just smiled and turned my back to him.

"You won't be smiling for long."

I left him behind.

"You won't be smiling when this is over!"

"Russell," I called, summoning my Unseelie warrior. "He's all yours."

Chapter Twelve

ELITHIEN

Rage filled me. Dark rage. *Violent rage.* A stabbing response as my past found me in my sleep. Memories slipped in like an assassin. One bite and I was in their grasp. I could feel it now, that growing darkness. Flickers of images, and a flash of pain...one so cruel it ripped my chest open.

NO!

My own roar echoed in my head, burning like acid along my throat. I was thrown back there, back in the void...back in the *memory.* Back where there was blood on my hands, and violence in my veins. Back when there was a seat at the Inner Circle on offer...but it wasn't an offer for me.

I wasn't worthy...nothing more than a weapon...*nothing more than a result.*

Blood soaked into my shirt...blood all around me. Loyal blood. *Royal* blood. Blood of my sire and their side before that. And I knew in the abyss of my mind there was a shadow on the ground.

A shadow curled.

A shadow still.

Vacant eyes stared up at me...calling me. I don't want to turn my head. I don't want to see what's left. What's left of love. And loyalty. None of those things will undo what'd been done. None of those things will breathe life into those eyes. They stared at me now. Dull. Empty.

Dead.

There's only revenge inside me now.

Cold and hard. A cutting edge, honed to a point from all these fucking years.

I will take from you, Elithien. I will take until there is nothing left to take. And then, and only then, will I abandon you on the highest cliff in darkest night...and you will wish you'd never heard my name...Then I will know I've won.

I've won...

I've won.

I opened my eyes to the darkness. Movement shifted all around me in this makeshift tomb. Night was coming. Night and an enemy I'd fought once before...and I'd lost. Lost what was precious to me...and what was precious to our line. I closed my eyes and clenched my jaw. If only Alliard had listened. If only his need for revenge hadn't cost me *everything I fucking loved.*

Not this time.

Not Ruth.

I pushed up from the small cot shoved hard against the wall and slowly rose. There was a change in me now. A subtle shift.

Dangerous tectonic plates realigned...unable to slip back where they once were. I felt the movement, where one edge wore at the other, until both sides cracked and caved. Caedes was here in this city and that was too close...*too fucking close to her.*

My fangs ached as that predatory side of my nature rose. It was a side I kept in control. A *beast* I never wanted to unleash. But it was pulling at the chains now, it was *testing* the cage I'd so carefully constructed around it. It was searching for a way out.

It'd find one. It'd slip its shackles and roam these streets. It'd become the thing mortals feared. It'd become the thing *Caedes* feared...for her.

I lifted my gaze to the steel barrier between us. The scent of Ruth invaded me. A raw, tormenting compulsion. I couldn't get enough of her...couldn't see past that hunger she triggered in me. Couldn't see anything but her pale, dripping body in my arms as I'd pulled her from the river. I'd made her enemies mine, made her existence *personal.*

I was driven by desperation and that insatiable need to own...to bite...*to claim.* She was mine...mine to touch. Mine to have. Mine to watch while my men cared for her and protected her.

They'd protect her now.

Fists curled at my sides as night closed in. I needed her, needed her like I couldn't breathe. My body trembled, my muscles clenched. I closed my eyes and drew in the faint scent of her

"You're fucking dead!" The lawyer still screamed, his voice harsh and raw. "I can't wait until you're done, Vampire *whore.*"

I licked my lips and tasted blood. My blood, not his. *Not yet.* But soon. Soon this would be over once and for all.

"You're scaring me."

I winced at the words and pulled away from her as Hurrow rose from his bed.

"I thought you had a leash on that thing."

"I do." I chose my words carefully. *For now.*

"He triggers you...and so does she. You're like a keg of gunpowder searching for a fucking match. I can't protect you... not like this."

I opened my eyes as the steel door gave a *click* and the locks disengaged. "Then don't." I answered. "Protect her instead."

The stench of death and blood assaulted me. It was a scent I was born in...a scent I'd grown accustomed to over the years. A scent I'd wear again.

But not yet...*not until I'd had my fill of her.*

The rattling of chains sounded. I glanced at the sniveling imbecile standing on a chair and felt that animal inside me rattle its cage. Someone had grown weak. Someone had given in and relieved the bastard of his torture. I knew just who it was.

One scan of the space, and I found her. She stood in the half-finished kitchen, just a stove, sink, and an old, well-used table. She was dressed in jeans and a long-sleeved blouse. I cut a gaze right, and found a navy blue hoodie draped over the back of a chair.

The salty scent of food still lingered. She'd eaten, hours ago now and, judging by the sofa pushed into the shadows and the newly arrived thick blankets, I was willing to bet she'd slept, as well.

She turned as though by instinct, then running steps left nothing behind. She was in my arms before I knew it, her warm skin under my hands.

"Elithien?" I closed my eyes as she called my name.

That savageness rose inside me as I lifted her, pushing her back against the table.

"Elithien?" the Unseelie growled. A warning. But I was far too gone for that.

Her fingers tangled in my hair. Her breasts pressed against my chest. I was thrown back into that alley where the beast had first risen for her. Bodies lay all around me and the smell of death clung to the air. They were still now...*they were all so very still.* Except for her.

I watched her chest rise in shudders as blood dripped from my hands. I watched as her fingers opened and closed, searching for the baseball bat to use as a weapon. I watched her eyes flutter open and try desperately to focus on me as I stepped out of the shadows. She was hurt...*badly.* Frantic steps rang out behind me. Her father's screams followed. He'd gotten there fast...*good.*

I was done here...finished what I came to do.

I'd met the woman who drew me out of the shadows and into the light. *Ruth Costello*...I pulled away from the memory now and lowered my head, her warm lips on mine. The woman in the photographs...the woman her father had warned me to stay away from...*as if I could.*

"What the fuck," the lawyer spat, standing on that fucking chair, the cuffs wound over the meat hook above him.

She wound her arms around me, letting the beast take what it needed. I grasped her waist and lifted, pushing her backwards onto the table.

"It's okay," she murmured. "I'm fine. I'm here. *Take what you need from me.*"

I did. I buried my face against the side of her neck, fangs scraping over the flutter in her vein. She gave into me. Never fighting. Never resisting. Letting me reach up between us and open the buttons of her blouse one at a time.

She smelled of death…she smelled of fear. She smelled of *goddamn* Unseelie. That savage sound rattled around in the back of my throat. She smelled of every other thing *but me.*

"E." Hurrow was behind me. "You're scaring her."

I froze and pulled away, finding her lips parted…and her pulse racing under my lips. Her blouse was open, her breasts bare. Had I done that? *I see you,* she'd said before in the car when the beast woke. She said the same thing now…just with her gaze.

"It's okay," she whispered. "You need to touch me, need to make sure I'm safe. Is that it?"

This wasn't the man she was used to. This wasn't the man *I was.* This beast was savage and predatory. This beast was anything but kind.

"Kiss me," she demanded. "Soft and slow. Bring back the Vampire I love."

I reached up with trembling hands and cupped her face. She stared into my soul. "Why are you so full of rage?" she asked.

She had to ask that? *Didn't she know?* Couldn't she see the monster in my eyes roamed for her? Killed for her…*would die for her.* The violence of that fueled me, burning through what was left of my soul. I took a step backwards as the beast inside threw its head back and roared. "Why?" I repeated. She flinched from the sound. It was savage. *I was savage. "Why?"*

I turned to the steel wall and caught the smug sparkle in the blue eyes of the mortal.

Whywhywhywhy? WHY?

I spun at the last second, cocked my fist, and drove it through the wall. Steel buckled, tearing at the last minute. I just stood there, head bowed, *breathing.* "Because you, my mortal," I answered, "are so full of grief."

She didn't hate me. *Why didn't she hate me?*

I lifted my gaze, then unfurled my fingers and pulled them through the torn, buckled metal, desperate and horrified to look at her. "Don't you see? Everything that happened to you was because of me."

Her brow furrowed in an instant. There was a slight curl of her lips before she shook her head. "No, I don't believe that."

It didn't matter *what* she believed. The truth was the fucking truth, no matter who's skin it wore.

A snigger came from the pathetic *gnat.* "He's going to take everything," the lawyer taunted.

I jerked my gaze toward him as Justice and Rule stepped out of their rooms. Slow. Careful. Flanking me on all sides. Cautious, that's what they were. So fucking cautious. *They should be.*

"What did you say?" I growled. Cold plunged through me, chilling me to the bone, like I was newly dead all over again.

The bastard just smiled, blue eyes shimmering as every fucking male in the room zeroed in on him. "He'll take her first. Maybe he'll even let me keep her?" He met my gaze. "She fucks like she's dead anyway."

I caught the flinch in the corner of my eye, and the subtle shift of her gaze. He hurt her...

Rage spilled over.

The piece of shit. Images invaded, merciless and wretched. Caedes was fucking her. Holding her hands over her head, her wrists trapped in his as he thrust between her thighs.

She'd fight, my Ruthless. She'd kick and scream, buck and howl. But it wouldn't matter. She'd be trapped in the confines of her own head, held prisoner by the will of a powerful Vampire. Caedes was too strong mentally and physically...he'd violate her *over and over and over again* until she was dead. Agony roared through my chest, slammed home by panic.

I lunged for him, grabbed the *fucking dead mortal* by the throat and lifted. Blue eyes widened. Terror claimed him as I curled my lips and bared my teeth.

"Elithien, *no!*" Hurrow roared. *"We need him!"*

Hands were around my arms, pulling me away. But they weren't strong enough. They weren't anywhere near strong enough. Not against me...*or against Caedes.*

Darkness pushed in around me, washing over the walls and climbing over the ceiling, and that infernal *Unseelie* power cut through me like a blade. *We need him.* The power pushed against my mind. *He'll be dead soon enough anyway.*

I jerked my gaze over my shoulder, past Hurrow, to the male who stood in the center of the room. The male whose presence unnerved me...whose very fucking *existence* unnerved me. The bodyguard turned his head and met my gaze. There was a knowing there...a dark, infernal fucking thing. He was getting stronger...*in leaps and fucking bounds,* swallowing this goddamn room, cramming his forbidding fucking darkness into each crack and crevice...just like he was trying to shove it into me.

Get the fuck out of my head, I snarled, watching him flinch and pull away.

But it worked. The hatred and fear that choked me eased. I stared at my fingertips against the scumbag's jugular, one fucking twitch and I'd tear his throat out. He'd never speak... never live. The image bloomed inside me, sweeter than a deadly rose.

"You will die tonight," I promised with a curl of my lips as he fought for air. "But Caedes will die first."

Chapter Thirteen

You will die tonight. I shivered at the words as Elithien backed away from me with a careful glance.

But he wouldn't quite meet my eyes, as though he was hiding from me...hiding who he truly was—*as if I hadn't seen him at all.*

I pushed off the table, stood on trembling legs, and reached for my open blouse. Elithien's gaze snapped toward me once more. Those midnight eyes fixed on the open neckline and the swell of one breast as the shirt gaped. Heavy breaths made his chest rise hard before it fell. I lowered my hands, letting him see me.

"E," Hurrow urged once more, and took a step. "You need to leash this if she's going to survive."

Elithien swallowed hard and that shimmer of rage dulled.

"You go to war like you are now and we're all as good as dead.," his second warned.

Justice watched Elithien, and Rule watched me, taking one slow step toward me. He lifted his hand slowly, his fingers grazing my breast as he worked the buttons closed.

"Get him down," Elithien commanded, his voice deep and dangerous. "And set up the meet. I want it open...and public...*and far away from her,*" he barked, stabbing a finger in my direction.

Alex coughed and choked, wheezing as he sucked in huge gulps of air.

They all moved around me, snarling and savage. I was the eye in this storm; still, frozen, not a blade of grass moved in my world as I stared into the chaos of men. Alex was lifted and pulled down from the hook. I'd shoved a chair under his feet, unable to take one more second of that grating gnash of chains. It was that chair he was shoved into by Justice.

"Do not fucking look at her," the towering Vampire warned as he leaned over him. "Or I'll fucking end you myself."

Russell stood in Alex's line of sight like a wall. The effect couldn't have been clearer. As of right then, Alex ceased to exist for me. I shifted my gaze to Rule as he buttoned the last button on my blouse and leaned in to kiss me. His hand cupped my cheek before he pulled away.

"What's going on here," I whispered, and glanced at Elithien. "Tell me he's okay."

"He's," the Vampire winced, forcing the word. "*Fragile.*"

The way he said it made my pulse race. Was he talking about PMSing or was he talking about lethal, unstoppable wrath? They were worried. They were *all* worried. Elithien stepped away, watching Alex. I was worried more than anyone.

"You heard him." Justice slipped a new SIM card into a phone. "Somewhere public, and you say anything other than the location and you'll be dead before your next breath."

"I think we need to plan this," Hurrow growled, and paced.

"There's nothing to think about. I upheld a pact...that pact expired as soon as Alliard was dead." Elithien's words were cold, lifeless...*dead.* "Caedes wants me dead, and I want revenge."

"And the rest of us?" Hurrow snapped. "Where the fuck do you think that leaves us?"

Elithien didn't answer, just gave a nod to Justice. Panic filled me as the massive Vampire released Alex's cuffs and thrust out the phone. "Call."

But it wasn't Alex I cared about anymore. *She fucks like she's dead anyway.* His words burned inside me like a slap. Something was brewing here, some dark undercurrent of bloodlust that was swelling with a rising ride, threatening to drown us all. Elithien said this was all about him, and my mind raced to piece it all together as the cell phone rang through the speaker.

My family had been connected to the Prince's death...a man Elithien had loved and respected. A man that was connected to whatever was happening now. This...*Caedes* was part of the Inner Circle. But I still had no idea who *or what* they were.

"I've been waiting for your call." The voice seemed to resonate through the open space, sending shivers along my spine. My pulse quickened, making me feel out of control.

"I want to meet," Alex mumbled.

But I couldn't focus on them. I had to piece this all together, and as I watched Elithien's dark eyes turn stony with rage, I knew in my heart there was something else going on here. It was too...*simple.*

If it's easy, kid...then look deeper. My father's voice echoed in my mind.

"The Jewel at midnight." The voice on the other end of the phone commanded. "One thing, Alex. Ask Elithien if it's his Prince he misses...or the Princess' bed?"

I flinched at the words. My heart was stabbed, bleeding from the unseen wounds as I swallowed hard. Oh, I understood now. *Now it all made perfect sense.* I couldn't stop the chill from tearing through me, and the pain that followed. Elithien had been in love with her.

Elithien had been in love...with her.

He was a blur of speed, midnight eyes wide, fangs bared, his face a mask of savage rage as he lunged for the phone. "I'll fucking *kill you!*"

Laughter spilled through the speaker a heartbeat before Elithien crushed it in his hand. Bits of plastic and shattered glass went flying, and I felt like them for the flicker of a second, crushed, and shattered. *Get it together, you're no one special, Ruth.*

"Say goodbye to your Vampire, Ruthy," Alex chuckled. It was his words I heard in my head. His words over and over. *You're not special, Ruth. It's over.* "He's now a walking dead man."

A choked sob tore free. I tried to clamp my lips down, tried to swallow the sound.

Elithien whirled, speared him with a chilling stare, then lunged. Alex was in the air before I knew it, legs dangling, his face turning red with the unmerciful grip around his throat. Harsh breaths punctured Elithien's words. "You think this is a game, mortal? You think this is going to end with you alive? Either way, your life is over..."

He stilled then, and turned his head to stare at the floor. I knew he was aware of me...of my pain, of my presence. He dropped Alex, just let him crash to the floor, his legs buckling under him.

"Let's go," Justice snarled, grabbing him by the collar and yanking him to stand.

"He's dead...*you're all fucking dead.*" Alex's blue eyes blazed with madness.

Heartbreak was one thing. Death, that was as final as it came. *Know your enemy,* Dad always said. *Know him better than he knows himself.* "I want to know everything, Rule." I turned to my Vampire. "And I want to know it now."

There was a wince as Elithien raised his head. "You want to know about Caedes?" There was torment in his eyes and danger on his lips as he lifted his hand toward me. "Then come, I'll tell you all you want to know."

I gave a careful look toward Rule as Hurrow jerked his gaze to Russell. "Unseelie, you're with me."

Russell gave me a thoughtful glance over his shoulder before he left, that smear of blood still on his cheek. I knew my family was dirty, knew there were things I shouldn't ask about. I knew 'deals' and 'handshakes' weren't always in both sides' favor, buy still I'd had to carve out a slice of the business for me, forever turning a blind eye to the terror we caused.

But that was *nothing* compared to this. I followed Elithien as he led me out of the smooth steel door and into the main slaughterhouse once more. There was no touching between us, no comfort, just cold, bitter silence.

*He's going to break my heart here...*the thought ripped through me like his seduction. He was both pleasure and pain, this man...and I had fallen for him deeper than I ever expected.

"You weren't supposed to hear that," he finally murmured, standing there with his back to me. "I apologize."

"You apologize?" I whispered.

I'd never tried to control him...let him do what he wanted to do...touch me the way he wanted to touch me. Let him love me that way, too. That was the way it was between us. He was all hate and fangs and lust. I was nothing in his world, an ember already darkening as I floated away. I'd grow cold without him...*I'd be nothing without the fire.*

"You think I wanted this?" He spoke to the wall. I braced myself for the oncoming pain. "We're all fucking collateral damage, Ruth, we always have been."

Collateral damage...destroyed in the wake of the blast.

Yet right now, *right here,* in this moment, we were still standing.

Know your enemy, the words drove me forward. I reached out and touched his shoulder. He stiffened with the touch, then sagged, head lowering, defeated. "Is he unkillable?" I asked. "If he isn't, then we have a chance. You tell me what to do and I'll do it. But we're fighters, Elithien. You and every Vampire and Unseelie in that room. We aren't here to be *collateral,* we're here to survive. If that cold, fucking river taught me anything, it's that. Find us a way to survive, Elithien. Find us a way to walk away from this alive."

"He thinks I'm a threat for his seat on the Circle." His words stopped me cold. He turned then, and I met the steel of truth in his eyes. "That's what this is about, money, power. *Control.*"

"And the Princess?" I whispered. "Was that about control?"

He flinched at her title. "No. That wasn't."

My breath caught in my chest. I wailed inside for those crushing words...*I loved her...still love her.* No matter the circumstances, I couldn't help but feel that flash of agony tear through my chest.

"But she is in the past, Ruth." He came forward, but he never touched me. Instead, his fingers trembled at his sides. Chest to chest...I stared into his eyes.

These Immortal creatures woke something inside me. A beast of my own. It was that beast that rose to the surface. That beast that wanted to bite, and mark, and fuck, to stake her claim. That beast that ached with savage purpose. I was powerless here...and so was he. There was only one way I could give him that power back. Only one way I knew how. "How long until you have to leave?" I asked.

The glint in his eye shone for a very different reason now. "You want to do this here?" His voice deepened. "In this stench of blood and death?"

My pulse sped as he stepped closer. I straightened my spine, flinching as he grasped my hips with both hands. "Yes," I answered.

I didn't care where we were. All I saw was him. His pain. His need.

Energy hummed through my body, making me flinch as he slowly sank to his knees. He lifted one foot and removed my boot, followed by the other, working without a sound.

My jeans were gone in an instant, sliding down my thighs, leaving me in a black lace thong and my blouse. The cool touch of his fingers warmed against my skin. But it was the look in his eyes that made me shiver with anticipation. Cold. *Carnal.*

His fangs shone in the dim light as he smiled. It was a wicked smile...*a knowing smile.* "If you could see yourself right now." His thumbs slipped under the thin band at my hips. Lace rolled as he slowly dragged them lower. "I didn't bring the rope." His gaze was riveted between my thighs. I shifted, opening my stance, as he slipped one leg of my panties free, then the other.

"You're going to ruin them, aren't you?"

He met my gaze, delight sparkling like a star in the night. "I sure fucking hope so."

It'd become a thing with these Vampires. The sheer fabric of my underwear torn, shredded by fingers and fangs, left sodden with the musky remnants of our desire. It was going to cost them a small fortune to keep me supplied with underwear...*however long that lasted.*

He lifted his hand, fingers sweeping up the inside of my thigh until he drew a touch along my crease. A sound rumbled in the back of his throat, deadly...*inviting,* as the steel door opened behind us and Rule stepped out.

"Hurrow wants to go over—"

"Not now." His fingers pushed inwards to the first knuckle, his gaze fixed on mine.

"But he—"

Elithien snapped his gaze toward him, lips curled, fangs bared. "I said *not now.*"

Only then did the Vampire look down to where his Alpha knelt, fingers driving into the center of me, working my clit with the brush of his thumb.

"Her panties," Elithien growled, and tossed them to Rule. "Wind them around her wrists."

The Vampire's eyes widened. He looked my way, the words, *are you sure?* all over his face. But I was already lifting my hands, wrists pressed together, as Elithien's fingers slipped deeper, tearing a shudder of desire through me.

Blood. Death. All around me—and sex, pure, animalistic sex. I looked down at him...at this *monster* with his slick fingers working deeper. Elastic bit into my wrists as Rule reached upwards, grabbing one of the hooks from above, and slipped the middle of my panties over the end.

"Not quite satin sheets and a soft bed." Elithien rose slowly, sleek muscles rippling as he lifted his hands and worked the buttons of his shirt. "But it'll do for tonight."

"You *will* come back to me." I demanded. "You will take care of business, then you'll take care of me."

He just chuckled and lowered his hands to the buckle of his belt.

"I think he likes you being demanding," Rule whispered, taking his time unbuttoning my blouse. "He likes it when you show some teeth."

I smiled right back at Elithien. It was a sinister smile, tinged with my own kind of savagery. "You forget who I am."

"Never." The smile slipped as pure devotion shone in his gaze. "You just forgot who *you* were...welcome back, *my* Ruthless."

With a surge, he gripped my waist and lifted. I clung to the steel hook above my head and wrapped my legs around his waist. Rule spread out his fingers and cupped my breast, moving behind me. But all I saw was my Alpha. All I felt was the brutal thrust as he plunged deep.

I closed my eyes, focused on the perfect pain. "You will come back for me," I growled. "You will take care of your fucking business and come back."

White fangs shone as he gripped my hips and thrust hilt-deep, slamming all the way home. I opened my eyes to hardness...to driven, lethal focus.

"Do you hear me, Vampire?" I commanded, my tone every bit as threatening as his gaze.

He didn't answer. But the feral curl of his lips said all I needed to know. He moved closer, wrapped his arms around me, and buried his face in my neck.

"Do it."

His breaths were hard and heavy, cock driving higher...*higher*, taking me to that peak once more. I bucked my hips, driving harder and harder against him. *"Fucking do it!"*

With a savage roar, he jerked his head backwards, and struck.

I clung onto that hook, riding his release on the wave of my own as he sucked at my neck. Waves of delirium crashed against my shore. Warmth spilled from me between my thighs and at my neck until, with utmost care, Elithien licked the bite mark and pulled away.

I clenched when he slipped from me, and helped ease my feet to the floor. Still I shook there, blouse gaping, breast peeking out of the cup of my bra. I could still feel him wet between my thighs, already feel the loss of him.

He met my gaze, taking in the fire of my hunger, then lowered his gaze, sweeping down my body to linger between my thighs. "Thank you," he sighed, and lifted his focus once more. "For reminding me what I have to lose."

"And gain," I promised.

There was a smile before he glanced at Rule. "You'll take care of her the entire time. I want you at her side, you and the Unseelie. She goes nowhere without you."

Rule just lifted his hand and turned my head, staring into my eyes. "Hear that, Princess? This ass is mine."

I'd never seen someone so damn happy about the prospect. I remembered our last time together, my hand on the roof of the car, his fangs at my core as I bucked against his mouth. Jesus, if I wasn't turned on again! He knew it, too. The curl of his lips in a knowing smile promising so much more.

"Now," Elithien murmured, the coldness slipping into his tone once more. "I have a meeting to attend. I want you somewhere safe. Not here. It's too far away."

I knew the city. I knew the Jewel. Bright lights and wide-open streets. At midnight, it'd be bustling with late night dinners and the throbbing beat of Crown's nightclubs. All of it not too far away from the heart of the city. *My heart.* "My building." I met his gaze. "Assuming I can still get in."

Darkness sparkled as he gave a nod. "Yes, close enough, and yet secure." He glanced at Rule, giving unspoken commands before leaning close to kiss me. "Stay close to them, my Ruthless."

He left me then, with the smell of desire mingling with the smell of death.

I wondered if this would be my new perfume. If blood-lust and slaughter were my new Chanel No. 5? Rule reached up, his fingers grazing down my thumb, but made no move to untie me. I turned to the Vampire, desperate for the truth. "Will Caedes kill him?"

That cocky glint dulled in his eyes. "No, not yet. He'll torture him, though bring out the darkness...it's what Immortals like Caedes do best." He lifted the elastic of my thong and pulled it from the steel hook.

Gone was the charged excitement fueled by lust. It had turned to something harder, something *deeper*. I needed answers. Rule stared at my panties as he circled in front of me and kneeled. "The Inner Circle, what can you tell me about it?"

He let out a chuckle. Somehow, I didn't think it was because the question was funny. "Careful, Ruth. There are monsters you want to tangle with...and one's you run away from in terror."

"Which one are you?"

He lifted his head, his perfect lips curled in a smile revealing the tips of his white fangs. "It depends who it is."

God, he was the perfect predator, midnight tousled hair, pale skin, and perfect lips. He had a body to die for, muscled and taut...a body built for fighting...and fucking. *I'm gonna make it my life's goddamn purpose to fuck you senseless every opportunity I get.* His words returned to me.

"Why me?" The words slipped free as I lifted one leg for him to slide my panties on.

"Princess, if I have to answer that, then you wouldn't believe me even if I told you." My jeans were next, then my boots. I fumbled with my zipper as he rose. "You are every bit as worthy as anyone else. You are the one we want...the one we'll protect...*the one we claim.*"

My heart thundered as a muffled bark of anger echoed from inside the steel room.

"We'd better save them from themselves," Rule suggested, his finger grazing my chin before he turned my head toward him. "You think this started for us in the alley? Ruth, you have no idea."

He leaned forward then, kissing me softly before he strode away.

I was stunned by his words. My thoughts were slow to process, dissolving me molecule by molecule as I was taken back to that alley, to the cold bricks against my back and the feel of

Elithien's fingers at my temple...*More,* my own desperation filled my head. I'd wanted him, *ached* for him.

The stranger in the shadows.

My very own mafia monster.

What did Rule mean, it didn't start in the alley? That was the first time I'd met them...

I was sure of it...

Chapter Fourteen

They were at each other's throats. Fighting. Cursing. Glaring at each other from across the space in the slaughterhouse. It was all a bad idea, Hurrow snarled. *Very bad,* Justice added. Elithien was to meet with that *Caedes* in a crowded room at the Jewel, his second Hurrow, and protector, Justice, at his side, leaving Rule, Russell, and me hiding with Alexander in the empty Costello building no more than three blocks away in the heart of the city.

I didn't like it. None of us did. But the Wolves weren't answering their phones and the Fae were 'mysteriously' busy. I was starting to understand the players now, picking up on bits of information.

The Inner Circle consisted of the Immortal ones, representatives of their lines. Powerful and controlling. There was the Outer Circle, those with smaller bloodlines and claims to the bounty cells like the one across the river afforded them. But the main players, the ones who had the biggest stake of all...*they* were the Inner Circle; Vampire, Wolf, Fae. The three competing Immortal creatures, all just as savage as each other... who controlled the bigger cut of the fortune that flowed like a vein to fill their greed.

I stood back, watching them, as drops of information slipped into their rage.

In the end, Elithien won. He was the one Caedes wanted. He was the one who'd find out what the other Immortals of the Inner Circle knew about the betrayal of Alliard. He'd get it, one way or another.

He didn't want to involve *'the Breeds'* any more than they were already. Something about them fighting their own battle. My mind slipped to that night in the warehouse. That night where my past and present had collided. We all had our battles. I turned my head, seeing the smug asshole sitting there, still pale and shaken, but his eyes alight as he watched them snarl and fight amongst themselves.

God, I couldn't remember what I'd seen in him. How fucking stupid and naive I'd been. Revulsion filed me as I pushed off the counter. "I'm going to get a shower."

"Not on your own," Russell protested, then winced.

"The fucking *hell you are, Unseelie,*" Justice snapped. Yes, the air in the slaughterhouse was just ripe for a fucking war. "If anyone's going to watch her back in the fucking shower, it'll be me."

I glanced at Russell, who took a step forward, and glared. "You're starting to piss me off, Vampire. I'd be careful if I were you, *real fucking careful.*"

"Yeah?" Justice snarled, meeting him midway across the room. "Just because you fucking lust after her like a goddamn rutting dog, doesn't give you *any* fucking right to her at all."

The hairs rose on the back of my neck as the temperature in the room plummeted.

"Justice—" I started.

"At least I'm there when she needs me," Russell growled. "Can't say the same for you..."

Teeth were bared, and hate raged.

"Shut him the fuck up, Elithien," Justice warned. "Or I'll take the Unseelie outside and we'll be looking for a new bodyguard."

"Fuck that," Russell sneered, his lips curled into a venomous smile. "Let him take me...I'd like to see him try."

"Enough," Elithien yelled. "You think we have time for this bullshit?"

"I see the way you look at her," Russell barked, his lips curled in a cruel sneer. "Looks like she won't fuck you, either."

Justice moved fast. One minute, he wasn't within swinging distance and the next, his fist was tangled in Russell's shirt.

Darkness pressed in all around us, dulling the overhead lights until we stood in the fading glare of a dying bulb as my Vampire protector leaned in close. "At least I know what she looks like when she fucks, which is more than you can say."

"She's going to be mine, bloodsucker." Russell leaned closer, and the room darkened just that little bit more. "One way or another. Learn to deal with it, or *fucking leave.*"

"Stop," I pleaded. Pain roared through my chest. *"Just stop it!"* My love was killing us...a slow, agonizing death. "You know what?" I snapped. "Fuck you all. I'll shower on my own."

I turned then, strode toward my duffel bag, and lifted it from the old sofa in the darkness. "And Russell...*turn on the goddamn lights.*"

The room brightened in an instant. I knew there had to be a block of showers and I was in no mood to listen to the petty squabbles of horny men. I found it, deep in the original part of the building. The lights flickered before they stayed on. Footsteps echoed behind me. I didn't even bother to turn as I stepped inside.

"The Unseelie's getting unpredictable," Hurrow warned. "Unstable. His powers eclipse his control. *That's a problem.*"

I froze at the sound of his voice, then dropped my bag to the row of seats between the banks of lockers. "The *Unseelie* has been through an unbelievable life-changing experience, so cut him some fucking slack."

I tracked the slow steps Hurrow made, my hand delving into the open zipper of my bag for underwear, jeans, and a shirt. A chest of steel pressed against my back. He was hard, predatory...riding the killing edge. I stilled, and let myself press back against him.

He lifted his hand as I dropped my head to the side. His fingers grazed along my neck, making my body tremble.

"Shower, Ruth," he murmured. "Dress warm, it's going to be a cold, endless fucking night. I'll keep watch for you."

I pulled the Sig from the small of my back, then unbuttoned my shirt and kicked off my boots before stepping away. His gaze was like a phantom touch along my body as I undressed. Smooth, seductive...trailing down my spine to the curve of my ass. He liked my ass, liked watching it...liked touching it.

A *clink* rang out in the dressing room, the sparkle of gold flashed against the concert floor.

"What the hell is that?" Hurrow moved fast, bending to grasp the ring from the floor and lift it into the dull overhead light. The ruby barely glowed, turning black in the dim light as he turned the heavy thing in his grip. "Why on earth do you have your father's ring in your pocket?"

I flinched at the question. "How the hell did you know it was my father's?"

There was something about the ring. Sparks collided in his eyes as that ominous chill swept through me once more. I knew that cold...had sensed it crawling under my skin as I'd sat on the bed in Russell's bedroom. I jerked my gaze to the corners of the room as my heart pounded.

"What is it?" he asked, following my gaze.

Panic punched higher as I shook my head. My throat tightened, strangled by an unseen fist. I couldn't get the words out.

He jerked that unflinching stare back to me, meeting my gaze. "Where did you get this, Ruth?"

I waited for that hooded figure to come...as I finally gave in. "It was on my desk in my office."

He was silent, brooding, *thinking*. "You didn't think to tell us about it earlier?"

"You mean when you were asleep and I was trying not to think about being five steps away from the man who'd tried to kill me? No. I didn't."

I grabbed my bodywash and headed for the showers. Fuck the ring and his pissy inquisition. I had enough shit to deal with… but even as the sting of my anger faded, I knew it was a lie.

The ring worried me.

It wore at me.

That damn barb. I still felt the damn ache from the sting on my finger. I knew there was hot water plumbed in from testing the temperature at the sink in the half-finished kitchen. I wasn't disappointed. Heat rushed through the spray. I stepped under, lifting my gaze to Hurrow as I turned.

My nipples hardened as I washed, soapsuds racing down my body. I chased them with my hands, cupping my breasts, then dipped lower to my stomach. That predatory gaze followed, even if he was still pissy. I had no doubt he was listening for a pin to drop in the entire building.

Heat burned in his gaze when I turned, switched off the spray, grabbed a towel, and hurried to dry. It was cold in here amongst the concrete and steel. I dressed, grabbed my things, and headed for the door, stopping when Hurrow gripped the other side of the doorway, blocking my view.

"Tomorrow, Ruth. When this is all over…you and I are going to take a stroll down memory lane."

The image he pushed inside my head was us. My hands against the wall outside the nightclub while he fucked me from behind. I'd been waiting for it, for him to come to me. My pulse raced at the thought. Hurrow wasn't like the others, he was a little colder...a little harder. He liked to dominate a little more...the only difference was, this time, I liked it. "It's about time, Vampire," I replied. "I was starting to think you didn't want me anymore."

The bark of laughter was sudden. "Woman, you have no idea how far from the truth that statement is."

I ducked under his hand, leaving him behind. "Then I'll enjoy it when you prove me wrong."

They were silent when I pushed through the steel door. Justice brooded on one side of the room, tucking a Glock into his shoulder holster strapped across a neatly pressed midnight blue shirt. He lifted his gaze and looked at me, that aching desperation lingering in his eyes.

He wanted me...*they both fucking wanted me.* And I wanted them just as badly.

But I was starting to understand that Vampires were a breed of their own...*and they didn't play well with others.*

They kept themselves busy while Elithien paced. I went to him, desperate to ease his pain. He cupped my cheek, those dark eyes boring into mine as he spoke. "Whatever happens tonight, I need you to promise you'll stay with Russell and Rule."

Caedes won't kill him...I clung to those words, swallowed hard, and nodded, meeting his gaze. I hated him going out there without me...hated that I felt so fucking *mortal.* "You tell that...*motherfucker*," I whisper-snarled, pretending to fix his collar. "If he lays one hand on you, I'm coming for him."

He smiled then, those perfect lips flattening against his fangs. "My Ruthless."

"E," Justice growled as he stepped toward me.

My heart thundered as he turned his head.

"Time to go," my protector declared as he grabbed me, yanking me hard against his body. "But not before one last kiss."

His lips met mine, taking, tasting. His fangs scraped the inside of my lip, making me melt with the memory of him. He was all aggression...all cold steel wrapped up in the body of a giant. My hands went behind him, gripping him, *pulling him.* Heat flared between us, coupling with the pounding of my heart before he broke the kiss and pulled away. "When I get back, Ruth, I better find you naked."

There was a sly glance toward Russell, followed by a smirk, before the Vampire pulled away.

Don't go! The words were a gunshot in my head. But there was no waiting, not for someone like Elithien. In an instant, I was back in my family's world...where you didn't ask questions... and you didn't look weak. Not in front of your family...and *especially* not in front of your enemy.

I'd learned that the hard way.

Justice met my gaze again as Hurrow shrugged on his coat and followed. But the look from the protector said it all...*don't worry, he's safe with me.*

"Ruth," Rule muttered behind me. I hadn't even heard him moving.

"Walk," Russell snarled.

Alex stumbled forward, grinning as he went.

"I think I liked you better when I couldn't see your face," I snapped, grasped my thick jacket, and followed. "You *fucking disgust me.*"

"Didn't disgust you when I was—" His head cracked backward as his body slammed forward, careening into the steel door with a *thud.*

"Whoops," Russell exclaimed, the heavy thud of his boots echoing.

Alex staggered, worked his jaw, and said nothing as we made our way out of the slaughterhouse into the pitch-black night.

It was early, by the shiver that coursed across my skin and the silver moonlight, I guessed ten o'clock. The Explorer blinked as the doors unlocked. Alex was shoved into the back seat.

"Up front, Ruth," Rule directed. "I'm not having you sitting next to that piece of shit."

I climbed in as Russell slid behind the wheel. One look at me, then he started the engine and backed out of the space. It was all so quiet, so very fucking quiet. There was a different energy around us, impending, toxic, and silent.

The growl of the engine and the harsh, raspy breaths from Alex filled the space. Elithien was headed to this meeting without the one thing Caedes wanted. Maybe that'd been Caedes' plan all along? I tried not to think of all the ways this could go wrong and stared out the window as we left the slaughterhouse and headed back to the glittering lights of the city.

We were hungry tonight. That predatory feeling grew stronger the closer we came to the towering high-rises. My senses were on fire, nerves jumpy, as the sudden piercing wail of a siren came from behind us. Red and blue flashed in an instant, slamming my heart against my ribs, until the ambulance pulled out around us and roared past.

My nails had pierced the stitching of the armrest. My breaths were strangled and hard, like a hard lump in the center of my chest. All I could hear was that gasping wheeze from me as the stunning glint of the Costello Corporation building came into view.

I'd loved it once. Loved the thrum and the pretense. But the heartbeat that had brought the company to life was no longer there. It had died on the day my father died. Still, I held onto hope that one day I'd rebuild...one day I'd take back what was mine.

"Never." The throaty groan came from the back seat.

"What the fuck did you say, dead man?" Rule snarled, narrowing in on the piece of shit behind me.

But Alex was silent now. Still, that word crawled under my skin, wearing away at the walls of my heart. *Never.* That word wanted in...wanted to take up space inside my mind and give birth to a whole new set of demons. I had enough demons already. I didn't need any more.

I flexed my nails and clung to the hope instead of the stitching of Elithien's car, and ground my teeth as we grew closer, winding our way through the city streets until my building towered over us.

"You think the code will still work for the parking garage?" Russell wondered, glancing my way.

"It's worth a try."

There was a snigger from the back seat before a hiss of movement came. A *thud* was followed by a low groan.

"Keep it up," Rule warned. "You have to be alive, that's all. There's plenty of gray area there. Remember that."

We nosed into the entrance, pulling up at the lowered boom gate. It wasn't a surprise that the keypad sensor glowed red. But that wasn't the only thing stopping us. "Russell." I jerked my gaze to the thick chain wrapped around the end of the boom gate, holding it in place. "We'll have to park out front."

"I don't think so," my bodyguard growled as he opened the driver's door and climbed out.

Headlights splashed against his powerful body as he strode toward the chain and the post. Darkness pushed in all around him, dulling the headlights, leaving him in the shadows.

The Unseelie's getting unpredictable. Hurrow's words floated to the surface of my mind. The shadows moved differently around him now. They clung to him like a forlorn lover, desperate to taste...to touch...*to have him touch them.* My breath caught in my chest as he moved, sleek and powerful, predatory in his own way. A surge of pride tore through me. Here was a man who could have any woman he wanted.

Here was a man standing against four powerful Vampires.

A man not afraid to put everything on the line...for me.

Pride turned into something darker, something savage and possessive. He jerked the chain, snapping it from the post, and cast it aside before he turned his head. Darkness shimmered in his gaze as he found me through the windshield. Ebony black. A starless midnight sky. Drawing me in as he held my gaze for a second.

It was as though he felt that hunger awaken. A beast in reaction to his beast. I swallowed hard and shifted my gaze to the empty parking garage. Heat rose to my cheeks, making my heart thunder. I tracked his movement as he strode back to the open driver's door and climbed in.

We said nothing as he pulled the Explorer around to park near the elevators. We'd agreed the top corporate offices were as safe a place as any as long as my code still worked.

"Wait here while I check," Russell ordered, glancing over his shoulder at Alex.

There was no reaction, just a guttural draw of breath before my bodyguard climbed out once more.

"It'll all be over soon," Rule reassured.

I wanted this to be done...I wanted it *all* to be done. The truth waited for me. Truth about my mother...*and my father.* The truth about my company and all the dirty little secrets my family'd hidden.

It was time to kick that nest of vipers...and see what came out.

The elevator doors opened in front of Russell. He was striding back to us in a heartbeat. Rule shoved his door open and climbed out. His phone gave a beep, drawing my gaze. One glance at the screen, and Rule jerked his gaze toward Russell and gave a nod.

"Out," my bodyguard snarled. "Make one fucking move, and I'll end you."

I followed them, climbing out of the car and walking to the elevator. Russell walked beside me, a wall of Unseelie muscle between me and the man I'd once loved. The elevator doors opened again, and we strode through. Distorted images reflected back at me from the stainless steel walls. Yet I couldn't care about them now, could only close my eyes as that heady feeling carried me higher...and higher...rising above *everything*.

I was finally home.

Chapter Fifteen

ELITHIEN

I stepped out of the Explorer, buttoned my jacket, and scanned the lingering crowd waiting to get inside the Jewel. Finery and diamonds sparkled. Women and men walked arm in arm, dressed in tuxedos and floor-length shimmering gowns. Ruth's world. That's what this was. *Once was, at least—until I came into her life.*

"We'll take a look around," Hurrow declared, his hard gaze searching.

I gave a nod, shifting my focus to the alley. The memory of her rose like a predator lying in wait. I knew that predator. *I'd fucked that predator...*still had the taste of that predator on my tongue. Still, it wasn't enough.

It wasn't nearly enough.

Her blood raced through me, dark, exciting, blooming like a savage rose inside me thorns and all, as I tore my gaze from the trash-filled alley. Soon. Soon I'd have the rest of her life to ease my hunger. My cock twitched, thickening with the thought. Who the fuck was I kidding? I'd never ease. Never fill. Never grow fucking tired.

She made me violent with lust, that one.

And sometimes just plain fucking violent.

Voices crowded my ears, making me wince. Laughter. Mortals. Too many sights and sounds. I wanted to leave this place. Go back across the river. Back with the beasts.

"All clear." Hurrow was suddenly at my side. "He's not here."

But there was something bugging him. He cocked his head and turned to watch them as they climbed the stairs and disappeared through the glass doors. He was on edge. *We all were.*

He shifted his body, turning to a couple as they exited.

"What is it?" I asked.

Silence greeted me as the couple suddenly stopped two steps outside the bar. Confusion crowded their expressions. There was a flicker of...*was that pain?*

"Let's go back inside," the male murmured. His companion just nodded and turned as they both hurried inside.

Justice strode toward us, coming from the opposite side of the building. "Two blocks are clean, I searched every car and every alleyway," he growled, then stilled, narrowing in on Hurrow's expression before he followed my second's gaze. "What is it?"

"Not sure," Hurrow muttered, and stepped forward.

I followed as he strode toward the steps of the Jewel and climbed. Justice closed in behind me. There was something *off* about the place, something I couldn't quite put my finger on. Hurrow pushed ahead, hand rising to his chest, flingers sliding under his jacket to the shoulder holster.

My gut tightened. My senses were on fire.

There was no laughter from the Jewel. No roar of those inside. If I knew anything about mortals...it was that they were fucking noisy. Laughing. Crying. *Screaming*. But as I stepped up to the glass door and stepped inside, I heard none of that.

The hairs at the nape of my neck rose as I followed Hurrow inside and checked my watch. Fifteen minutes until Caedes was due to arrive. Plenty of time. An older couple strode toward us as we headed toward the open doors inside the foyer. I watched them as they came to a stop inside the door.

"Wait..." the elegant gray-haired woman murmured, and stopped. Confusion flared on her face for a second before she murmured, "I'm not ready to go yet."

"Are you sure?" Her date moved closer. "We can—"

"I'm sure." She turned to him, catching my gaze. "I'm sure I don't want to go."

"What the fuck?" Justice muttered behind me.

He saw it, too...*we all saw it.*

"Some kind of magic," Hurrow scowled. "Fae magic."

I inhaled deeply, catching the faint scent of something malicious and malevolent. Fae. The place fucking reeked of them.

"Shrike's stench is all over this place," Hurrow curled his lip. "No wonder the place is packed."

I had to wonder what the price was for money. Blood? Sacrifice? The kind of magic the Fae dealt in was *never* worth the price. And yet poor mortal saps like the guys who owned the Jewel thought it was worth it. Money forever, more money than you can spend. But money is worthless...

Love. Now that's what I'd sell a piece of my soul for.

Endless love.

To be with Ruth forever. To be...her Immortal.

I glanced at Hurrow. *One* of her Immortals, anyway.

I strode toward the door of the restaurant as Hurrow, slowed by the maitre d', curled his lips, and bared his teeth. The poor mortal flinched, nodded, and lifted his hand, leaving the wait stand behind.

I was worried bringing Ruth into the coven. Worried that four of us would be too much...*Vampire* for her. But then the woman had to go and get herself an Unseelie, dooming herself for the rest of eternity to jealously and possessiveness.

Still, we need the Unseelie, needed him now more than ever.

I didn't like that feeling...*needing someone.*

Glasses clinked. Low voices murmured. I picked up on normal, boring conversations, sex, money, children, more sex. On and on it went as we walked through the front bar area to the more exclusive section in the back.

A whisper of fear skated across my mind. To bring me back here was an outright threat. *I know what she means to you,* is what this said. That beast inside rattled its cage. *Easy,* I calmed.

"I want to know everything about him," I murmured softly. "Every flinch, every fucking whisper of his mind."

Hurrow gave a small nod in response as the waiter stopped at the rear door and ushered us through. In a heartbeat, I was back here, in this time and this place. Stepping inside and watching as Denzel Costello sat in the darkened corner of the room... waiting for me. Was it our second meeting...or our fourth? I tried to remember. The fourth. Definitely the fourth.

He'd had what I wanted...and I was more than patient enough to play the game.

She's too much fire for you, Vampire. You'll only get yourself burned...

Those words echoed inside me as I scanned the elite. Men and women, bored, confused expressions plastered all over their faces. That chill grew colder at my back, snaking its way through my belly. Something didn't *feel* right. Maybe we should...

"Mr. Venadi." The waitress stepped out from the darkness. "We've been waiting for you. If you'll follow me."

She led us to a table in the middle of the room. Soft lights spilled over the round table. One chair on either side. I checked my watch. Five minutes. I calmed the pang in my chest, taking the chair she offered.

"Can I get you something from the bar?"

"Scotch," I answered. "Neat, top shelf."

One nod and she was gone, as were Hurrow and Justice, sinking into the shadows. My phone beeped, drawing my focus. I wrenched it free, and stared at the screen.

All clear.

Caller Unknown

I tucked the cell phone back into my pocket as the waitress returned, slid a neat white coaster onto the table, and followed it with a glass of amber liquid. I watched those around me, and saw the confusion in their eyes, the constant reaching under their jackets before they pulled their hands sharply away. I saw the women reaching for their purses on the table before deciding against it and sliding their hands to their laps.

I saw magic. A whole lot of fucking magic. But none of it made sense. You wanted a compulsion spell to sweep across every part of the city and invite them to your establishment, where you make them eat and drink. You make them laugh and spend. You make them *feel.* What were they feeling now? Constrained. Fearful. *Confusion?* "I don't like this."

Hurrow's rage blasted through my mind a second before I was slammed with a wave of power. One so unmerciful, it made me catch my breath. Abominable and wretched, the stench of something fetid preceded him as the governor of the Vampires...the Lord Master, stepped into the Jewel.

They all felt it. Every mortal...and Immortal, and there were a few.

They flinched, freezing.

There was a predator in their midst. One unlike they'd ever felt before.

One more powerful than I was...*but not as savage...*that, *I had in spades.*

Sly glances turned toward me, eyes widened in response. I met their gazes and gave a slow nod. *Easy,* my mind whispered as I readied for the assault. But as the door to the exclusive half of the Jewel opened, I felt the wave of power from the Immortal diminish.

He was masking himself, blending in with his environment...*a foul, merciless, chameleon.* Brown eyes flashed to mine as he neared. He looked just the same as I remembered. Tall, slim. *Acidic.* His pinched nose twitched when he caught my scent. I unnerved him. *Good.* I glanced at his companion and stiffened. *Unseelie?* Tall, powerful...and not one of ours.

I swallowed my surprise and made myself relax, lazy...a small smirk as I reached for my glass and lifted the rim to my lips.

"Elithien."

"Caedes." I forced his name through clenched teeth and motioned to the chair. "Only one chair, I'm afraid."

His eyes glittered as he smiled. "We won't be staying long. The mortal..." One scan behind me and that sparkle in his eyes dulled. "He's not dead, so where is he?"

"Safe," I answered, and motioned to the chair once more. He was on *my* turf here. "I see you brought...*a friend.*" I met the Unseelie's gaze.

Thickset, bestial. Runes were inked along the corded muscles of his arms, and even under the long-sleeved black shirt, they glowed that deep emerald green of their world. He reeked of war, this one. Savage, unending war. I wondered from under which rock this one had crawled? And I wondered what Shrike would do about the invasion of his turf? Flip his shit, I imagined. Maybe the Fae would back me now?

"You think I came here for you? You think too highly of yourself, Elithien," Caedes snarled, still standing on the other side of the table. The air shimmered around him, something darker danced around him.

"Then what? You came for the fucking mortal...is he worth that much to you?" I emptied my glass and lifted it, catching the bartender's gaze. The whole room seemed to quake, like a foreshock to the grand finale.

There was a curl of his lips, a sneer, and I met the bloodlust in his eyes with the full force of my own rage. Death. That's all that lingered between us...the Princess, the Prince. His. *Mine.* "Why are you really here, Caedes?"

"For the mortal...of course," he answered, taking a look around the room.

Something was happening here...something unseen. Something that crawled along my skin, making me freeze with chilling clarity.

"One last time, mercenary," Caedes warned in a whisper. "Give me the mortal. His soul belongs to me."

He lifted a hand and, in an instant, those runes blazed under the Fae's shirt. Everyone in the exclusive part of the Jewel rose then. Every man. Every woman.

I jerked my gaze toward the door to the front section as it was thrown wide. They spilled into the space, pushed and shoved. They were no longer mortals...*they were controlled.*

Glazed eyes stared back at me from every mortal as they pushed toward me. I was the only one sitting...the eye of the storm. I smothered a flinch and lifted my gaze to Caedes as the first glint of a gun shone under the soft overhead lights. It was followed by another...then another. Until the room gleamed with a circle of steel.

E? Hurrow pressed inside my head. I slid the empty glass from my fingers as the Fae took a step backwards. Runes glowed...his lips curled. I knew what the compulsion spell was now...and it had nothing to do with greed *and everything to do with revenge.*

"Is he worth that much to you?"

"The lawyer?" Caedes stepped backwards as that darkness around him glowed emerald green. "I couldn't care less if he lives or dies. It's not him I'm after."

"Then who the fuck is it?" I pushed upwards, standing on my side of the table.

Movement all around me, flanking me on both sides as Hurrow and Justice came closer. But that Unseelie glow pulsed and throbbed around the Vampire, coming from the runes glowing on the other's arms. The bastard was using the Unseelie.

"WHO THE FUCK IS IT?" I roared as that green pulsed.

The answer hit me harder than any bullet could. I saw it all...

It wasn't the lawyer he was after, at all.

It was Ruth.

"No!" I roared and lunged, but the second I moved, he was gone...as though he hadn't been here at all.

"E!" Hurrow bellowed.

The first shot tore through the air with a *crack!* Followed by another, then another. I flinched and ducked. Hurrow went down.

Blood bloomed against his crisp white shirt. Justice was a blur of brute strength, opening his arms wide, shielding me as the room exploded with the deafening roar of gunfire.

Chapter Sixteen

"STOP STARING AT HER. NOT GONNA TELL YOU AGAIN," Russell warned, and shifted that infernal Unseelie gaze to him. He didn't just meet Alex's stare...but towered over him, making the pathetic excuse for a man cower like the sack of shit he was.

Alex turned away as the elevator came to an abrupt stop at the top. But the second we were out, I felt that sickening touch on the back of my neck return. I reached up, rubbed the knotted muscle at my nape, and kept on walking. I wanted him gone... gone from this building and gone from my life. Snuffed out...I'd do it myself, if I could. One shot was all it'd take.

I worked my shoulders as I walked, boots thudding on the glistening tiles. There was a hunger growing inside me. A darkness, where a second ago there'd been fear. Caged. *Desperate.* That feeling crept over my skin, whispering lies as it went. *Something's happened. Something bad.*

I sucked in a hard breath and strode to the keypad on the front doors, pressing my thumb to the scanner. The red light blinked green. Of course they hadn't removed my details from the system...because, for all intents and purposes, *I was fucking dead!*

"Hey," Rule said as he reached out and replaced my fingers with his as he rubbed my neck. "You okay?"

I flinched, forced a smile, and nodded. "Yeah. Just, demons, you know?"

His dark eyes sparkled, whispering, *this will all be over soon. Hang in there.*

I pushed the door wide and strode into the darkness, treading on pages tossed on the carpeted floor. I flicked on lights, just enough to brighten the space, and saw the carnage of what was left of my company.

There was nothing. Not a computer...not even a fucking chair. Pain plunged deep, tearing a jagged line across my chest, flaying me open...and laying me bare. It was me who turned to him now. Me who bored my animalistic hatred into his stare. Hard breaths consumed me.

All my life.

All my father's fucking life.

Gone.

Russell moved around the floor, checking rooms behind closed doors as Rule stepped away to stare out into the city.

"Won't be long now," Alex's words were a whisper.

Rule and Russell snapped their gazes toward him, but it was me he stared at...

"I told you before," Russell growled, locking on...striding across the floor like a missile toward Alex as a tremor tore through the building. The floor shuddered. The city lights blurred through the floor-to-ceiling windows. I stumbled sideways and threw out my hand as a deep green glow came from a corner of the room.

A man followed, glowing, hulking. The green glow seemed to pulse from what looked like a line of markings along his arms as he lifted his hand. Dark Unseelie eyes met mine before he smiled. Alex lunged a second before a *boom* cracked through the air. Russell went flying backwards, a missile of muscle and rage, until he hit the office partition with a *crunch*.

I jerked my gaze toward Rule as a figure strode from the other end of the space...one that led to the outside of the building. *That can't be right.* He was tall, graceful. Images flashed inside my head, morphing with one another *here...Russell's bedroom... the alleyway* as I huddled against the Explorer, and those flashing lights...*those sickening flashing lights beat at the darkness of the alley.*

It was him. My stranger in the dark...here, coming toward me

"No," I cried out as Alex grabbed me and swung.

His hand was around my throat in an instant. The past collided with the present as I was dragged backwards, his snarl in my ear. "I fucking warned you, Ruth. But you didn't listen."

I screamed then, punching my boots down, driving him backwards faster than he could drag me. Rage erupted, spewing out of me like a volcano. I kicked and punched, turning in his grip to ram him into the open glass door with a *crack*.

"RUTH! *RUN!*" Rule roared. Alex stumbled and fell as the glass shattered.

Shock filled me. Panic. *Thunderous.* Roaring through my head as I did the only thing I could...*I left them behind.* Footsteps slammed behind me as I tore out of the top floor offices and raced, heading for the stairs.

"Ruth!" Alex roared. *"Ruth, get back here!"*

A sob tore free as I slammed the handle of the stairwell and stumbled into the dim light. Panic made me turn my head at the last second...Alex was wide-eyed, filled with rage. But behind him...*behind him came the monster from the dark.*

He grabbed Alex by the back of his neck and lifted him like he was *nothing* before hurling him through the air. Alex's screams came toward me, tearing through the gap in the stairwell door before it slammed shut with a *clang!*

I ran, gripped the steel banister with trembling hands, and lunged down the stairs. Howls of rage came from above, terrifying howls...howls that shook the building and flickered the lights.

Jagged breaths burned along the back of my throat as I tried the handle on the next level. Locked. Desperation tore from my lips in a bark of rage. I kept running, taking the stairs two and three at a time as the stairwell lights flickered and snuffed out.

Darkness consumed me. Inky black making me fall instead of lunge. I missed a step and rolled my ankle until pain bloomed. Terror and pain.

RUTH! Elithien roared through my mind, making me stumble again in the dark...making me slam my shoulder against something hard, something that bit into my side. I spun, yanked my hand up to kick and punch, and smashed the steel handle of a door.

A handle that gave way before it came to rest. I fumbled, and gripped the handle as the door opened before me. Heavy footsteps thundered as I eased the door open and closed it behind me as the door above slammed shut.

Faint light from the emergency exit sign splashed crimson across my eyes. I stumbled and cried out at the pain in my ankle as I tried to find my bearings. *Hutonstation Lawyers* was still painted on the glass front doors. I stumbled forward, staring into the empty foyer.

The entire building was empty. Floor after floor. Lawyers. Financial Consultants, rooms and rooms of the best now gone. That Unseelie roar came from the stairwell, making me turn and back away.

I wanted to run and hide...I wanted to find somewhere safe. But there *was* nowhere safe. Not from monsters...and not from my past. The stairwell door flung open as I stumbled backwards and in that sickening blood-red glow was Alex. Slick wet shone on the side of his head. He stumbled, and then swayed, narrowing in on me.

"I told you..." he slurred. "Told you what would happen. You didn't believe me."

Boom! The floor shuddered under my feet. Something plunged down out in the darkness. I watched through the window as it fell, then jerked my gaze back to Alex. "You don't want to do this, Alex." I hated the tremble in my voice. "You don't want to—"

The door wrenched open behind him and in spilled the night. Alex was gripped and lifted shoulder high. All I saw were shadows.

"Get down, Ruth." the darkness that was Russell growled.

I dropped instantly, listening to the sickening *snap* of bones before Alex hit the floor...and that's where he stayed.

Hard gasps, a savage bellow of air. That darkness trembled... and shook. It wasn't the man I knew...it wasn't even the kind of Unseelie I knew. Malice spilled from every cell of his body as the beast that was my bodyguard strode forward, bared blackened fangs, and roared.

I threw my hand up as a cry tore free. That same deep green glow pulsed inside him like a heartbeat. But it was darker than the other male and didn't come from any markings. It pulsed from deep inside the pit of his belly. He lunged through the air, unbridled and unforgiving, leaping over me, and hit something hard behind me.

A sickening hiss came from the hard wall he crashed into. The green glow spilled from the darkness, growing brighter and brighter. Terrifying sounds came from them. Unmerciful thuds were followed by howls of agony. I didn't know who was who. I didn't know anything, other than that my heart ripped from my chest at the sound.

Russell...RUSSELL...

"The time has come, Ruth." The cold, menacing voice came from above me.

I flinched, kicked my good foot out, and shoved away as that figure rose above me, the man from the shadows...my unescapable nightmare. I scurried, lower than a cockroach...

then shoved upwards, hobbled, and clenched my fists. "Stay the fuck away from me."

A *boom* ripped through the space as the unleashed savagery behind me took out a wall. Russell rose above the glow of green, lifted the darkened blur of a fist, and roared. The air-splitting howl sent an icy torrent of rage through the air, hitting me like a punch to the chest.

I sprawled forwards, lifting my gaze to the window and the lights sparkling far down below. The blur...the blur from outside the window...*had that been Rule?* Panic filled me.

I spun, pushing a trembling hand behind me as that beast from the shadows came closer.

"You belong to me, Ruth," he commanded, looking at me like I was a *thing*. "You look so much like her. Come to me."

"You f-fucking s-stay right there," I stuttered as my fingers clenched around the grip of my gun and I pulled it free.

He looked at me like he was disappointed. Like I'd fucking *disappointed* him. So I squeezed the trigger. *Boom!* The shot tore free. The bastard barely flinched. His dark eyes glittered with madness. His lips curled, revealing long white fangs.

"You shouldn't have done that." He met my gaze.

I caught motion behind him as the door was opened and a blur of movement came. "Get the fuck away from her, Caedes," Rule gasped, and stumbled toward me.

My heart lunged at the sight. He was hurt...*really hurt*. His arm hung low...too low, and he weaved when he walked. Bones crunched as he stumbled forward and bared his fangs. "You'll have to kill me first."

A sickening hiss followed as the foul creature in front of me spun. "That *can be ARRANGED!*" He boomed.

I squeezed the trigger on instinct, feeling the kick of the gun in my grip. All I saw was Rule...and all I felt was unending hatred. *"Get the fuck away from him!"*

BOOM. BOOM. BOOM.

I squeezed until there was nothing but the buck of the steel. No more...no more. He's not going to hurt them. He's not going to—

The elevator opened with a *ding*...drawing my gaze...and out of the blinding white light of the elevator came Elithien, Hurrow, and Justice...*and they were pissed.*

Blood—I felt the room tilt—all I saw was blood...

Blood on their shredded shirts.

Blood smeared across their faces.

Their fangs were bared, and hands soaked in crimson rose as my Vampires lunged through the air toward us. Justice reached him first, claws slashing the air as he unleashed his rage.

The infernal creature in front of me threw his head backwards, letting out a ferocious sound, and before Justice could collide, he was gone...in an instant.

Russell roared as the consuming darkness lunged forward and spun.

"Where is he?" Justice raged, and whirled, scanning the space. *"WHERE THE FUCK IS HE?"*

I just stood there, gun still in my grip, the *click...click...click* echoing in the space.

"Ruth," Elithien murmured. I flinched at the call of my name. "It's okay now."

But the gun was still in my hand, and my finger was squeezing...*squeezing...squeezing...* Justice stepped closer, his infernal eye glittering with unquenched hunger. "Easy now, my little warrior, easy." He slowly reached up, gripped the gun in my hand. and reached for me.

Until the roar of darkness cut through the space.

I flinched at the sound, and screamed. Russell was a blur. A thunderous, unleashed force that slammed into the walls and ripped the door behind me from its hinges. Wood splintered as Justice left my side and stepped forward.

"Easy now," he called to the infernal midnight beast.

The beast that was my bodyguard...

That darkness seemed to rise with Justice's presence, swelling and consuming until the faint emergency lights were snuffed out, plunging us into pitch blackness.

My heart boomed, and panic punched into my chest.

"You're scaring her, Unseelie," Elithien cautioned.

I tracked the sound, breaths panting, filling my head with the sound.

"Look at her," Elithien insisted. *"Feel her. Taste her fear.* The threat's gone now. You've done your job, soldier." I tracked the sound of his words as he moved. "You've done your job."

Dull red glowed through the suffocating darkness, until slowly, the faint red glow of the emergency lights shone. Still the beast wasn't sated. It snarled and howled. Piercing howls that ripped through my head, making me clap my hands over my ears.

His rage was consuming, lashing and splintering something inside me. Tearing into my heart as it slammed home all the memories we'd had.

Russell, reaching across for me after my father's funeral, clicking the seatbelt home before he drove me out of there, taking me to somewhere special. Somewhere I could be *normal* and drink malted marshmallow milkshakes and laugh way too hard.

Russell, as he reared above me as I cowered against the Explorer...*you're safe, Ruth. You're safe with me.*

Hard breaths. Panicked breaths. Still that unmerciful piercing shriek tore from Russell...*and it* was *Russell...even as a demented, shadowed beast.* I stumbled forward, crying out as agony ripped through my foot...and slowly, I stumbled into the opening.

In the blood red glow of the emergency lights, I saw him, saw him for what he truly was, and it both chilled me to the bone and swelled my heart. He was terrifying. He was beautiful. He was torment. He was mesmerizing. The same deep green glow that came from the other Unseelie before also came from him.

But it was deep inside him. Swirling like waves of hunger in the pit of his belly.

Unblessed, that's what I'd heard Justice call the Fae. Malignant. *Evil.*

I stepped forward, barely feeling the flare of pain now. The man I knew wasn't evil. He was anything but. I lifted my hand, my voice trembling. "You said I was safe with you."

The beast raged and snarled, casting lashings of darkness like a whip to steal the red glow of the lights once more.

Darkness.

Lights.

Darkness.

Lights...

As though the beast couldn't make up his mind. *No.* The thought stilled me as I stared into the pit of madness...*as though the beast and the man were at war.*

A tortured sound came from the swirling blackness. He was forming now, slowly. Arms and legs, his body lashing the air as the beast consumed the space.

"Don't...want to...hurt you." The words were agonized.

Pure agony. Tortured and guttural.

"You won't hurt me," I soothed, and slowly took another step.

The beast threw its head back and roared. The building trembled. City lights shimmered once more as the deafening boom rattled the windows.

"Ruth," Elithien warned.

I could feel them all behind me. Terrified. *Savage with their own rage.* But this was Russell...this was the man who gave his life for mine. This was the man who, against everything, tore himself apart just to be the beast he was—*for me.*

I stepped closer, even as a warning growl from Justice slipped into the air. "Don't..." my protector urged.

But I stepped again, moving closer to the beast. Cold, consuming breaths blew against my face and fluttered my hair. I stood at the edge of the abyss here. One step away from madness. I stared into that hate and rage, and felt nothing but...*love.*

The beast lowered his head, stilling as I flinched with the hard blast of his breath.

"Need...you," he groaned. Those midnight eyes danced with deep Unseelie green.

"What the fuck," Justice barked.

"Need...*something,*" Russell snarled, and stared into my eyes. "I can't stop...*this.*"

My own breaths rose in sympathy. My breasts pressed against my shirt, drawing the beast's gaze lower...*lower,* until a shudder tore free in response.

"He needs me." I breathed.

"The *fuck he does,*" Justice protested. "Not like that he doesn't—"

"He's unleashed," Elithien answered. His voice was cold, rigid, not a hint of rage. Still, I felt it like the press of a blade against my skin. "The beast, or the man. He can't be both."

"Yes, he can," I corrected. Blue eyes sparkled in my memory. His smile. His touch. Russell was in there, but swallowed down into the pit of his belly like that savage, unmerciful, Unseelie green. "He's in there, and he needs me. I can be his anchor. I can tame his beast."

"You become that for him, and there's no going back. You sure you want that?" Elithien asked. "Take a good, hard look at what he is, Ruth. That is no mortal...and no fucking Vampire, either."

I turned to him...to my *Alpha*. Sadness shone in Elithien's eyes, the kind of pain I understood now.

"Would this break our bond?" I questioned. *Will you accept him,* was what I was asking.

A small smile played across his lips as Elithien looked at the Unseelie creature behind me, then met my gaze. "No, it won't break our bond, Ruth. He laid claim to you before us...and I'll honor that claim. But *if* the Unseelie wants to share your bed... then there *are* conditions."

"Conditions." My stomach tightened with the dangerous glint in his eyes, and a snarl of hunger spilled from the infernal creature behind me. "What kind of conditions?"

Elithien held my stare. "That's between me and the beast."

Chapter Seventeen

"Princess," Rule called, lifting a hand to me as he stepped forward. "Let's leave the Alphas to chat."

Elithien stepped nearer the towering shadowed creature. Dark eyes seized mine before Russell lowered his gaze to the Vampire.

This was the second time Rule had pulled me away when the men around me wanted to 'chat'. The last time, the warehouse had trembled and shuddered and what sounded like a bomb exploded inside before Russell stalked out with blood on his cheek. It didn't take a genius to see what was going on here. I'd been in the center of pissing contests all my damned life. Why should this be any different?

Only it *was* different. I knew that the instant I met Elithien's stony gaze.

These weren't men...these were monsters.

There were rules to follow...*especially where I was concerned.*

I couldn't hear what they were saying. White fangs flashed in the dark and that savage, unending snarl slipped from the Unseelie beast's lips. But Elithien commanded his attention with that low, unyielding tone.

"Come over here," Rule murmured. "And let me tell you how it feels to be thrown from a fifty-story building for love."

"Sixty," I corrected, tearing my gaze from Elithien as he stepped closer to Russell's Unseelie beast. "It's sixty floors."

"Well, then," he gave me a cocky smile, then winced. "That's why it hurt like a bitch at the bottom."

A sudden bark of laughter tore from me. The way he limped and grinned made it funnier.

"Ow," he moaned, and lifted his good arm for me. "That hurts. Come over here and let me whisper all the nasty things I'm going to do to you when I'm better."

He was such an idiot. I couldn't help but smile and limp into his arms. "And when do you think that's going to be?" I joked.

He leaned closer, lips kissing along my jaw as he whispered, "In about three point two seconds."

A chuckle spilled from me... then died away as I caught sight of the shadow on the floor, long, curled...*unmoving*. "Hold that thought," I muttered. It didn't take long for that savage side of me to push to the surface.

Didn't take long at all.

I barely limped. Hate was all I needed. I stepped out of Rule's arms and took three steps before I stopped, balanced on my aching ankle, and wrenched my foot backwards before I unleashed as hard as I could.

A sickening *thud* rang out as I drove my boot into Alex's body. I did it once more for good measure, taking a soul-deep satisfaction in the hollow *thump* my boot made as it connected. "Come back from that, you piece of fucking shit." Hard breaths claimed me as I stared at the body, then lifted my gaze to Rule.

Pride shone in the steel shimmer of his eyes.

I still remembered the feel of the gun kicking in my hand, still see the flinches in the crazy Vampire's face as the bullets found their mark. I still saw Russell as he snapped Alex's neck and let his body fall.

In this moment we were all beasts and beasts alike.

I'd kill the fucking world to save them...just as they would for me.

"Okay." Elithien's voice snapped me out of the moment. I shifted my gaze to the hard steel of his eyes, then the rageful Unseelie beast. "We've come to an agreement. I will allow this...*mating.*"

Justice snarled and bared his teeth.

"On a number of conditions," Elithien continued. "The main one being, if this happens...then we're to supervise."

My body clenched tight. I jerked my gaze to Russell, who was as still as the night. "*Supervise?* What the hell does that even mean?" I was out of my depth here, trying to understand how that could even work.

Elithien stoppled in front of me, captured my chin, and tilted my gaze to his. "This is not just fucking, Ruth. Not for the beast...and it won't be for you. To tether an Unseelie's power like that is...*not without risks.* Risks I don't plan on taking, not when it comes to you. Which is why this is going to happen with the beast chained...and us watching his every fucking move."

My pulse spiked as I stared into those steely eyes and saw the truth. Elithien was scared...*no, he was downright terrified.* Somehow, I think me falling in love with the Unseelie had been the last thing on his mind.

But as that terrifying thought took hold, Russell shook his head from side to side...and the darkness laid waste his last remaining hold. A roar resounded, making me tremble...making me fear.

As the deafening sound echoed and then fell silent, I licked my arid lips and whispered. "Tell me what to do."

Chapter Eighteen

"You want to do *WHAT?*" I barked, and jerked my gaze from Elithien to the shadowed Unseelie. Russell snarled and lashed the air, throwing himself from one side of the room to the other in an attempt to ease his own torment.

"It's the only way. We can't trust it," he said calmly.

We can't trust it.

It.

The Vampire still saw my bodyguard as the enemy. I stared into those bottomless dark eyes of my Vampire. He saw Russell as not just a threat to my safety.... *Was that jealousy burning in his eyes?* A clench of his jaw told me all I needed to know. "I'm not doing it." I shook my head.

"It's the *only* fucking way, Ruth. We can't have the—"

"No." I cut him off. "I'm not mating him. I choose you, every fucking time, I choose you. If this is causing you pain, then I'd be a pretty shitty girlfriend to go ahead with anything like this."

One brow rose in an instant and that guttural voice deepened. "Girlfriend?"

I took a step closer, drawn by the *hunger* between us. "What do you want me to be, Vampire?"

"Mine," he grabbed the back of my neck with brute strength and dragged me against his hard chest. "All fucking day and night. I want to be buried hilt fucking deep inside you and I want to look into your eyes when I fuck you. Until time no longer exists. Until *I* no longer exist. You understand me?"

My heart thundered. My mouth went dry.

I nodded, it was all I could do as the *Alpha* stared into my soul.

"But that can't happen. Not while you're still mortal and I'm not ready to give up on that. I'm not ready to see you change who you are. So, that leaves you unprotected, *vulnerable*." His gaze sank lower, lingering on my lips as he said the word. A shiver raced through me at the sight. "So we need the beast to protect you...and there's only one way that's going to happen."

"Elithien," Justice argued. "No."

"He needs to mate with you, needs to tie his Unseelie fucking soul to yours...needs to feel that unending savagery, so that every fucking blip on your radar is annihilated before it even begins. That fucking hunger that rides him whenever you're near." *Just like I do.* The words echoed in his eyes.

Heat flared inside me as rage cracked like a whip from Justice.

"I need him to be a weapon, Ruth." His fingers speared deeper into my hair, tilting my head as he met my gaze. "I need him to be violent and unending. So this *will happen.*"

The rage that came from the Vampire behind me was chilling. Goosebumps raced along my arms as Elithien shifted his gaze to Justice. Rage sparkled in his eyes, crystal clear. "You want her to fucking die? You want to force her to become what we are?"

"No," Justice answered.

"Then make fucking peace with it," Elithien barked. *Like we all have to make peace.* My Alpha curled his lips and bared his teeth.

That bone-jarring cold seemed to ease. Still, shivers tore along my spine as Elithien turned to Russell as he thrashed and howled, making me jump and flinch.

"So, if you're willing to go ahead," Elithien met my gaze. "the beast needs to be in chains. Warded chains...and us in the room while it happens."

I swallowed hard and shifted my gaze to the infernal creature as it stilled. Heavy breaths claimed him...*controlled him* as he stared into my eyes. Chained. Warded...*watched.*

*Please...*those infernal eyes begged. *Please end this.*

"Okay," I answered. "Tell me what to do."

"You," Elithien murmured, "will let the beast ride you."

Russell came forward, shadows lashing the air like whips before Elithien jerked his head toward the movement. "You know where, Unseelie. The only place warded with enough strength to withstand you."

My Vampire pulled his phone from his pocket. Blood-smeared, the soaked front of his shirt stuck against his skin. The metallic scent of fresh blood filled my nose, making me catch my breath and still. My heart pounded, my senses raced. I closed my eyes and felt the sway.

"Ruth?" Elithien questioned.

It was all too much. The blood. The attack. *Death hovering on the surface.* Their pain...all their pain. "I'm okay." I opened my eyes and forced myself to breathe, then nodded. "I'm okay. Let's just get this over with."

A sad smile crossed his lips. "Not very romantic, I'm afraid."

Who the hell had time for romance when it came to ending rage and agony? I licked my lips. "Make the call, Elithien."

He gave a nod, slid his thumb across the smear of blood on the screen, and stepped away. I shuddered with the cold, wrapped my arms around my body, and lifted my gaze to Justice. He was so still, nothing more than an outline in the dim red glow. Hate was a battering of fists inside me as he turned his head, refusing to meet my gaze.

"Do you think my love it that fragile?" I whispered, catching the flinch at the corner of his eye. I limped closer, lifting my hand to cup his cheek. "You love me like no other. You protect me *like no other.* I will want you...like no other."

He shifted that midnight eye to mine. He was a wound...an open fucking wound, raw and bleeding.

"This changes nothing," I insisted.

"You're wrong," he answered. "It changes everything."

It was my turn to wince. I dropped my hand. "Will I lose you over this?"

"No, Ruth," he growled, his tone unyielding. "But you can fucking believe I'll mark my territory every fucking chance I get."

A shiver tore through me at the ravening, feral longing in his eye. Elithien's voice echoed in the background, but I couldn't catch the words. All I saw was Justice all over me, stretching my arms above me as he fucked me in the shower from behind. Images assaulted me, erotic images, carnal and perfect.

"And that, Ruth…" he warned, "will be just the start."

"Okay." Elithien drew my gaze as he tucked the phone away and turned to that ravening shadowed beast. "Back in the cage, Unseelie. We'll meet you there."

Russell jerked that unmerciful gaze to mine. I thought I saw sadness for a second but there was nothing either of us could do. He was untethered and dangerous, to himself and the rest of the world.

"Ruth," Elithien called, and held out his hand. "It's time." He lowered his gaze to my ankle. "First, there's one thing I need to do."

He came close, lifted his hand, and grazed his fingers along my cheek before he kissed me...*hard.* The metallic tag of blood bloomed in my mouth, taking me by surprise. My heart thundered...pounding harder than ever before.

His blood. Vampire blood.

Power rushed through me, making my eyes flutter closed. I was ripped apart, even though I never moved. I held onto him as my mind was taken far from this place and cast into the midnight sky. I was his world here...I was his universe and, as I drank him down...he became mine.

My muscles tightened, then relaxed. Synapses fired. Atoms exploded and were reborn again. Like I was reborn. Unstitched and put back together. He flinched and tore his lips from mine. Hard, sawing breaths expanded his chest.

*More...*a savage voice growled inside me.

"No, Ruth." Elithien's brows furrowed as he stared at me. Surprise detonated in the steel of his eyes.

I took a step forward, no longer limping. "More, Elithien."

Darkness collided with desire. He dragged his fangs across his bleeding lip. He wanted me...

Wanted me more than ever before.

I lifted my hands, fingers fumbling with the buttons on my blouse. I wanted him, too.

His fangs on my skin...their lips on my body.

Hunger echoed around me as the air came alive with savage growls of desire. Steel glinted from my Vampire's eyes before Elithien stepped closer and grasped my hand, stilling it as I opened one button and moved to the next. "Save it, Ruth. You're going to need all the strength you have."

I sucked in the cold night air.

Drew their power deep inside me, and gave a nod.

I followed them out of what was left of the destroyed office floor, glancing one last time at Alex's still, dead body as I left. Bright lights from the elevators made me wince and close my eyes. But the pain in my ankle was fading now to nothing more than a twinge.

By the time we hit the parking garage floor, it didn't hurt at all.

We climbed into the Explorer with Justice behind the wheel, leaving Hurrow and Rule flanking me.

"He's going to come back, isn't he?" I asked, glancing at Elithien as we drove out through the boom gate and into the city streets. "That *Caedes.*"

He said nothing for a long while, then finally, "Yes. But you won't need to worry about that. Not anymore."

"First Alex, and now a fucking Master Vampire with an Unseelie as his guard. I'm starting to reconsider the whole *mortal* weakness thing right about now."

There was no comment, just the surge of the Explorer as we tore through the night. The closer we came to the other side of the river, the more my thoughts turned to what lay ahead. I was to have sex...only in the most unromantic way.

Satin ropes and foreplay turned me on. But chains and an untethered beast? The whole thing terrified me. Justice grew quieter and more distant the closer we came. The familiar *thud...thud...thud* of the plate seams on the bridge competed with the boom of my heart.

We were on the other side and tearing past the Hunting Ground before I knew it. My stomach tightened as the Explorer slowed and nosed into the parking area of the warehouse. For some reason, the Unseelie terrified me...even more than the Wolves.

The lights were on. Shadows consumed the glow, standing outside...waiting for us. *No, they were waiting for me.* A green glow pulsed once around the warehouse, pushing out into the darkest night, like this place was a heartbeat for the city. One that was alive with power.

We pulled up hard outside the building and climbed out.

"Mojin," Elithien nodded.

Suddenly, I was aware of everything. Every whisper...every look.

"It's the blood," Rule whispered beside me. "You're going to be okay, Princess. We're not going to let anything happen to you."

"Then why do I suddenly feel fucking terrified?" I responded.

"Because," he smiled, pulled me closer, wrapped his arms around me, and finished. "You're smart."

"He's in chains, like you wanted," the Unseelie said to Elithien. "But I gotta warn you against this, Vampire."

"Warn all you want. It's going to happen...unless she decides otherwise." Elithien glanced toward me.

A howl of rage came from inside. The steel walls trembled until they creaked and shook. This entire place was a predator...*a beast lying in wait.*

I stepped away from Rule and moved nearer, lifting my gaze to the forbidding building. "Take me to him."

The Unseelie gave a nod and turned, striding to the corner and disappearing. Elithien followed, then me, Rule, and Justice. The door closed behind us with a *boom,* making me jump in my skin. I glanced at the middle of the warehouse where Alex had once sat...now he was nothing more than a carcass...

He was dead...and all because of the beast that waited for me. The monster in chains...the one who'd do anything to keep me safe. I climbed the stairs, and the closer I came, the further I left fear behind.

This, to me, was purpose.

This was love.

Death. Sex. Bonding.

The Unseelie stepped through the door at the top of the stairs and we all followed. Power hummed through the air. Power that seemed to suck the air out of me, like a vacuum...*or a void.* I stumbled. Hands grabbed me, pulling me upright. Silver eyes flashed in front of me.

"Are...you...okay?" Warped words seemed to dance over me. I couldn't focus...couldn't think. I couldn't feel anything but that gravitational pull.

My belly rolled with the feeling as I tried to focus on the Vampire in front of me. Rule's face sharpened in my vision. Concern flared in his eyes as he lifted his gaze to Elithien and spoke. But I couldn't catch the words, not over the roaring inside my head.

My mouth moved. Words were empty, or so I thought. Rule jerked his gaze toward me. His lips moved. All I could do was nod and pray he understood me. I was okay. *I was okay... Russell...I had to get to Russell.*

Darkness crowded his eyes. He gave a nod and lifted me, pulling me against his chest. I wound my arms around his neck and clung tight as he carried me through that unending pull toward a hallway.

Green glowed from inside a room further along the hall, darkening to almost black. That dark eerie glow pulsed, brightening and darkening, and with every brightening of that Unseelie heart, the power grew hungrier.

Hairs stood on my arms. My heart pulsed in time, as though it also belonged to the Fae, and as I was carried into that room...I knew just how powerful these Fae truly were.

There were three of them. Three mammoth males dressed in skintight black pants, their chests bare and glistening with sweat as they stood at each wall. Markings glowed along their arms, just as the attacker's had in my building. I stared at the markings as they ebbed and surged, throwing that sickening green glow against the walls.

I glanced at Rule as he lowered my feet to the floor. Still, he kept one arm around me, and for that I was grateful. Russell stood in the middle of the room, that same dark, shadowed energy lashing the air. He was naked...*very naked*. His head was lowered, his muscles rippling. Faint wisps of darkness danced across his groin, the only thing keeping him from being fully exposed.

But it was the Fae moving around him that drew my focus. They were doing something to the walls of the room, pressing their hands against the steel plates, lowering their heads as those glowing markings throbbed and spilled from their arms into the walls.

Thick chains that hung from steel connections welded to the corners of the room led to Russell's limbs, reminding me of the steel ropes in the shipping yard. But here, the chains weren't meant to tether a twelve-hundred-foot cargo ship...they were meant to restrain Russell.

My Russell...well, soon to be mine.

I swallowed hard as all three of the towering Fae straightened at the same time. Sweat poured down their backs, making their skin ripple. Hard, sleek muscles tensed and flexed. The biggest of the Fae lifted his head, and turned.

Inhuman...*animalistic.* That's what he was. Something inside me trembled...something inside screamed for me to run. This wasn't just another Immortal, this was an enslaver. Malicious and malevolent...and he looked at me like I was in his way.

"Shrike." Elithien looked at the shadowed beast. "Will it hold?"

The Fae glanced at Russell as the infernal beast turned toward him. A low snarl slipped from my bodyguard's lips. He hated his existence in that moment...and it was all my fault.

"Who the fuck knows?" the Unseelie Alpha answered, his gaze boring into me. "I'd say good luck, but there's just not enough in the world that'll get you through this."

He turned toward the others then, and that emerald green glow dulled to a low shimmer. Air rushed into my lungs, and filled my ears until they popped. I swallowed and swallowed again as the three Fae strode from the room, giving me a look of pure distaste before they closed the door.

Then there was just us.

Just Russell, chained.

Just my four Vampires, watching me with a mixture of pride and terror.

I stepped toward the center of the room, lifted my hands... fingers trembling...*and began to undress.*

Chapter Nineteen

Bitter, cold air danced across my skin. My fingers trembled as my blouse dropped to the floor with a whisper of fabric. The beast in front of me was still.

Too still.

Hard breaths punctured the air as he watched me. That consuming whoosh of air was the only sound in the room —*apart from the panicked racing of my heart.* I licked arid lips and reached around my back, worked the clasp of my bra, and let it fall free.

"Not the most seductive atmosphere, I'm afraid," I murmured, feeling a little like a rabbit trying to seduce a Wolf. He just watched me. Those predatory midnight eyes missed nothing as I balanced on one foot, stepped on the back of my heel, and stepped out of my boot. "Could have at least brought candles, right?" I hated how fucking awkward this was. "Maybe champagne and roses."

Was I even doing this right?

Did he even care I was here?

"Ruth," Justice muttered, drawing my focus.

The shadowed beast whipped his gaze toward the Vampire and let out an inhuman sound. It ripped through the air, low, guttural...*warning*. Making me freeze.

"Do *not* make a fucking sound," Elithien commanded. "Unless you want us all to die this night."

Lips curled on the savage beast in front of me. Those consuming eyes were piercing. Barely controlled rage sparkled and flashed like a severed live wire. I fought that uncontrollable need to run and lowered my hands to the button of my jeans. "Don't even worry about them," I urged, hoping to draw his focus back to me with the slow slide of my zipper. "They aren't even here."

The beast tracked the sound, pitch-black eyes following my fingers as that strange emerald glow ebbed and pulsed from the walls, casting the strange hue across my skin.

"That's it," I encouraged, taking a step in front of him. He towered above me, casting that consuming darkness across the walls and ceiling, just like Kapre had that night at the docks. I shoved my jeans down and stepped free. My nipples tightened to hard peaks. "They aren't even in our world." I met the beast's gaze. "It's just you and me...*just you and me.*"

Thunder echoed from his chest, fierce and erotic, like a purr of the most dangerous kind. I was the woman in front of the lion... one lathered with blood.

Sheer black panties the only thing keeping him from seeing me.

But he did see me.

Those eyes traveled down my body, stopping at my breasts.

I tried to picture the man in front of me and not the beast. Blue eyes sparkled in my memory, but no matter how hard I clutched hold of the image...it slipped through my grasp. He wasn't just the man anymore...nor was he the beast. He was both. Both safe and unmerciful. Both lover and protector.

I slid my fingers under the edge of the elastic. Tension crackled through the room behind me...like a bomb ready to explode. *Justice, please...control it.* I sent the plea through my mind and out into the darkness. In an instant, the Vampire froze before I slid my panties lower.

I could feel their eyes on me, dancing along my skin, lingering on my ass as I bent and slid my panties free. But it was the Unseelie in front of me that demanded all my attention as the shadows drew closer around him. His fingers splayed open, then clenched into a fist as he pulled against the inch-thick shackles around his wrist.

"You want to touch me?" I moved closer. So close I could feel his breath on my skin. "Is that what you want?"

The beast stared into my eyes, savage, *ferocious.* I swallowed hard, tore my gaze from his, and stepped to the side. That massive fist clenched once more before his fingers unfurled. He lowered his head, nostrils flaring as he drew in my scent.

I focused on those fingers as the Unseelie glow brightened. Runes pulsed in the walls. I had a strange feeling they were dampening him, smothering his power...a little at least. All that force...three powerful Fae to infuse their power into the walls... I turned my gaze to his—all because he wanted to fuck me.

No, not *fuck*. I stepped up to his hand and closed my eyes. *Mate*. That's what this was...a ritual, a *binding*. He was 'unleashed', that's what Elithien had called it. Unleashed, untethered. A force barely constrained. His touch was so gentle, power thrummed against my breast and tore through my body. But he was constrained with me, subjecting himself to shackles and wards.

That hard, *heavy* rush of breath stilled as he brushed my nipple.

A trapped breath escaped, tearing from me with a shudder.

Mine...

It boomed like thunder inside my head. I opened my eyes and met his gaze. Russell was in there...somewhere. It was his voice that echoed, his words that claimed me.

Mine. His fingers curled around my breast...his low, needy growl demanded more.

I turned my body, letting his palm engulf my breast, fingers sliding over my ribs as his thumb skimmed across my nipple. Heat rushed at the sensation. Power mingled with desire...

I saw the creature now. Imposing. *Consuming.* I saw remnants of the shadowed beast called Kapre, and a whole lot of danger all wrapped up in one Immortal being. I lowered my arm, fingers trembling until they cupped the back of his hand.

He flinched at the touch, then that purr deepened. I lowered my head, swallowed a shiver from the cold, then lifted his hand and kissed his fingers. He'd saved me. No matter how terrified I was right now...I knew the threat would *never* be him.

Cold brushed my lips as I breathed in. Dark energy moved inside me...making me tremble, but this time for a whole different reason.

Want...to...kiss you.

The words bloomed inside my head. I opened my eyes and met his imploring gaze. I left his hand, moving to stand directly in front of him again. He was towering and hulking. The shackles around his outstretched hands made it impossible for him to move. He lowered his head until the steel links snapped taut and the markings on the wall blazed.

But I couldn't reach his mouth, could only slide my hands along his chest. Power stung my fingers with the connection as I slid my hands upwards over thick shoulders until I rose on my toes...

"Justice," Elithien spoke, making me flinch at the interruption. "Lift her for the Unseelie."

"You've got to be shitting me!"

The low thrum from the shadowy beast turned into a growl as he moved that hostile stare to the Vampire.

"You want to kiss me, right?" I drew his gaze to me once more. "Unless you want the shackles removed, there's only one way that can happen."

The infernal creature's lips curled as the heavy thud of footsteps sounded. But Justice was slow, careful, making sure he didn't provoke the creature as he gripped me by the waist and lifted. The beast sank into a squat, giving me his thick, muscular thighs to stand on.

Cold hands lingered at my waist. I wanted to close my hand over Justice's to reassure him. But I didn't dare, not unless I wanted the beast unchained. I stood on his powerful thighs, rising above him as I wound my arms around his neck and Justice stepped away.

Kiss...the word echoed inside my head as I bent closer. I meant to dip lower, to meet his lips with mine...until I realized it wasn't my lips he wanted to claim. His dark eyes glittered, fixed on the sway of my breast. I leaned closer, arching my back to his need.

That tingle of power licked me, making me shiver.

"Oh..." I closed my eyes with a tremor as the whisper of cold turned into something else.

Something hungry...

Something caged.

I speared my fingers through his midnight hair and cupped the back of his neck, drawing him against me. He took more of me into his mouth. That heavy purr was back again, spilling along his throat to close around my nipple with the graze of sharp teeth.

"Oh, fuck me." My eyes fluttered and my hips rocked.

I was enthralled with the sensation. Links snapped taut as the beast wanted more. Those wards against the walls blazed brighter, filling the room with the glaring green glow. I felt them pulsing against me now, felt their magic press in deep. Like how I wanted him.

More...he growled inside my head.

I balanced on his powerful thighs, gripped his shoulders, and slid down against his chest. His eyes closed with the sensation, nostrils flaring as that heat tore through me. Wards. *Hunger.* Blinding me.

Something groaned from both sides of the room. The groan turned into a howl...and all of a sudden, the Vampires were there.

"Ruth!" Elithien snarled, coming closer. "Step away from the beast *now.*"

The savage growl that tore from my midnight beast was feral. Power hummed through his body as that howl of steel turned to shrieks.

I heard my Vampire, and felt his fear press against my mind. But the glow of the wards consumed me, taking me under, past the fear...down to where desire raged. I wanted my Unseelie. Wanted him like I'd never wanted anything before.

"I want to fuck," I groaned, and sank down to rock my hips against him. "I need..."

"It's the goddamn steel...*it's not going to hold!*" Elithien bellowed as I rocked my hips against my beast's massive cock. The girth of him made me tremble. I'd never had anything so...*huge.* I rubbed myself along the throbbing veins of his length, and reached down.

"It's okay." I heard my own whisper sounding hollow and strange. "It was never meant to."

I knew what was to happen now...knew there weren't enough wards in the word to hold my Unseelie at bay. I knew deep inside that they'd never stood a chance. He was playing with them, making them believe something as pathetic as steel and markings made a lick of difference. When the only difference in a creature like him...*was his will.*

I twisted at my waist and dropped my head backwards, letting my body slide down his until I fell the short distance and hit the floor.

Crack! One of the steel connections snapped, the thick chain lashing the air like a whip, as the heavy links slammed into the wall near Rule's head. The Vampire jerked his gaze toward the beast, silver eyes glinting with rage as he bared his fangs.

"WHAT THE FUCK!" the Fae boomed, and threw the door open.

I felt the beast stiffen behind me, wrench his head toward the intrusion, and howl his rage. The sound was deafening. The vibration slammed through the room, rocking the building...I tasted his power. But the sound didn't hurt me. Instead, that pulse inside me pushed the thunderous roar away. I was in that void I'd felt before, that consuming, undeniable void. I knew what it was now...that vacuum didn't come from the wards pressed into the walls, or the power of the Fae, *it came from my malevolent creature.*

The walls shook. My Vampires lunged, and Elithien drove the Fae out of the room, slamming the door behind them.

There was fear in his eyes as he turned to me. Real fear, as the second girder snapped with a shriek of tortured steel. I was lifted by thick, shadowed hands and carried. Air buffeted me, casting strands of my hair against my cheek before I was pressed against the far wall.

That power hummed inside me, swallowing me in the vibration. The green Unseelie glow pulsed as the enormous shadowed creature loomed above me. All that darkness...at the tips of my fingers. He closed that powerful body around me, wrapping those midnight tendrils around me like a shield. Hiding my nakedness...as though it was only for him—*all for him*. His hands gripped my wrists and lifted them high above me, pinning them to the wall. Chains clinking was all I heard. Steel still shackled his thick, monstrous wrists as he slid a knee between mine and gently forced my legs open.

Mine. The word resounded inside my head. *Mine...forever.*

The head of his cock slid along my slit. I dropped my head and shuddered with the sensation as he found my entrance. Movement came at the edge of my focus as markings spilled along my skin before they sank, fading away. That darkness sank deeper, claiming me, turning me into something else. I jerked my gaze toward the blur of movement and bared my teeth. *Stay away*...that savagery warned. *Mine.*

Night swept in around me. Dark, sacred night. I was consumed by that void. Swept away in that euphoric vibration as that thick head slowly slipped inside me.

I stiffened, breathing hard, as he stretched me.

That monstrous vein along his shaft pulsed. Heat spilled into me. A delicious heat, tearing a moan from the back of my throat. He made me feel savage in this moment. Made me feel like this was forever...this moment—*this need.*

"Mine," I cried, staking my claim. "You hear me, Russell? *You are mine.* Beast and all."

His hands left mine, grabbed me by the waist, and lifted. I wrapped my legs around the monstrous creature's hips as he pushed in deeper. Inch by inch, thrusting slowly...then making my body shudder with need as he withdrew.

A snarl of impatience rumbled in the back of my throat as I rocked my hips forward...*seeking*. I lifted my head as he drove deeper, and found my Vampires on the other side of the room. I saw myself in their eyes, clinging to the midnight beast as he drove inside me, lifting me, making my eyelids flutter...making my hips buck. The Unseelie savage fucked me as my Vampires stood immobile and watched.

This was what I wanted.

This was what I *needed*.

My arms shuddered, unable to hold me as the first wave of ecstasy same barreling into me. Heavy hands gripped me. Fingers spread wide over my breasts as he impaled me with his cock. But his hands were no longer midnight. I turned my gaze to his...and this was no longer the beast.

Russell moved inside me, fucking...*bonding*. And when he came...*he roared*.

Chapter Twenty

My heart hammered...breaths deepened. I lay there, curled against his chest on the floor in the middle of his cell as that Unseelie glow pulsed darker from the walls, illuminating with just enough light for me to see. Shorn metal girders lay all around me, some still embedded three inches into the floor. Wards bled like thick tears down the walls until they seeped into the cracks of the floor. Still I was here, *alive...*

"You sure you're okay?"

I forced a smile, listening to the battle still raging outside the door between my Vampires and the Fae, and answered for the hundredth time. "I'm fine, Russell. Don't worry, you didn't hurt me."

I felt him relax. His breath was warm on the back of my neck as he inhaled. Slowly, question after question, he was returning to me, slipping from the beast's hold. A shudder coursed through me. Little white lies, that's all they were. I'd tell monstrous black ones if it meant he didn't tear himself apart.

"Think we should rescue them?" he asked.

I dreaded this moment. Still, I nodded. "Yeah, I think maybe we should."

Cold licked along my spine as he climbed to his feet. A savage twinge flared between my thighs as I pushed upwards.

"Here." He held out his hand to me. I stared at that hand. Thick, pink fingers. Powerful arms. Not the shadowed beast...

"Thanks." I swallowed the panic and lifted my hand. It wasn't the ache I cared about. That was almost delicious, a reminder of how he felt inside me. No, that wasn't what made me tremble at all.

I rose carefully, warmth wet between my thighs. Russell looked down at the glistening sheen. There was a flicker of the beast in his eyes...a flare of satisfaction and pride. As I watched, his cock grew thick and hard, ready for me once more.

"Leash it, bodyguard," I said with a smile. "For a little while at least."

His smile was radiant, beautiful, his lips stretching over his teeth as he chuckled. "Looking at you like that...makes me want to tear apart the world."

I stepped closer, lifted my hand to the back of his neck, and drew him down to me. Our lips met, tasting, taking, but inside, I shivered at his words...*because that's exactly what I was afraid of.*

"—you want to talk about consequences *now?*" Elithien snapped, drawing my focus. "I need allies, Mojin. If I have none here, then I'll find them any way I can."

I broke away from the kiss and turned to the roar of voices spilling through the closed door. We were alone now...but that hadn't been the case earlier. I tried to rearrange the fragments of what'd happened in the moment Russell's shadowed beast bonded to me. The door flew open...and rage spilled out. That's all I remembered...maybe that's all I wanted to remember.

I reached down, grasped my panties, and slipped them back on. There was a *crack* from outside. Something thudded against the wall. I hurried, yanking on my jeans, and didn't even bother with my bra. Instead, I shoved it into my pocket, my finger skimming the cold band of my father's ring before I pulled on my blouse and my boots once more.

The door opened and rage walked through. Cold rage. *Vampire rage.* Elithien met my gaze, those steely eyes taking in every inch of me before he spoke. "Can you walk?"

I swallowed hard and nodded. "Yes."

"Good, because *we're going the fuck home.*"

Relief washed through me. "Home as in this side of the river?"

His smile was chilling. "Yes, my love. Unless there was another home you wanted?"

He shifted his gaze to Russell behind me and all of a sudden, that smile was deadly. Another home? Did he think I wanted to go home with Russell?

I swallowed hard and crossed the room. He flinched at my movement, raw, flayed to the bone. He'd just stood there and watched another man ride me...watched another man have what was his. He might've consented to the Unseelie...but that didn't mean he had to like it. I crossed the room as Justice, Hurrow, and Rule slipped into the room.

"I want to go home with you. *Our* home. *All of us.*" I stood in front of him, desperate to reach out to him...to have him accept me even with the smell of another man all over my skin. This was what it came down to, wasn't it? All the rage and the cold, hard steel.

"You told me this wasn't going to break us." I looked into his eyes, my voice so small.

Jesus, my heart clenched tight, wrapped in razor wire and covered in thorns. I could feel the bands cinching and twisting until the shards bit deep.

"I just watched another man fuck you," his voice guttural and menacing. "One who isn't part of my coven. You were..." sparks danced in his eyes. "Breathtaking. Now the bodyguard *stays* with us...no exceptions. He lives, fights, and *fucks* under my roof or not at all."

"Understood," Russell answered behind me.

"Get your things," Elithien commanded, staring at me. "We're leaving."

My Vampire reached out his hand for mine. I felt Russell stiffen, that forbidding creature still too close to the surface. But he leashed it, just like I knew he would. I slid my hand into Elithien's and followed, feeling the ache between my thighs as we walked out of the ruined room and into the hallway.

The walls outside were bowed, the door frames buckled. "Holy shit," I whispered.

Elithien turned his head, his gray eyes sparkling. "Yes, holy shit."

The Alpha of the Unseelie Fae just stood there, arms crossed over his chest, watching me as I followed Elithien. I had no friends here...that was plain to see. His lips curled, baring his teeth. Hate raged in his eyes. I thought for a second I'd feel the sting of his words, until the towering male jerked his gaze behind me...and my bodyguard stepped closer to me.

Something unspoken passed between them. Fear. Rage. A battleground of stares as we left. Justice was waiting for us at the open door. The overhead lights of the warehouse bled into the gloom of the space. We were out, striding down the stairs. I gripped the railing, feeling the quiver in my knees. My body had used too much energy, fighting, *fucking*, taming a beast at midnight.

I still felt that remnant of the Unseelie settling inside me, finding the cracks in my soul like I was a living, breathing Kintsugi art piece. But instead of gold, it was the darkness I tasted. That limitless power spilling into me, until it *became me*. I pulled away from that brush of power, following my Vampire down to the warehouse floor and across to the door.

Hurrow was waiting for us, and Rule stood just outside. None of my Vampires said a word as we hurried toward the four-wheel drives and climbed inside. Elithien never once let go of my hand, opening the door for me, waiting until I climbed inside before he followed. There was no more room in the back seat for anyone else. It was just him and me.

"Home," I said, and felt relief roll around inside me. "Hurrow... take me home."

"Thought you'd never ask," the Vampire growled, starting the engine.

We were rolling out of the driveway, speeding along the street past the Wolves' clubs, and turning before I knew it. "What kind of trouble are you in with the Fae?"

"Too deep for me to explain," Elithien answered as he turned to me. "But that's not the issue we should be concerned about, Ruth. We have bigger enemies to fight. That Vampire tonight, the one who came after you, have you seen him before?"

Memories flashed inside my head, and even though my body was exhausted, fear still kicked in. "Twice."

"I want you to tell me everything...leave nothing out."

I told him about the man in the corner of the room at Russell's place, and in the alley when we were pulled over by the police. He listened intently. Glances in the rear-view mirror said Hurrow heard every word, as well.

"And you said you were looking at articles about your mother when he appeared?" Elithien asked.

"I mean, I was sitting there with my finger bleeding from Dad's ring and he—"

"The same damn ring I saw before?" Hurrow growled.

"Yes." I shifted to the side, shoved my fingers into my pocket, and yanked it out. Elithien stared at the thick jewel in my hand before he reached out. "Your blood," he murmured. "You said your blood hit the ring before he stepped out of the doorway."

"That's right," I agreed as a chill broke out across my skin. "It's my father's ring, Elithien...just a ring."

"Just a ring," he repeated, but something flittered across his eyes as he lifted his gaze to mine. "And yet you saw this ring on your father's finger before he was buried."

"My uncle—" I started.

"Needs to be paid a visit," he finished, and turned his gaze to the early morning sky. "It's too late now. There's no time left."

"I can go," I protested, glancing at Hurrow. "I'll take Russell, find out what I can, and come back."

Elithien lifted his head and met Hurrow's gaze. The Alpha's second was silent for a moment before he spoke. "He proved himself tonight. We need him...and we need Ruth."

"I want you to be careful," Elithien warned. "Do *not* leave the Unseelie's side, not for anything, not until I can track Caedes down and end him."

Track him down...I knew war when I heard it whispered. I wanted to fight.

I *would* fight...for him.

Alex was gone now, so there was one less monster in my world. Only, a bigger one was coming now, barreling toward us with a Fae. "Did they do this, betray you? Those Fae at the warehouse?"

"Shrike? No...but he knows who did."

I swallowed hard as we turned into the driveway and the headlights of the Explorer washed across the house. "And this is how it ends."

Elithien was already reaching for his phone as the screen lit up. "Not *your* goddamn end, that's for sure."

He climbed out as we came to a stop. Commands were barked, but I was too tired to care. Hurrow climbed out of the car and was at my door in an instant as the others pulled up behind us.

Movement came at the edge of the driveway, figures slinking from the trees and drawing my gaze.

"He'll keep you safe," Hurrow reassured as men stepped from the darkness. "If you can't trust anything, you can trust that."

But these weren't just any kind of men. They were midnight giants, at least ten of them, stopping at the edge of the clearing and waiting. "Who are they?"

"No one you want to tangle with. You want to stay close to the bodyguard now, Ruth," Hurrow insisted, staring at the new arrivals. "And whatever you do...don't wander off on your own."

Elithien strode across the driveway as one of them stepped forward. Ebony skin shone in the moonlight. He moved with the grace of a hunter, all sleek muscles and long strides.

"They smell like death," Russell growled, stepping closer.

"That's because they are," Hurrow muttered, and pushed me into Russell's arms. "Inside, Ruth."

My bodyguard was there, pulling me close as he led me to the open door of the house. Rule was already inside, moving from room to room. I listened to the echo of his footsteps as I stepped inside.

"Sleep." Russell gave me a gentle push toward the Vampires' side of house, the haunted expression in his eyes clinging tightly. "When you wake up, we'll see your uncle and get the answers you've been looking for." Russell turned toward the other side of the house.

We all needed sleep, and food, and comfort.

None more so than my Unseelie.

Rule stepped out of the kitchen doorway with a plate of food. A heaping sandwich sat in the middle, slices of canned fruit to the side. "It was the best I could come up with in a hurry, I'm afraid."

My belly howled at the sight, and my mouth watered. "It's perfect." I stepped close, taking the plate. "Thank you." I kissed him, sliding my hands over his shoulders to pull him close.

He glanced toward the window when I pulled back. Even he was unnerved by the intruders. I grabbed the sandwich, took the biggest bite of my life, and chewed before I swallowed and spoke. "Who are they?"

"Who did Hurrow say they were?"

"Not fair." I bit again, chewed, and swallowed, almost moaning with delight. "Don't you know it's rude to answer a question with a question?"

"In this case," he said, sliding his hand along the back of my arm and herding me toward Elithien's bedroom, "it's perfectly acceptable. They're mercenaries, Ruth. They will cut you down and ask questions later. Elithien said he'd protect you and he's making good on that promise. So now you can sleep and rest that stunning brain of yours. Because we need to stay alert, especially after tonight."

I let him guide me as I slipped the last slices of pear into my mouth. He punched in the code, waited as the steel door slid open, then took the plate with a kiss on my cheek. "Shower, sleep. Elithien will be beside you soon."

I did as he said, took my time under the steaming spray, and crawled into bed, still a little damp but utterly exhausted. I tried to wait for Elithien, desperate to hear the hiss of the door and feel the dip of the mattress next to me. But there was no more waiting for the emptiness...there was no keeping the beast of sleep at bay.

I tumbled into the darkness, swallowed down into the nothing... and slept.

Chapter Twenty-One

"You okay?" Russell asked, and glanced at the sprawling white mansion set back off the street.

"Sure," I lied, staring at the familiar grounds.

"We've been sitting here for an hour now. I don't want to push you, or anything."

He didn't want to push. I knew that. But some things took time. Some things festered before they broke the surface and you could get them out. This was one of those times. Memories assaulted me every time I came back to this place. The tug of war inside me between loyalty and betrayal almost tore me apart. I hated, and yet *needed*.

Both weak and strong.

Can a person be both at the same time?

It was simple...*they can't*. Not if they wanted to stay sane...and alive. I had to make a decision here. Use...*take*. And decide how much of myself I left behind. Blood was blood. I got that. I'd been force fed those words my entire life. But blood could be spilled. Blood could be forgotten...just as well as any betrayer. But also, blood could almost be sacred. Blood could be the thing that held me together in the end. The only question was... which one would it be?

"I'm ready," I declared, *finally*.

He started the car in an instant, steered out from the shoulder on the other side of the road, and pulled the car into the circular driveway that led us to the house. The last time I was here, before my uncle knew I was alive, the police had been involved. Threats were howled in rage. I'd thought they were behind the threats left on my windshield and the ones in my office. My cousins, Judah and Blane, may not be the most honest of people, but it hadn't been them who'd set me up.

Images of Alex's dead body surfaced as we pulled up outside the house. Russell was out of the car in an instant and striding around the front. I opened the passenger's door, making him frown. "I was going to get that for you."

"You're my lover, and my protector," I answered. "Not an employee."

"You think I only opened your door because you paid me to?" One brow rose and he glared at me. Flickers of the shadowed beast rose in his eyes. "I did it because it made me feel good to treat you with honor. Don't take that from me."

I stopped as he neared and lifted his hand, waiting for mine. He did treat me with honor...and also lust. The wave of that slammed into me as he neared, boxing me in as I stood inside the open door. *I could take you...right now. Open your zipper. Fingers sliding into your panties...*

"Jesus." The word tore free from my mouth as the front door opened and my uncle stepped out.

Russell's smile was quick...and cocky, curling the corners of his lips higher as he stepped to the side, letting me out. *Just remember who's really in charge here, Ruth. I can have you any time I want. Mine,* that guttural voice inside my head commanded. *Mine.*

"'Bout time you came. I was getting a damn crooked neck watching you two sit in your car over there. What the hell were you doing, anyway? Trying to map the entire fucking constellation?"

"Nice to see you, too, Uncle," I muttered, and climbed the stairs. He looked older than the last time I saw him. His hair was turning a lighter shade of gray. "Almost white-haired there, I taunted, stepping into his arms.

It was awkward, like being slammed into a bowed plank of wood as he chuckled. "I have you and your father to thank for that." He released his hold, giving me two hard thumps on the back before he turned his attention to Russell. "The bodyguard can stay out here."

"The *bodyguard* can go where he damn well pleases," Russell responded, climbing the stairs to stand beside me...maybe a little close.

The male wanted to stake his claim, and he succeeded as my uncle looked from him to me. All I could do was smile.

"Right," Jerry grumbled, shuffling as he turned and headed back inside.

Tires squealed from out in the street. I turned my head as a blur of midnight blue tore along the driveway, the sleek engine roaring before it died.

"Goddammit. Fucking kid can't leave us the hell alone," my uncle groaned as Judah climbed out of the sports car. "Hurry inside, maybe I can lock the door and pretend no one's here."

The screen door swing closed with a *bang*. We were inside and moving toward the far end of the house before the heavy thud of steps came from the front.

"I see you, old man!" my cousin snapped. "You can't run from me."

"Money," Jerry snapped. "It's the only time he comes around. That and when his mother is cooking a roast."

It felt strange to see them like this. Bantering and snarling, almost like a real family. *Almost like the one we could've had.* Fuck, that hurt. The punch was bare knuckles into my sternum, making me swallow hard and feel the ache.

"Ruth?" Russell asked beside me.

I winced and met his gaze as my cousin strode up and grabbed me in a hug from behind. "Well, look who decided to come back from the dead."

The reaction from Russell was instant, the growl low and terrifying. Night found us as we stood in the back room of my uncle's house. The same house where I'd suffered repeated threats and bullying all my damn life.

"Get your fucking hands off her before I tear them off and shove them up your ass," my lover threatened as he stepped closer. Shadows crawled along the wall and over the ceiling.

Judah's hold eased instantly, leaving me to turn and shove him away with a punch to the shoulder. "Do that again, cousin, and you might just find yourself in serious trouble."

He didn't speak, just stared at the towering male beside me as the walls trembled and the floor shook.

"I'm not someone you can touch and prod and bully anymore," I warned. "You want to touch me...you'd better be asking for permission first."

"Jesus, okay, I get it," Judah snapped, his face going red. "Call off the dog, Ruthy."

Rage boiled to the surface. I closed the distance, my fists tangled in his shirt before I knew it. I yanked him close, so close I saw my own spittle smack his cheek. "*You're* the fucking *dog* here, cousin. My entire fucking family is. You want to talk about loyalty and honor like you understand what they fucking mean? You have no idea." I shoved him away from me, disgusted. "They've bled for me. They've protected me...they saved me from the river while our company was being torn to shreds. Where the fuck were you? Snorting crack with some random hooker you paid for in lines."

I stepped backwards, not taking my eyes off the shell of a man until I pressed against Russell's chest. He wasn't my bodyguard, or my *dog*. He was the man who'd saved me when no one else could.

"Apologize." I jerked my gaze toward my uncle as he looked from me to Judah. "I said, *apologize*."

"Fine," Judah snapped, and dragged his fingers through his thick hair. "I didn't mean anything by it...I was just glad to see you alive, is all. *I'm sorry for grabbing you.* Won't happen again."

I waited, staring at him like he'd sprouted two heads. Like both of them had.

"Why are you here, Judah?" Jerry demanded, glaring at him.

"I'm bored, and fucking lonely, okay, old man? Give me a break," he snarled.

Holy shit. What the actual fuck was happening here? "You're lonely?" I repeated. "And bored?"

Seems like I wasn't the only one hurting with the company gone.

"Why the hell are *you* here?" Judah sneered my way.

My uncle glanced at me, and waited. It was now or never. I dropped my hand to the thick outline of the ring in my pocket. "I came for answers."

"Then let's have them." Judah opened his arms and turned to his dad. "Let's finally fucking hear some truth for once. Or have you forgotten what that is?"

"Fuck you," my uncle snapped, and forced a smile.

But I could hear the tremble of fear in his voice. He walked with a limp, favoring his right side as he headed toward the sitting area. "If we're gonna dig up the dead, then I'll need a goddamn drink."

I followed him to the room where only the 'men' were welcome. The women of my uncle's house were left to chatter in the kitchen...and gossip in the pergola, out of earshot. It hit me then, how very disappointed they must've been when I was born, then their hopes dying when my mother died.

Did my uncle secretly wait for my dad to find a new wife? To give this family the sons it deserved? I could almost see that hope dying as he waited year after year for my father to move on. But Dad never did. God, that must've pinched.

He sat down hard with a groan and motioned Judah toward the Scotch. At least my cousin knew his way around the bar...he'd enjoyed enough of them. Amber was poured, a deep draw through thick lips, and my uncle closed his eyes with a groan.

"You know, I've been dreading this moment ever since your father told me he wasn't going to make it. I fucking knew." He opened his eyes and stared at me. "And I fucking told him. I said, '*I ain't gonna lie to her. The kid comes to me, and I'm gonna tell her the truth.*' So, kid. Here we are."

"Here we are," I repeated as a shudder coursed across me. "I want to know about her."

He chuckled and shook his head. "I don't know much...hell, none of us knew that much when it came to Cassandra."

"But you tried, didn't you?" I didn't need to ask the question. "It's what you do, right? Dig up dirt. Find something to use against them, if not now...whenever you damn well wanted."

I shifted my gaze to Judah, remembering the USB and the nice little video they'd taken of Harlequin Greenholme, balls deep in some hooker's pussy as she called his name and got the money shot. And a money shot it had been... an image of his watch, his face, and the urgency in his voice as he called her name. They'd taken the man's company out from under him. I shook my head and turned to my uncle as he still spoke. Like father, like sons. Thank fucking God mine had been the best of them.

"We looked. I did, at least. Had my best guys on it for months, tracking her life down. But there was nothing on Cassandra Eastman, as she was back then before your father became smitten. There was just *poof,* and there she was. Perfect, stunning, radiant. Your father was a done man the moment he laid eyes on her. Then there was you, Ruthy. And you were everything your father dreamed of."

I winced at the words as that hidden letter reared up to punch me in the face.

Russell shifted closer, even though I hadn't seen him move.

The back of his hand brushed my fingers. The thick, corded muscles of his arms pressed against mine. Reassuring me... giving me strength. I tried to breathe, tried to feel like my life wasn't one big fucking lie as I listened about how my father was enamored with his brand-new baby girl...*that he hadn't fathered.*

Had he known?

Of course not.

But he started to suspect at some point.

Enough to steal my DNA and have it tested.

What was it? The way I walked, talked? The way I looked? What was it about me that rubbed him raw...enough to think maybe I wasn't his? *Jesus.* I jerked away from the thought and tried to focus as my uncle chattered on.

"—didn't know what was going on. She wasn't talking. Your father followed her, then there was that night. The night it all happened."

"What?" I questioned. "Go back a bit. Can you repeat all that?"

He looked at me with so much sadness, those same blue eyes my father'd had, shimmering with tears. "I tried to reach out to her in those last few months, Ruthy. You have to believe me about that. But she pulled away from us. She even pulled away from your father. She was hiding something, changing right before our eyes."

"Changing how?" That cold shiver moved deeper, probing my defenses...searching for a way in.

"She was lying to your father, that I knew for certain. He came to me one night, distraught. I'd never seen him so shaken. It was the first and only time I ever saw your father cry. He stood right there." He turned his head toward the fireplace, his voice thick and husky, reliving the moment of despair. "Stood right there and sobbed his damn heart out."

My heart hammered as that bitter cold slipped deep, finding a crack unguarded...and slipped into my soul. "Why? Why was he crying?"

My uncle shook his head. "He wouldn't tell me. But he paced like a damn lion, broken-hearted, soul-fucking crushed. But you know us Costellos, we don't stay down for long."

There was a hardness in his last words, an edge I'd heard many times before.

"He went to work, Pops," Judah muttered.

There was a glint in my cousin's eye. A hunger. He went to work.

"Yes, eventually he did."

"And you have no idea what happened between him and… *mom?*" I asked.

Jerry shook his head and gave a shrug. "No. He refused to talk about it, and after a while I stopped asking." His hands trembled when he drained the last of his Scotch and nodded toward Judah. "I told you all I know on that. Anything else there is to know won't come from me."

Judah grabbed his glass, splashed amber into the bottom, and returned to where his dad sat.

But the glass wasn't lifted to his lips right away. Instead, he rolled the tumbler in his hands. His voice was low as he spoke. "What happened at the Jewel last night, Ruthy?"

I flinched and swallowed hard. Memories flashed, filling my head with terror, rage…and sex. The kind of sex that made me heady thinking about it…and the kind of terror that filled me with dread. I lifted my head, lies on the tip of my tongue.

"I worry about you," my uncle murmured. "You're so much like her. All the secrets and the lies. You'd think us Costellos would be used to them. But there are just some you can't get past, Ruth. There are some that shake not just the foundation of your world…but *the* world."

My foundation was shaken…and I wasn't the only one telling lies. I reached onto my pocket and pulled out my father's ring, keeping my finger from sliding over the barb. "You want to talk about lies, Uncle? Want to explain why this was on my desk?"

His blue eyes sharpened, narrowing on the shine of gold in my hand before he met my gaze. "Where did you get that?"

I took a step closer and leaned down. "Where you left it for me."

Anger flared in those arctic blue eyes. "Where *I* left it for you? I left it on your father's goddamn finger, *that's where I left it.*"

Scotch splashed against the sides of the tumbler as he pushed up from the chair and forced me backwards. He reached out and snatched the ring from my hand, lips curled in a savage sneer. I'd never seen such a visceral reaction from him before. He was usually a snake, a cruel, patient snake. But this was all lion...all *Wolf.*

"This?" He lifted it into the air and stared hard, scowling before he turned it around and stared at the barb. "This isn't your father's."

"Of course it's his," I snapped. "Look at the damn stone."

"It's too dark. Your father's wasn't that dark, and it didn't have as many loops and swirls like this one has. Judah, fetch mine on the nightstand next to my bed."

My cousin left, his steps ringing out as he made his way along the hallway and returned. "Here, Pops." He held out a thick ring, identical to my father's.

Both men crowded over the thing, peering without saying a word, until my uncle straightened and handed them both to me. "I told you it wasn't your father's. See how the stone is darker, and the pattern is different?"

I stared at the damn thing and at first, I couldn't see any difference...until I looked deeper. The ring with the barb had a darker-colored stone, almost blood red compared to the brighter one in Jerry's, and the pattern, while swirling...was different. My own blood still clung to the edges of the ring I'd thought was my father's. Relief swept through me. "So Dad's..."

"—is still on his damn finger. Anyone who touches that will get his fucking hand removed."

I didn't know why I took comfort in the sting of rage in his tone. But it was there, stopping that tremble as I closed my eyes and breathed deep. "Okay...that's good."

"Still doesn't answer the damn question, Ruthy. Who's ring is that...and why the hell was it in your house?"

I jerked open my eyes, staring down at the damn thing before I handed Jerry's back to him. In my head, all I could see was the Vampire striding out of the corner of the room toward me as I sat on Russell's bed. "I don't know. But I intend to find out."

"When you do, let me know...Judah and me will pay him a damn visit." That serpent reared in his eyes, and he was a Costello once more.

"I will." I slipped the ring into my pocket. I didn't want to. Didn't want the damn thing anywhere near me. Not anymore. "I need one more thing from you."

"Go ahead., Jerry urged.

I lifted my gaze to his. "I want a list of everyone who bought pieces of my company."

"Won't do any good," he muttered. "There's too many of them.

"Haven't you heard?" I gave him a smile of my own. "I'm not about being *good* anymore...I'm about getting *even*."

He chuckled then, and shook his head before he finally stopped. This time, when that glint shone in his blue eyes...it danced like fire. I left him then, carrying the tainted ring with me as I walked to the door.

"Ruthy," he called, stopping me. I glanced over my shoulder at him as he came out of the sitting room and stopped in the doorway. "I want you to come to me if you're in trouble. We're family. We're blood. While I haven't always been there for you, I want you to know I'm here now."

So many years...*so many goddamn years I'd waited to hear those words.*

My throat thickened as I gave a small nod.

It was all that was needed.

I climbed back into the Explorer as Russell slipped behind the wheel. Too many things raced through my mind as we drove out of the driveway. The ring. My mother. *My dad.* Sunlight glinted off the nondescript midnight blue sedan parked across the street from my uncle's house. I turned my head as we passed, meeting Carina Chase's steely gaze.

Her eyes widened as she saw me...this time it was my turn to smile.

I'd risen from the dead, ready to spill blood and claw my way back.

Only this time, I had an army by my side. I reached across the seat and gripped Russell's hand.

An army they'd never see coming.

Chapter Twenty-Two

ELITHIEN

DEATH FILLED MY DREAMS AND, AS I SURFACED, HUNGER followed. I sucked in a harsh breath and felt that hunger shift under my skin. I needed blood...but it was more than that.

I rose quietly and looked around the room. It wasn't my room... not the one I shared with Ruth, at least. But a darker room. A quieter one. One hidden in the back of the house, protected by steel and memories. One where the beast could hide from her.

I didn't trust him, not that vile part of my nature. The one debased and corrupt. The one who wanted to hunt.

I flicked on the light and stared at her. Pictures of another woman. Her pale skin, her perfect smile. Her bare shoulder leaning into the light. That hungry gaze in her eyes as Morgana stared into the lens of the camera and into my soul.

It was a picture taken a long time ago. When we were happy...*and she was alive.*

I lifted my hand and tugged on the frame, placing it face down on the desk before I turned to the next one. She stood in front of the Louvre in Paris, head down, smile seductive. And another, as she danced at a gala, hair swept up, looking every bit the Princess in a stunning midnight gown.

Pain tore through my chest at the sight. I pulled every image of her from the wall, stacking them neatly before stowing them away in a cupboard in the corner of the room.

The walls were bare now, just pale patches in the paintwork where my life had once been. But not anymore. My life was alive, beating with a mortal heart in the other wing of the house. She was warm and safe, sitting on the sofa with the bodyguard.

Now it was my job to keep it that way.

Keep her safe.

No matter what it took

I turned away and headed for the small dark bathroom, not bothering with the light.

A craving filled me, making my skin itch and my nerves strained. I hit the shower handle and stepped into the freezing cold spray, hissing as the cold made me feel even colder...and more animal. Fangs cut through my gums as I tipped my head back and washed my hair. I didn't want Ruth to see me like this. Not now when the beast shifted under my skin far too close to the surface.

I reached down, running the slick bar of soap across my stomach before I fisted my cock.

The Unseelie. Memories found their way into my head. Stabbing memories. *Carnal memories* as the midnight beast fucked her against the wall. She was just as brutal in that moment...just as much the malevolent creature as he was.

I couldn't stop myself from moving toward her as the green Unseelie power filled the room. Couldn't stop myself from staring into her unfocused gaze as she bared her fangs. She wanted him as much as she wanted me.

Flesh.

Blood.

Sex.

My cock hardened under my hand. But I didn't take the release. It wouldn't matter, even if I did. The mortal was under my skin and deep inside my veins. I wanted her more than I'd wanted any other woman in this unnatural goddamn life. I couldn't get enough, not of her scent or her body.

Or of her blood.

An ache spread through my body. I was too close to the beast now. Too *savage* to go to her. I didn't want her to see me like this. I had to prowl and hunt and feed that sickness inside me. I had to come to her a man, and not a monster...maybe then I could think straight. Maybe then I could do what needed to be done.

Find Caedes.

Kill him.

Protect her...like I hadn't protected her before.

I switched off the shower and stepped onto the tiled floor. Water ran down my spine, but I couldn't stand the feel of the towel against my skin. I dressed without drying, pants, shirt, buttoning as it stuck to my damp skin. I yanked on socks and boots and was out the door as darkness settled. There was no waiting for the others, no taking her to my bed. The truth was, I didn't trust myself. Not when I was this close to hunger...not when I was this close to the edge. I grabbed the car keys and strode outside, then hit the button for the sleek, dark Audi and slipped inside.

I wanted to disappear, to blend into the shadows. My headlights cut through the darkness, splashing over painted skin. Ancient eyes glinted as one of the Feralis strode through the grounds to disappear on the other side.

Feralis exercitus. An army of the dead, although they were very much alive. Mercenaries to the core. They'd keep Ruth safe...as long as she stayed with the Unseelie and away from the grounds. They'd protect her until I found a way out of this mess.

I shoved the car into gear and pulled out of the parking area, making my way around the house before I hit the drive and headed toward the other side of the city.

You're running, the beast snarled inside my head. *Running away from her and your responsibilities.*

"Shut the fuck up," I snarled, and punched the accelerator.

Darkness swept past as the white lines blurred. There were no police here. Mortals had given up trying to make us yield to their petty laws, that's why we stayed on this side of the river— where sparkling lights beckoned—*most of the time, anyway.*

I hit the on-ramp for the bridge and wove my way through the traffic to the other side of the city. My mind raced, haunted by those I was about to betray. I steered the Audi onto the off-ramp and pulled up at the set of lights. A heavy beat thudded against the window. Movement drew my gaze to the Lamborghini next to me. Young women dancing in their seats, arms failing as they sang and partied. Life. Raw and fleeting.

One of the young women turned her head and looked my way. Her words stuttered, lips moving in a mumble as our gazes connected. She was pretty and young. Glossy lips, long auburn hair, and wide brown eyes that tore from mine. She prodded her companion and jerked her gaze over her shoulder before glancing my way again.

"Fuck me, you're beautiful!" she howled through the open window.

I turned my head back to the street ahead as the lights changed from red to green, and floored the Audi. Lights were nearly blinding as they passed. I left the vibrant young women far behind. Part of me wanted to run...and keep on running. But another part of me was desperate to stay...to kill, and finally bring this to an end once and for all.

I wasn't what they saw...not really.

No...not beautiful. Damaged. Diseased. A monster. I jerked the wheel, spearing off the main streets to back streets and dark alleys, then pulled the sports car up hard. Heavy breaths claimed me, tearing from my chest, sounding harsh in the quiet. My headlights shone against overflowing trashcans and a homeless man with his dirty yellow tent and a shopping cart filled with belongings.

He lifted his hand, shielding his eyes, before I pulled back out into the street, this time driving more slowly. Hunger burned in my veins, making that beast inside writhe and shift, snarling as it filled me with hate. *Fucking feed me.*

I licked my lips. Maybe if I just drove...and kept on driving. Maybe then that itch would disappear. Bright lights, fast lanes. I punched the pedal and felt that roar in my veins. The beast's midnight eyes stared back at me from the rear-view mirror. Her laughter rang in my head, guttural, secretive. Ruth. She was everywhere, like a drug racing through my body.

I'm not going back to that fuck pad.

I winced at the memory of her voice and felt my cock grow hard. I wanted her back in that...*fuck pad,* wrists bound with red satin, breasts jiggling with each catch of her breath. I wanted that flare of surprise in her eyes as I fucked her. I wanted her slick, wet, and hungry, the way only Ruth could hunger...with the look of *fuck you* in her eyes.

I wanted my Mafia Princess...my goddamn Ruthless Queen.

I jerked the wheel on instinct. There was a place that catered for those like me. A bar run by Phantom, one that catered to darker desires. Knife's Edge was more than a strip club and more than a brothel. Mortals with an itch came there. Women looking for something a little more *savage.* Sex was what they wanted. But there were those who came to feel the bite, those whose idea of ecstasy was feeding beasts like me.

Ruth's face filled me. I licked my lips and turned the car into another street. Hate was cold and hard in the pit of my stomach. It was a shotgun cocked and loaded, ready to tear me apart. Just keep going. Keep driving. Find somewhere else where the air wasn't thick with need.

I drove until the streets blurred, hands strangling the wheel, praying I had another fucking option. But in the end, there was none. Just a taste was all I needed. Enough to sate the monster. Just enough to safely go back home to her.

I doubled back, making my way to familiar streets and pulled up outside an alley. The Knife's Edge was already lively. Metal bars across the doorway, the bouncer an Unseelie I knew. I killed the engine and shoved open the door. The stench of desire assaulted me, thick and heady...like syrup on the back of my tongue. I shut the door behind me and stepped into the darkness.

With every stride, I sank deeper and deeper into that waiting pit of despair.

Feed, my monster whispered. *Choose, or I will.*

I winced at the words and strode along the street to the darkened entrance.

"Elithien." Dark eyes glittered from the Unseelie, reminding me a little too much of last night.

I gave a nod as he opened the battered steel door and stepped to the side. I sank into the emptiness and strode down the stairs. Sparkling white floor lights revealed the path taking me all the way to the bar. Wolves tendered here. The silver glint of their eyes followed me as I stood at the edge and surveyed the room.

"Hey, I know you, right?" The woman's voice came from behind me, followed by a giggle. "Yeah, I know you, dreamboat."

"E," the bartender called, placing a glass on the bar. But he didn't pour, not until he turned and grabbed a bottle from the top shelf. I'd been here enough times for them to know me by name...and for me to know them. I met the bartender's gaze and nodded.

"Noah," I responded as the bartender pushed a glass of Scotch my way.

"Don't tell me you don't remember, dreamboat," the woman murmured, her voice heavy with intoxication. "Am I that easy to forget?"

I clenched my jaw and turned, staring into her big brown eyes. I knew exactly who it was. The pretty young woman from the Lamborghini. She smiled at me, lips pursed, breasts pushed out.

"I remember." I lifted the glass to my lips, never once taking my eyes from her.

She was beautiful. Cheerleader perfect, isn't that what they said? Vibrant, flush with life...and not my type.

"You come here often?" she asked, cocking her hip and smoothing down her mid-thigh dress. Her friend behind her was too busy eyeing the shirtless Wolf behind the bar. Thick muscles stretched and strained as he worked the drying cloth.

"Isn't that normally the guy's line?" I drained the Scotch and played with the empty tumbler. She wasn't Ruth, didn't look anything like her. Maybe she was different enough for me to...

No. The warning tore free inside my head. *Not her.*

I turned away, leaving her swaying at the edge of the bar. "Hey." Surprise flared in her brown eyes as I left. "Where you going?"

Movement was all around me. Lovers. Dancers. Bright lights flashed on the dance floor, blinding me for an instant. I blinked and saw Ruth there, swaying in that floor-length blood-red dress. Hurrow was behind her, hands on her hips as he looked at me across the room. I blinked again and they were gone. The tips of my fangs cut deeper and that ache turned to a roar. Mortals danced in front of me. Girls stripped high up on platforms, twisting and turning their bodies around a pole.

I spun, gaze searching for the brunette once more. The desperate howling of my beast was driving me to the edge. I scanned every woman...finding her friend tongue-deep in some other guy. Light slipped in further along the bar. Movement came, long hair fanned out as someone stepped out of the fire door into the alley. A male followed...his own need in the driver's seat. I turned away as the door swung closed. It was too late now. Too late for me to take her blood.

But there was something about the memory...something that nagged at me.

I left the dance floor behind and headed deeper into the club, slowing at the fire door now latched closed.

"Wait...don't do that."

A voice filled my ears. Her voice, the cheerleader outside. I strode forward, pushed through the door, and scanned the shadows, finding them. They were further along the alley. Her back was against the wall, and he was all over her, kissing her deeply, his hands roaming over her body.

Not your business...

I looked away and kept on walking, steering as close to the other side of the alley as I could, and left them behind.

"Hey...I don't think you should—" Her voice was slurred, smothered by his kiss.

I ground my teeth as her muffled whimpers turned frantic. *Not my problem. Not my fight. Just keep walking.*

"Wait," she groaned, that voice familiar. "Don't...that hurts. *Please don't do this!*"

Hey, I know you right? Her voice filled my head from before, soft...seductive. Nothing like it was now. There was fear in her voice now, a sharpening of her senses. I kept walking, leaving them behind, and turned the corner.

"Stop it...*I said stop. You're hurting me!*"

I stopped at the desperation in her voice. My fangs punched downward, my fists curled at my sides I was turning before I knew it, striding back into the darkness. The piece of shit never stood a chance. His eyes widened, his hand tore from under her dress before she stumbled away. Her eyes were wide, *haunted.* Fear was a rag shoved down my throat. *Her fear.*

That beast inside me broke free, savage and wild, finding in his eyes all those who'd betrayed me...and all those I'd betrayed.

"*Do not hurt a woman like that!*" I roared, then stopped.

Hard breaths punctured the air as I stared into his wide, frantic gaze.

He was Alliard.

He was Shrike.

He was Phantom...

And he was Caedes.

Caedes, standing over the body of the woman I'd once loved...

Caedes, striding across that floor in the Costello building, threatening to take everything from me again. *Yes...*the monster inside whispered. *Feed.*

I wrenched the piece of shit closer, opened my mouth wide, and struck. He was big and tall...powerful, with long arms that fell to his sides as his blood splashed into my mouth. The male froze for a second, until fear kicked in. Fight or flight. The panic didn't last. Not for him. Not anymore. He bucked in my grasp, fists slamming into my shoulders. The scent of the woman still on his fingers only made me savage. I bit harder, my fangs sank deeper, cutting through flesh and veins to the bone underneath. The monster in me hungered for something more than blood. The monster in me was rage. I reached up, my fingers finding the bones of his skull before I twisted.

The *snap* filled my ears as I let him fall. She was still there...the pretty young brunette. Her spine was pressed against the wall, looking at me with the same look Ruth had...when I'd pulled her from the river. "Leave," I snarled, my voice thick with feral need. "And don't ever come back."

She stumbled and fell, skinning her knees. The scent of her blood bloomed in the air before she ran. Still, the beast inside me wanted her, wanted more than blood and death. "No," I choked out the word, and stumbled to the middle of the alley.

My demons came for me, rising up from the ashes of my mind.

Alliard waited in the darkness...Alliard, with his morals and his spite. Alliard, who'd dragged me into this mess with him... then died. Hate rushed through me, cold and arctic and never-ending. The alley swayed around me as I fell to my knees.

The roar was unmerciful, tearing along my throat to bounce off the walls. Desperation. Hate...so much hate. It poured out of me like a volcano, hot and bitter and raw.

Blood on my hands.

Blood in my throat.

Warm and vital.

My stomach clamped down even as my throat constricted. But it was all too late. I heaved and wretched, throwing myself forward until my palms smashed against the filthy alley floor. Warmth splashed on the concrete in front of me and that heady, metallic scent filled my nose.

In that blinding moment of desperation, she was there. Her red hair gleaming in the light, her perfect brown eyes searching mine. Her sigh echoed in my ears as the memory slipped into my head.

My Ruth.

My Ruthless.

Feed, the monster urged inside me. Only one woman would do.

Headlights shone against the bloody mess behind me. The pungent stench of fear lingered in my nose as I turned toward the end of the alley. I left the blood and terror behind. *Feed,* the beast urged as I took a step. *Feed now...*

Movement came from the end of the alley, drawing my gaze. I drew in a deep breath, tasting the fetid stench of foulness. A warning bloomed in the back of my throat, then a rumble spilled out as my lips curled and I stopped walking. "Forllen."

The Vampire froze just inside the alley, cloaked in shadows, the high collar of his jacket covering most of his face. But I'd know that cockroach anywhere. My fingers curled, the scent of blood still ripe and fresh...what was one more kill to the count?

"Easy, Elithien," the piece of shit murmured. "I'm not here to fight you." He lifted his head. Bright headlights of a passing car cut across a strong jaw and piercing eyes. His lips curled into a wry smile as he finished. "I'm here to offer you a way out."

An unmerciful sound came to life and spilled from my lips. Betrayer. *Corrupt.* I'd never in a million years align myself with someone like him.

"You do want information on the Inner Circle, don't you?" The Vampire shifted his gaze, trying to look nonchalant, not willing to meet my gaze. "Caedes has always taken quite an interest in you."

"What the fuck do you want, Forllen?"

His lips moved into a smile that was more of a smirk as he met my gaze once more. "I want only what you want, Elithien," he offered. "I want the Circle to break."

"So, treason," I responded, keeping the edge of fear from my tone. There were others around him. One across the street, another at my right. If he'd wanted me dead, I'd be dead already. But that wasn't Forllen's style, was it? He was a mako swimming in a pool of great whites. Killers. Hunters. Sharks. Caring about nothing but themselves.

"You call it treason, I call it an opportunity. I've heard your new mortal is..."

That warning burned in the center of my chest. *"Don't you fucking talk about her."*

"Feisty." His smirk grew wider. "You were always touchy when it came to love, weren't you? Which is why we make the perfect team...for love."

"What do you know about love? You can't see past your own reflection," I snarled.

The dark pools of his eyes sparkled that little bit harder. "Oh, I think you'd be surprised when it came to love and me. But this is not about me, it's about *you*. You want what I can get. Information."

I waited, hatred brewing inside me like an arctic storm.

"You want to know who ordered the hit, don't you?"

I flinched at the words.

"...and you want to know how to get rid of Caedes once and for all." The bastard took a step closer. "Look at you." Those glittering eyes drifted up and down me. "So much torture... endless torture. No Princess...no Prince, and soon to be, no heady mortal love."

His words rocked me. The beast inside writhed with ravening need. I flinched at the blare of a horn in the distance. Harsh breaths punched from my chest. My words rolled out like thunder. "And in exchange?"

"I want to make a statement, Elithien. I want to make a stand. Hit them right where it hurts. I know you have a pickup coming tomorrow night...and I want to intercept that pickup."

"Money?" The word burned in the back of my throat. "You want me to become like you for *fucking money?*"

"It's not just any money though, is it? It's a slap in the face...a big *fuck you* to the governors," Forllen insisted, fangs exposed by his smile. "I want to send a message, Elithien, and I want to make it loud and clear."

And use me to do it.

But was it just him? I doubted it. There were other players here. *Dangerous players.* The great whites were circling...and I was bait.

All the ramifications came to life inside my head. He wanted me down there playing in the muck of our Immortal world with him, with blood on my hands, and betrayer as my name. "You realize what that will do to Shrike and Phantom when they find out?"

"Spoils of war, my friend." He took a step backwards. "Spoils of war."

"I am *not* your friend," I bit back.

The scuff of a shoe behind me drew my focus. I whipped my gaze over my shoulder. Silver shimmered in the darkness. The Wolf, Noah, standing there...*listening.*

Hate rolled off me. The storm finally came to life, rage, hopelessness...and finally cruel, cutting acceptance. The bartender held my gaze and backed away, heading for the propped-open fire door.

"What do you say, Elithien?" Forllen whispered, drawing my gaze again. "Do we have a deal?"

Chapter Twenty-Three

I TRIED TO REACH OUT TO HER IN THOSE LAST FEW MONTHS, Ruthy. But she pulled away from us. She even pulled away from your father. She was hiding something, changing right before our eyes.

"You okay? You've been jumpy all day."

I flinched at the words and jerked my gaze to Russell, who worked the towel around the rim of the glass. "I'm fine. Just a lot to think about."

Turmoil swept around me like a storm closing in. Secrets and lies. My family were steeped in them, but there'd never been lies amongst ourselves. Never deceit amongst thieves. Never blood turning away from blood. "I need to do something."

"We are doing something, we're drying dishes...and we're waiting for the Vampires to rise."

For Elithien to rise. The sudden starting of an engine at the rear of the house caught my breath. I left the sink and the kitchen behind and made my way to the front of the house. Headlights cut through the falling light of a brand-new night.

The sleek flash of the Audi was only a blur before it was gone, engine revving, tires kicking up bits of dirt as it raced through the entrance of the drive.

With Elithien behind the wheel.

A pang cut across my chest, my breath stuttering as it escaped. He'd left me...gone before I could even speak to him. "He's angry with me."

"With you?" Justice answered behind me. "No, never with you. Only with the demons riding his soul."

I spun and lifted my gaze. Justice was standing there, staring down...meeting my gaze. He consumed the room, every dam inch of it. All the air. All the space. All my heart. Movement came from behind him as Rule and Hurrow stepped into the room, hair still slick, all of them pale, jaws clenched—on edge.

"I can't just stand here and wash dishes," I protested, meeting Justice's gaze. "I can't play house."

"No one's asking you to."

Makes sense she'd spread her legs for you...must be fucked-up genetics, just like her whore of a mother. Alex's words reared inside my mind. I'd repeated those words all afternoon and while I did, I grew a new beast of my own. Now it was hungry for answers. One that could see the jumbled pieces of the puzzle...one who was determined to find their places and find answers.

"I need to get out of here," I announced. *Alex's smug expression was a fist in my throat.* "I want to go to the city."

"Not going to happen," Hurrow answered.

Heat flared deep inside, making me clench my fists.

"I'll go with her," Justice offered.

"And me," Russell growled, the tension between them sparking.

"No. None of you are going. We stay here and we come up with a plan," Hurrow declared. "What's so important?"

"I want to go to the apartment Alex had." *He had to have answers.*

"Pointless," Rule added, pouring himself a Scotch. "We went through that place, there's nothing left."

"Except the server," Justice said.

"*Server?*" I snapped, heart hammering. "*What* server?"

Rule just turned and lifted the glass before nodding to Justice. "The one he ripped from the shelf."

My pulse was thrumming, making my thoughts race. "And you have this server?" One nod from Justice was all it took. "I need it," I maintained. "I want to see all of it."

"Can't, it's encrypted," Justice explained. "I tried."

Ace...Ace would crack it. I stepped away from the front window. "Ace...Ace would crack it."

"What exactly do you think you're gonna find, anyway?" Rule asked, draining his glass and refilling it.

"I don't know." I shifted my gaze to Russell. "Everything he knew."

"Set up the meeting, then." Justice gave a shrug. "But it won't be you he's gonna meet...it'll be me."

He'll take one look at Justice and run...but not far, at least. "Tell the guy if he doesn't show, I'll get pissed...and we both know how that turns out."

I went to the study, flicked on the light, and sat down behind the desk. They had a server...a damn server. My fingers trembled as I wiggled the mouse and waited for the screen to open. By the time Justice strode through the door, I was already on the Pekingese website and logging a message.

"Tonight," Justice ordered.

"He's responded," I muttered and just stared at the screen for a moment before I met the Vampire's gaze. "He's ready to meet now...and he wants to come here."

Justice's lips curled in a smile...a chilling smile.

"Play nice, Vampire," I commanded, but the smile only grew.

"Don't I always?" he threw over his shoulder as he turned to leave. "Unless the asshole runs."

I tracked the thud of his steps all the way to the rear of the house before they died away.

"You think you're going to find something, don't you?" Russell crossed the room and stopped at the window. Headlights flared a second before the growl of the four-wheel drive's engine reached us. The Explorer was gone in a heartbeat, tearing through the night, just like Elithien had.

"I don't know," I answered, staring at the screen. "But the way Alex looked at me...told me only one thing."

"He had intel."

I gave a nod and met those midnight eyes. "I want to know what that was."

My hand went to my pocket as I rose from behind the desk. But the ring wasn't there. I'd left it in Elithien's bedroom, behind steel doors and in darkness. It wasn't my father's ring...and before I touched it again, I wanted to know who's ring it was.

"So we wait." Russell crossed the space and opened his arms.

I stepped into them, sighing, and pressed my face against his hard chest. "We wait."

I TRIED to keep busy and not watch for headlights in the night. But every second was excruciating and by the time headlights splashed across the front of the house, my nerves were wrecked. I blinked into the glare as the Explorer pulled up and the headlights died. *No Elithien...*I looked out into the night with a sinking feeling in my heart.

He was hurting, that I knew. Even the others were quiet and somber...*waiting.* Car doors opened and closed with *thuds.* Two sets of boots approached the front door. I rose from the sofa as the door opened and Justice strode in. Ace was right behind him, pausing for a moment as he scanned the area, then his gaze settled on me.

"You didn't leave the city." I uncrossed my arms. "I'm surprised."

"I thought about it," he muttered, looking around again. "So this is where you live your double life."

"Not a double," I corrected. "Just a better continuation than the one before."

One brow shot high as he glanced my way again. "Better, huh?"

"It seems hotshot here has made a few friends," Justice growled.

"More than a damn few. Your friend Carina Chase, to name one of them."

That deep-seated hatred rose. I could still hear her damn laughter ringing in my head. Fucking bitch. "Who else?" I met his gaze. "You said there were others, who else?"

"I don't know." He shifted from one foot to the other. "I never see a face. But they've been following me for days now. Every time I go to leave, someone's outside my damn door." *Because of you.*

He didn't need to say the words. I felt responsible enough. "I'm sorry, Ace."

He gave a shrug. "It is what it is. Now, you gonna chitchat or lead me to this server you need me to crack?"

It was just like him to brush off my ruining his life with a shrug. Still, I crossed the room and wrapped my arms around him. He was one of the few friends I had left, and that ache in my chest ate deeper. "Thank you." I clutched him tight. "Thank you for everything."

He shifted uncomfortably, his arms ramrod stiff at his sides until I released my hold and stepped back. All eyes were on us, Rule, Justice, Hurrow...and Russell. Their threatening stares made Ace's eyes widen in fear. "I'm just here for the server," he muttered. "Just get me the damn server."

"This way, Romeo." Rule nodded his head.

Ace hurried to catch up, disappearing into the back of the house with Rule. Justice gave me a glance, then followed, leaving Hurrow and Russell behind.

"He's coming back to you, Ruth." Hurrow glanced at the front windows, then back at me. "Just give him time."

He left, but instead of following the others, he headed for the back door and disappeared outside. It wasn't Ace the Vampire was talking about. I glanced once more at the night sky and followed the others, with Russell close behind.

Give him time, Hurrow had urged. But somehow, I felt that time wasn't really the issue here. I'd felt a coldness growing between us since that night at the warehouse when I'd pulled the gun and tried to end Alexander's life. Something had changed between us. Something more than the addition of Russell in my bed. It was a growing darkness, a hollowness in the pit of my stomach. One that consumed me more every second that slipped by.

Fight, the strength in me urged. I *would* fight...the only way I knew how.

With teeth and claws and information I could use.

I followed the sound of voices along the hallway to the back study. Russell stepped around me, watching the others as they powered up the server and connected it to a monitor. But it was the closed door on the other side of the hall that called me. Elithien's scent still clung to the hallway, sultry and seductive. I was stepping across the space before I knew it, then twisted the handle and stepped into the room.

A wave of grief slammed into me. Unforgiving, violent and bitter, choking in the back of my throat. I turned away from the darkness, lifting my hand to grip the doorframe...and froze. This was *his* grief. *His* pain. *His loneliness.* I could no more turn my back on his need than I could my own.

I reached further, flicked on the light, and stared at the small bed at the side of the room. It was an empty room...stark cream walls, a smaller bathroom than the one we shared. I left the sound of the others behind and moved deeper into the space. There were markings on the wall. Patches of brighter paint... like something had been hung there. I moved closer and dragged my finger along a discoloration.

It looked almost like images had been stuck on the walls. Lots and lots of images.

But they were gone now. Pain plunged like a knife in my chest.

"You okay?" Hurrow enquired from the doorway.

I flinched, dropped my hand, and turned toward him. "I honestly don't know. It's like I can't quite reach him. Not like I could before."

"He blames himself, for everything...especially you." Hurrow reached for my hand, his strong fingers capturing mine as he drew me close and kissed my knuckles, staring into my eyes. "He won't rest until you're safe."

"That file there," Russell said, leaning over Ace's shoulder. "Open it."

"Umm..." Ace hesitated, and looked to Justice. Something passed between the giant and my hacker. A shake of the head... a warning come up life. Something had happened between them before they'd walked in the door.

"There has to be more information than that," Russell snapped.

I left that room filled with heartbreak behind me, focusing on the growing anger in the study. "What's going on?"

"There is more..." Justice straightened and turned his head toward me. "But you're not going to like it."

All heads turned to me as I came closer. "What am I not going to like?"

"Ruth." Rule shook his head and came toward me. "I don't think—"

"What am I not going to like, Justice?" I bored my gaze into the Vampire.

"It's you," Justice answered, his tone cold, gaze even colder. "Alone, in bed..."

Me, alone in bed? Alex had a recording of that? A chill crept along my spine.

"You don't have to watch that," Rule urged, and turned his head to the others. "No one needs to watch that."

That feeling of disconnect swept over me. "I want to see it."

Justice let out a growl and wrenched his gaze away. Whatever recording they'd found upset him.

I stepped around Rule, dropping Hurrow's hand, and moved to stand behind Ace. "Play it, Ace." But there was no movement, just the cursor hovering over a file on the screen. "Ace..."

He swallowed hard, and clicked on the file. The screen came to life, dark at first. Shadows and pale light just a blur...until the image sharpened.

"Elithien..." my own moan of desire echoed through the speakers. *"Hurrow."* I rolled in the bed, hands under the sheets, between my thighs, my hips thrusting upwards.

I knew that night.

I knew this dream.

I stole a breath as the memory came to life, playing out for all to see. Ace shifted nervously in his seat and looked away. Justice and Rule stared at me, searching my gaze for every flicker of humiliation. But it was Russell who didn't turn away. He watched and listened as I called their names, seduced by the fantasy of my Immortal lovers...until Ace clicked the file and ended the sight.

The room was utterly silent.

"I killed him, right?" Russell muttered.

"Yeah, brother," Rule answered. "You killed him."

"I'm just checking..." Russell's fingers curled into a fist. "'Cause if I hadn't..."

I swallowed all that hate and rage and humiliation down into the pit of my stomach. "It doesn't matter."

Hate glinted in the midnight eyes as Russell jerked his gaze to mine. "He *recorded you.* He...*fucking watched you.* I want to break every fucking bone in his body. I *want* to make sure there's one less piece of shit in the world. One less..."

"Scum," Justice offered.

Russell jerked his focus to the Vampire. Something passed between them, purpose...acceptance. "Yeah, scum."

"I get that." I stepped closer, reached out to run my fingers over that clenched fist, and met his gaze. "But he can't hurt me anymore."

"Not after I'm through with this server, he won't," Ace promised. "There'll be no more files...nothing that can be uploaded. But it might take me a while."

"You'll need coffee then," Rule offered as he turned toward the door.

"Lots of it!" Ace called out before he turned his attention to Justice, laced his fingers and bent them backwards, stretching. "This might go a lot faster if you're not hovering."

"I don't...*hover*," Justice snapped, but reluctantly followed Rule before he tacked on, "Much."

I rolled my thumb across Russell's knuckles, taking comfort in the feel of him as Ace set to work. After a while, I paced, then took a seat on the sofa in the corner of the room. Rule brought coffee and, after a while, sandwiches, that he handed to me with a hard, breathtaking kiss.

They came and went while Ace sat in silence, searching through countless folders and files. Most of them involved shady dealings with men I cared little about, though some of them contained information on the Inner Circle. But it was information Justice and Rule already knew. Four hours passed in a blur. I found myself waiting alone on the sofa while the rest of my army tried to keep from acknowledging the growing truth...

Elithien still wasn't home.

"Ruth..." Ace called.

I jerked from my thoughts, and found Ace staring at me. "What did you say your mom's name was?"

That icy touch raced down my spine once more. "Cassandra...why?"

He frowned, glanced at the open door, then back at me. One silent jerk of his head, and I was slowly rising. I crossed the study, and stood behind him. There was a file called CC. Inside were videos, five, six, some left Untitled. Others, though...others were called 'Money Makers'.

Ace turned his gaze to me, and the ground seemed to open up and swallow me whole.

I gave a nod and prayed no one came in as the video played. A woman filled the screen, young...beautiful. Her eyes. *Jesus*. I couldn't help but stare. I'd know those eyes anywhere.

"You look *just* like her," Ace whispered, sounding amazed.

She stood at the corner of a building. For a moment, I couldn't quite work out the angle of the camera...until I realized what it was. This was a PI's camera. An investigator Dad must've hired to follow her. Headlights splashed across her face before the car drove past.

She cried out. The sound of her panic was like a shotgun blast to my chest. "I told you to stay away from me!"

A man's voice slipped from the speakers, low...muffled. "And if I did, what then?"

"Then I'd have some kind of life. This is it...this is over now. I have a family."

"And what a perfect little family you are, faithful husband, pretty daughter."

I tried to hear his voice. But for some reason, I couldn't quite grasp the tone.

He moved fast then, grabbing her arm and dragging her against him. Too fast...*inhumanly fast.* She resisted...at first, thrashing in his hold. Fighting and snarling until the sound was cut off as he kissed her with so much passion, I looked away...until I remembered what she was doing. She was betraying my father with another man.

"No..." she pleaded.

My blood ran cold.

I stumbled backward, my hand rising in the air.

"This has to stop. I don't want this anymore. You have to let me go. If Denzel ever found out..."

"You think I can't protect you? You think I give a fuck about that mortal *gnat.*"

"*I care about that mortal gnat!*" she cried, and pushed him away. "I love him. *I want him.* You have to *stop* this...it's been too long."

"For you." That warped, savage growl cut through the speakers. "It's been a blink of an eye for me. I won't stop, Cassandra. *I'll never stop...*"

"No," I whispered as the Vampire pulled my mother close and kissed her again.

After she stopped resisting, her arms went around his waist. Muffled moans of desire spilled into the room...she wanted him...that *Vampire.* She wanted him enough to betray my dad.

Chapter Twenty-Four

I want to send a message, Elithien, and I want to make it loud and clear.

I clenched the wheel and kept driving as Forllen's words rattled around inside my head. Headlights from the oncoming cars made me wince and look away. But no matter how fast I drove, I found myself turning toward home. "No," I muttered. "You can't go back, not now..."

Do we have a deal?

My jaw creaked. Fangs punched through the soft flesh of my gums as my cell phone vibrated and the horror of what I'd just done hit me. I reached onto my pocket, yanked my phone free, and glanced at the caller ID before casting it onto the passenger seat. The scent of blood still lingered from the splatter on my shirt and the smears on my skin.

The pretty cheerleader's wide eyes were haunting me as I left the mortal part of the city behind. Headlights bounced against the asphalt as the sleek Audi hit the off-ramp and merged into the lane.

Silver shone in the darkness as a blur came across two lanes of traffic and stopped in the middle of my lane. The brakes squealed and the tires screamed as the sports car skidded to a stop in the middle of the road. Phantom just stood there, head down, eyes fixed on the road until he lifted his gaze.

There was blood on his shirt, and streaked across his cheek... bloodied, bruised...but definitely not beaten. He strode toward me, his long legs eating the distance. His once-long hair had been cut short...it suited him.

I hit the button and lowered the window as bright headlights behind me filled the car. The oncoming traffic slowed, giving us a wide berth as Phantom stopped outside my door. "You ignoring my calls, E?"

There was a warning in those words. A carefulness. I forced my words through clenched teeth. "I'm not in the mood, Phantom."

"Then *change your goddamn mood*. The warehouse, E. Don't piss me off any more than you already have."

He turned then, and strode around the front of the car, shifting his gaze in the blinding glare of the headlights. He was a beast tonight, his skin too goddamn thin. He moved like a Wolf, long, languid movements striding away from the headlights, leaving the blood on his face to darken in the night.

Beasts.

We were all goddamn beasts tonight.

I turned the wheel, my gaze lingering on the streets that'd take me home—*to her*. A growl rumbled in the depth of my chest and spilled outwards. I punched the accelerator, leaving the backed-up line of cars behind, and headed for the warehouse.

Phantom was different tonight. Harder...*clipped.* His hair wasn't the only thing that'd changed. There had been a shift in the balance, a crack in the ether. One so subtle it could be missed. But I felt it...and Phantom did too.

Do we have a deal?

The words cleaved through my mind.

That fissure tore through my world, and all the cockroaches were scurrying out. I shot past the nightclubs and the brothels, leaving the glittering lights behind. It had all started with Caedes and it would end with him, too.

I pulled the Audi up outside the entrance to the warehouse and climbed out of the car. A shudder cut through me. I dragged my fingers through my hair and tried to force the beast back down.

Down into the darkness...

Where hunger felt like pain.

For a little while, at least.

Lights spilled out the open doorway and the bitter stench of rage followed. I stepped inside and closed the door behind me. Phantom and Shrike stood in the middle of the warehouse floor. One glance at the row of steel doors behind them, and that deep-seated ache came roaring back.

I wanted this over with...*all of it.* Caedes, Alliard...the Circle. "All I'm missing is the red carpet, it seems." I spoke, and my tone was a little more savage than I wanted. "Want to tell me what's so damn important?"

Phantom just stood there, his massive arms crossed over his chest. But Shrike, on the other hand... The Unseelie bored his unflinching gaze into mine, then took in the rest of me. "Heard you've had quite the night, what with mortals and meetings."

That crack in my world seemed to open wider, and a chilling draft swept through. My stomach clenched as I waited for him to get to the damn point. But as I stared into the Fae's eyes, I saw that shift plain as fucking day. Anger filled me, bitter, rancid anger. "You have something you want to ask me, then go ahead and ask."

"You were heard, Elithien," Phantom snarled, and shook his head. "There's no denying it."

"I wasn't going to."

The Wolf flinched and jerked his gaze to mine. That Immortal silver glinted like steel. The muscles of his jaw flexed with the clench. "So that's it then," he growled. "You betray us like that."

There it was, the slap in the fucking face. One so brutal, it rocked me where I stood.

I couldn't speak, couldn't stay a damn word.

"They'll come for us now," Shrike growled, stepping closer. "They'll fucking come."

"Then help me." I fought the rage. "We can break the Circle. We can end this."

"We can't end a damn thing, and if you honestly think that, then you're a fool." Shrike stabbed the words like a blade. "But then again...you always were a fool, weren't you, Elithien? A moral, loyal fucking fool. You killed yourself the moment you aligned yourself with Alliard and his fucking fantasy of living with the mortals, and you know it."

"And now you want to align yourself with Forllen." Phantom paced, his long legs eating the distance like his Wolf couldn't stand to be still. "You know what circles he runs in, E. They're reckless and fucking dangerous...even for us. We're not equipped to deal with that kind of danger. Those players...they don't play fair."

"Then help me," I pleaded softly.

"What's the saying? *Bed. Lie?*" Phantom growled.

That sinking feeling swallowed me. After all these years, they still didn't know me at all? My own fucking desperation was a whirlpool, sucking me under, tearing me apart. So this is what it felt like to drown?

"It won't be just me *lying* in it, Wolf." I met his gaze, then Shrike's. "They're coming either way and the sooner you get that through your thick canine skull the better we'll all be. We're stronger together."

"We're dead together," Shrike disagreed, hate raging in his eyes. "Fuck stronger."

I understood now. It didn't matter what I said, didn't matter how hard I pleaded my case. Didn't matter all the goddamn years I'd been by their fucking sides, feeding the Inner Circle their money. Their minds were already made up...and I was the betrayer.

I met their gazes, searing those sparks of rage into my mind, and turned away. Fuck stronger, indeed. I was on my own now. Maybe that's the way it was always meant to be?

I left the warehouse...left the money. Left my alliance behind and strode out of the building.

Do we have a deal?

I climbed into the Audi and started the engine as the scene replayed in my head. Forllen had been so sure I'd take the offer...so sure I'd give in...

I was, after all, full of goddamn self-loathing.

Riding that killing edge.

I could still feel my hands around his throat. Still see that sadistic shimmer of madness in his eyes as I'd answered. *Come to me with betrayal again...and I'll kill you my fucking self.*

Chapter Twenty-Five

"Stop the video." I winced at the broken sound of my voice. "Please."

Ace fumbled, smashing the button on the mouse. It didn't matter...it continued to play out inside my head. The secrecy... the betrayal. I backed away, untethered, *alone. Always alone... especially with the lies.*

Makes sense she'd spread her legs for you...must be fucked-up genetics, just like her whore of a mother

I clenched my eyes closed as the words invaded again, steadied myself, and opened them once more. "Delete it. Delete it all... every image. Everything. No one can know."

Even now I tried to protect our name...and myself.

Ace swallowed hard, his eyes bugging wide. "Okay," he stuttered. "Okay, Ruth."

My feet moved on their own, turning, stumbling through the house, not seeing a damn thing. Not the bright hallway lights.

Not the concerned faces of my lovers. Rule pressed in close, his lips moving as he caught my gaze. I smiled and nodded, not hearing a word he said.

I'll never stop...

The Vampire's words filled me.

I'll never stop...

My hands fluttered in the air, my own voice was detached and strained. Dull words spilled from my lips. I didn't know what I said. But it was something, enough to make Rule flinch and slowly nod his head. Justice and Russell were there in the background. I turned away before meeting their gazes. My steps carried me toward Elithien's bedroom...but that wasn't where I found myself.

No, that wasn't where I ended up, at all.

Chill night air hit me. My steps were silent, the hinges soundless as I closed the door behind me. *Not my father...not my father...not my—*

The night was so quiet, so *utterly* still. But inside my head I was screaming, howling with rage and fury...and loathing. For her as well as me.

She'd lied...

She'd *fucking* lied.

And I was a product of that lie. A slap in my father's face. A constant humiliation. No wonder he'd refused to tell my uncle. It's a miracle he hadn't hated me. *He hadn't hated me...had he?*

My knees trembled at the thought. I gripped the bricks, holding on with all I had as acid rose in the back of my throat. The ground was nothing more than a blur as a retch came. I coughed, heaved, and held on as the world swayed around me.

I'll never stop...those words echoed from the video. That voice... that muffled voice. I clenched my jaw and tried to remember. A Vampire...*Jesus*...a goddamn Vampire.

But what did that make me?

"Shouldn't have left the house, mortal." Movement came from the corner of my vision. Yellow eyes blazed in the night as the mercenary strode toward me. "Don't you know...it's dangerous out here." His gaze drifted over my body.

I flinched as my pulse stuttered, then boomed.

Stay inside, Ruth...whatever you do, stay inside. Elithien's warning rang in my head.

But it was too late. I straightened, swiped the back of my hand across my mouth, and stumbled backwards. It was all too late. "I..." I glanced at the house. "I didn't mean..."

"We're monsters," he growled, glancing to his right as another of them came from the shadows. Towering beasts, with yellow eyes and white fangs that extended when they smiled. "And you're the perfect fucking bait."

The closest one came for me, all leather and hunger. Sickening desire rolled off him in drugging waves. *Hurt...kill...take without asking...take and take and take.* The words assaulted me. He licked his lips, lowering those horrifying yellow eyes to drift down my body. Fear and revulsion turned my insides weak. I spun toward him, but my gaze shifted to the dark blur behind him...a blur that turned from black shadows to faint, dark green, and grew brighter in the blink of an eye.

Caedes came from that eerie green Unseelie glow, striding forward, even as the mercenaries whipped their gazes toward the intruder and bared their fangs.

"Still now," Caedes commanded with a sweep of his hand.

They froze, unable to lift a hand to save themselves.

He strode toward me, lifted his other hand, and shoved the hood from his face. Those haunting midnight eyes seized mine, and for a second, it was as though we were suspended in time and space. The world stood still in that moment, trapped in a void of power. The second between one heartbeat and the next that stretched.

"You?" I spat, harsh breaths burning in the middle of my chest. I scanned the mercenaries, searching their bodies for a weapon I could use. "Don't you come any closer."

"Or you'll do what?" he mocked, and looked at the mercenaries. "Sick your dogs onto me? If it's Vampire, Ruth," one twist of his hand, and the closest mercenary fell to his knees, "it belongs to me."

I shook my head and glanced at the house once more.

"Go on, scream," he urged. "And you'll never find the answers you need."

I whipped my gaze to his. "The only answer I need right now is how to fucking kill *you.*"

His lips curled and his dark eyes sparkled with a flash of...*pride?* The mercenary was struggling. His face twitched, his eyes slowly widened. Like this was some kind of spell and it was wearing away, or he was trying his damnedest to tear it away.

"Take one motherfucking step," I snarled, curling my fists up, and jerked my gaze back to him. Why the fuck didn't I carry my gun in the house?

"You don't need it." Caedes took a small step closer. "Guns are useless against me, anyway. If I wanted to hurt you, Ruth, I could have, many times over. I'm giving you an opportunity here. You want answers. I can provide those answers."

The Vampire from the video?

I stiffened at his words, that seething hatred burning inside me. I didn't want anything from him, not to fucking talk...only to die. "You want to give me answers? Fine, how can I kill you?"

The sadistic chuckle that slipped from his lips made me want to clutch my belly and moan.

"You will lose him, Ruth. You understand that." His smile fell away. It was all a facade anyway. A mask of humanity...nothing more than a plastic sheath melting away to reveal the monster inside. "The Vampire has become a...*problem.*"

The Vampire? My heart seemed to stutter and grow still. He meant Elithien. "You even look at him sideways, I'm gonna fuck you up." I straightened my spine, jutting my chin into the air. "You want Elithien...then you'll need to go through me."

"Is that an ultimatum?" One brow rose. "What is that worth to you? His life."

Everything...

The answer hit me like a splash of icy water. All the pieces slowly slid together. *I won't turn you into one of us...not yet.* Elithien's voice came roaring back to me. I froze...my heart hammering, as I stared into the dark. It wasn't Caedes I saw now. It was them...*my lovers.* The sight hit me like a shotgun blast to my chest.

I knew now why I hadn't made any effort to go back to my mortal life. Why I hadn't taken every opportunity to discount the tsunami of evidence that said I was dead. Why I'd stayed on this side of the city. In my...*home.* And my home had nothing to do with bricks and mortar. But *everything* to do with them.

Because I want them...

More than I want my company and my damn name.

I love them.

All of them.

Elithien's face burned in my mind. My first Vampire kiss...

"And what the fuck do you get?" I jerked my gaze to his. But inside I was panicking, desperate to do whatever it took.

"What I've always wanted...you, Ruth. I get you," Caedes answered as a snarl tore from the mercenary. "That's all I ever wanted. Your life for his. The alley of Sixth and James Street." He stepped back into that glow of green. "And Ruth, come alone, or your Vampire is ash."

Ruth? Rule's voice was urgent in my head.

I sagged against the garage as the last hold over the mercenary tore loose.

RUTH!

"I'm out here," I answered, closing my eyes.

The door smacked against the house with a *crack!* Rule, Justice, and Russell consumed the night, tearing across the grounds toward me.

"Get the fuck away from her!" Russell roared, and stepped onto the feral Vampire's path.

Savage yellow eyes glinted as they sized him up. But my bodyguard wasn't backing down, not even when long white fangs shone from under the curled lips.

"I'm gonna tear you apart, Unseelie," the mercenary growled, and stepped closer.

Two mercenaries became five and surrounded us, feral and unhinged. Madness shone in their eyes. Is that why Elithien hired them? Because they were nothing more than savages? Nothing more than...mindless beasts? I turned as movement came from behind me.

"Enough," Justice ordered. But even he watched them carefully. They weren't just Vampires, they were animals.

"No!" I whipped my gaze to the sound as Elithien stepped from around the corner of the house. He looked...*terrible*. His hair was matted...was that blood on his face? His eyes were haunted, more haunted than I'd ever seen. Agony cut through his gaze as he stared at me.

I'm sorry...

The words were a knife in my chest.

"Back to your jobs," he commanded, and cut the Vampire soldiers a glare.

One looked at the other before curled lips slid over pale fangs once more. They stepped backwards, like dogs obeying their master—until that master turned their back, at least.

"You okay?" I stepped toward Elithien.

He winced at the words, stopping me cold. "It's me who should be asking you that, Ruth." He glanced around at the others and the outside grounds. "What possessed you to come out here?"

The video...

Caedes. The warning.

Everything slammed into me.

Lie. The thought roared to the surface. *Lie to him...*

"I f-forgot," I stammered, heat rushing to my cheeks.

Elithien stepped closer, that inhuman silver shine glinting from his eyes in the faint light that spilled from the house. "You forgot?" he murmured, but there was something off in his tone, something that made him sound...*fragile.*

I swallowed hard under the spotlight of his gaze and realized that right here, with his entire focus on me...was a very dangerous place to be. "I saw the video."

Justice snarled and tore his gaze away. Russell grew still...so very still, as Elithien just held my gaze. "I'm sorry you had to see that." His voice broke as that glint sharpened like the honed edge of a blade. "I'd kill him a thousand times over, just for that. But you have to understand, I did what I did to protect you."

I was the one who stepped closer, drawn by the invisible current that churned and swelled inside me when he was near. "That I'll never doubt." He flinched as I lifted my hands.

So raw...so utterly raw.

He was hurting like I'd never seen another man hurt before. Torn apart and stitched back together, only the wounds were gaping and too much of him spilled out. He tilted his head as I cupped his cheek and brushed my thumb against his skin.

"Do you want to take me inside?" I whispered. *And make love to me.*

"I'd better take the geek home.," Justice commented, then my Vampire protector was gone, striding toward the rear of the house to disappear inside.

Elithien swallowed hard. I'd expected a nod at least, but not sadness.

"What happened, E?" Hurrow asked as he stepped closer.

"We're on our own now," he answered with the ghost of a smile. "I guess it'll be easier to defend ourselves, fewer alliances to be concerned about."

Hurrow froze, a savage flash of rage cutting across his face. "The Wolves and the Fae?"

"Gone." Elithien glanced at me, then at Russell and the others. "We need to plan., to strategize. We call everyone who's ever owed us in the past. I don't give a fuck what you do. Threaten, coerce...hold fucking captive, for all I care." He looked at me. "Whatever it takes." *To keep you safe.*

My world swayed...

You will lose him, Ruth. You understand that. The Vampire has become a...problem.

Caedes' words filled me, pushing and prodding, finding a place to settle down and worm their way into my soul. We were on our own now. On our own against an enemy that can command their very existence. How can we fight something like Caedes? How can we battle against an enemy that can bring us to our knees with a single flick of the wrist?

We couldn't...

That was the truth. We couldn't. Not when they controlled everything...*for Immortals.* But he didn't control me...or my family. "I have contacts."

The sadness still clung to his eyes even as he smiled. "That's my Mafia Princess."

He reached out his hand for me. It was instant, our connection, our love. I turned to Hurrow, then Rule, Justice...and Russell. They all gave a nod as Elithien headed for the house and took me with him.

This was it, the last stand. Caedes would come for us. That was without a doubt. We had tonight. Mere hours against an eternity of desire. By tomorrow...Caedes would have what he wanted...or what he'd come for. It was that simple, Elithien...or me.

And I was determined for it to be me.

He pushed through the back door of the house and we were inside. But it wasn't his bedroom he led me to...it was *that* room. The one which sent shivers down my spine. The room where I'd danced and fucked...

"I feel raw tonight, Ruth," Elithien murmured. "I won't be in control. I want to...*take.*"

The same hunger like from the mercenaries hit me. He was too much Vampire tonight. Too much *monster*. "Take whatever you need from me," I answered as he led me into that room and stopped at the side of the bed. "I trust you."

He looked at me with utter carnal devotion. His white fangs grew as the others came into the room behind him. My monsters...my beautiful, terrifying monsters. Hurrow went to the cupboard and opened a drawer.

Black leather and gleaming metal shone under the soft lights. I caught my breath at the sight of the harness and swallowed hard.

"Tonight," Elithien started, his inhuman gaze slipping lower, "I want to take you to the dark side and show you what your body was made for."

Chapter Twenty-Six

"Put it on her," Elithien growled. "I want to see her in leather."

A shiver coursed along my spine as Rule stepped closer. "You okay, Princess?" He reached up, caressed my cheek, and stared into my eyes. Chains clinked softly in Hurrow's grip, seizing my gaze.

Not rope this time...studded leather and chains...a dangerous combination where we were concerned. I swallowed hard, and nodded.

Rule reached down, grasped the bottom of my shirt, and lifted. Elithien was so still across the room. They all were. Every predatory gaze...every inhuman glint in their eyes...captured by me.

I lifted my arms as my shirt slipped free, my body trembling.

I was the prey...here.

Overpowered. Cornered.

The hunt over before it ever began. Who cared about running anyway? My shirt hit the floor with a soft flutter before I dropped my hands to the front of my jeans. The button released. The zipper slid low. I kicked off my boots, holding Elithien's gaze. He was a midnight storm brewing in the distance. Quiet, *seething*. On the verge of unleashing. One flash of lightning and we'd all go up in flames.

I kicked my boots away as Rule dropped to his knees in front of me.

"Rule?" I reached for his head, sliding my fingers through his thick, tousled locks.

"A true King will always kneel for his Queen, Ruth." He lifted his gaze to mine and slid his hands down the length of my thighs, taking my jeans with them.

This wasn't just sex. Not to them.

This was *worship*.

Mind, body, soul.

Hurrow came closer. Trust raged in his eyes, trust that I'd see him, that I'd see all of them. They weren't Vampires to me... maybe they never really had been. They were the missing pieces of my life. They were my *purpose*.

I saw that purpose now and it was blinding, burning me on the inside.

I held onto Rule and stepped out of my jeans before I reached around and unclasped my bra. The tremors stilled. There was a growing calmness inside me. Desire clashed with a longing of my own. I wanted to feel their love…wanted to bask in their devotion.

Hurrow's gaze slipped lower and my nipples tightened under his gaze. The points of his fangs slipped from between his blood red lips as he reached out. "Fuck me, you're beautiful," he whispered, and cupped my breast. "You ready for this, Princess?"

I glanced at the leather harness in his hand and nodded. "Yes."

Trust, that's what it came down to. Complete and utter trust. Trust with my heart, the same as they trusted me. He lowered his hand, giving the harness to Rule. A surge of excitement tore through me as I lifted one foot, stepping between the straps, and followed with the other. Leather creaked as it settled against me.

Rule leaned forward and kissed my thighs as the leather straps slid upwards, settling on either side of my thighs. Hurrow gripped the back of my neck, his fingers sliding through my hair. "Have I ever told you how much red hair turns me on?"

"Yes," I answered as Rule brushed the back of his finger along the leather straps and my crease. "But you can tell me again."

Hurrow's smile was fast as he grasped the strands and gently pulled them upwards as the chains and leather straps settled over my hips and around my waist, joining along my belly with metal buckles. I lifted my hands, eager once more to be bound… for them. As my pulse raced, Hurrow slid the harness over my arms and moved behind me. My breasts were bare, exposed. The leather strap nestled between then before splitting off into a higher choker that buckled at the back of my neck.

"Fuck me," Russell muttered, unable to look away. "You look…"

"Delicious," Elithien finished for him. "You look goddamn delicious." One quick glance at Rule, and the Vampire kneeling in front of me gripped my hips, His fangs flashing stark white in the darkened room as he smiled. He dipped his head as Hurrow pressed his chest to my back, taking my weight. I felt the brush of Hurrow's fingers down my arm as I reached up and over my shoulder, finding his strong neck. He dropped his head, kissing thae line of my vein all the way to behind my ear, and my body responded. My pulse…thready…panicky. *Desperate.*

I was already trembling as Rule gripped my knee and lifted, sliding it over his shoulder. I was exposed, trembling, and aching. Leather against my skin, cool breath and fire in his touch.

"No coming now, Princess," he ordered, dipping his head to lick between my folds.

"Oh, God." I closed my eyes and rocked my hips forward. I hadn't realized how much I needed this until this moment. I hadn't realized how much I needed them…their touch, their hunger.

Rule's finger slipped along my folds, gathering moisture, then slid all the way to circle my clit. The tremors moved deeper now, humming with an urgency in my veins. "Yes," I sighed as Rule reached around, gripped my ass, and dragged my core against his mouth.

This was what I needed. This…always this.

I tracked every touch, every gaze, and burned them into my memory as that delicious heat rushed through my body. His tongue speared deeper as he spread me with his fingers. The leather straps pulled taut as he slid his fingers underneath, using them as reins to pull me against his mouth. I was lost to that momentum, and that heat in my core burned hotter...until he pulled away. His lips glistened as he smiled. "Not yet, my Mafia Queen," he instructed as he rose, and kissed me.

Salty, ravenous desire. My own taste slipped into my mouth with a brush of Rule's tongue. I moaned and wound my arms around his neck, pulling him closer until Hurrow reached around, grasped my wrists, and unwound them from him.

Rule broke the kiss, watching as Hurrow's lips stayed against my neck, nuzzling that panicked thunder in my veins. "Fuck, I love you desperate and scared like this. You are a damn storm of emotions, Ruth. A beautiful, erotic storm of emotions," Hurrow complimented.

He pulled away then, his hand finding the back of my neck again. One sweep of his fingers and my hair fell to the side. So strong, not that I could fight him. He pressed between my shoulders, forcing me to bend at the waist. Just like the first time with us. My hands were against Rule instead of the wall, like hers had been outside the nightclub, as the sound of a zipper came from behind me.

His cock slid along my folds. I closed my eyes, savoring the feel of him as he entered me, stretching me, filling me. Chains rattled and clinked as he stoked that fire with a delicious thrust. "Are you desperate, Ruth?"

Fuck me.

I whimpered, knees trembling. My breaths came harder as he thrust deeper. I rocked back against him, my ass slapping against his thighs. The sound filled my ears as I shuddered with uncontrollable desire. "Harder," I growled, desperate and savage. "Fuck me harder."

But the moment I trembled and shook, he slid free, still hard and unspent.

I moaned, aching and needing. The hunger turned raw and menacing.

"You remember that night?" Elithien murmured, drawing my gaze. God, I ached for them...for every goddamn inch of them. Still, I lifted my gaze as Elithien took a step forward. My breath caught the light glistening on black leather as he worked the gloves over his fingers. "I do," he answered himself, and lifted his starving gaze to me. "I remember every catch of your breath...and every second. I remember the way you looked at me. So much desperation. You needed saving, Ruth. Just like now..."

He worked the buttons on his shirt, sliding it off until it hit the floor. Then he was across the room faster than I could follow, grasping me around the hips, lifting me until I wound my legs around his waist. "I'll always save you," he promised, those silver eyes glinting. "Until my last breath."

You will lose him, Ruth. You understand that. Caedes' words roared to the surface. My heart pounded as that thought took hold. My life without him...*The Vampire has become a...problem.*

My throat tightened as I wound my arms around his neck and kissed him like my life depended on it. *No, like* his *life depended on it.* His fangs scraped the inside of my lip. I took his tongue, moving deeper before I broke away to stare into his eyes. "As I would for you. You are mine, Elithien...*all* of you are mine."

He carried me to the bed and laid me down on the edge, the leather straps biting into my thighs as he looked at me. I shivered under that ravenous gaze. My skin trembled as he reached down, unbuckled his belt, and shed the rest of his clothes. The chains draped around my hips rattled as he moved, reaching out to grasp the metal buckle against my belly, then parted my thighs with his gloved hand.

One unforgiving thrust, and I cried out and gripped the bedspread. "Yes...*fuck me...yes.*"

He gripped the strap with one hand and slid his gloved hand along my body to cup my breast. Past and present collided. I was in that cold, dark alley once more, desperate and haunted by his touch. Begging...just as I did then. "More. Please, Elithien, more."

His growl slipped through the room, demanding...possessive.

"You got it wrong, mortal," he snarled, and leaned over me, his gloved hand sliding upwards to catch my wrists and pin them to the bed. "It's you who belongs to me...now and always."

Desperation and rage crackled through the room. Movement came from the corner of my eye. Shadows spilled through the room and crawled along the ceiling as Russell made his presence known.

"Leash it, Unseelie...if you want to be with her," Elithien commanded, never once taking his eyes from mine.

His fangs grew longer, sliding from between his lips. I knew what he wanted...I knew what he *needed*. Blood. *My blood.* I turned my gaze away from him, lifting my knees and tilting my hips...aching for him, for that bestial strength, for that unforgiving power, and as he let loose a roar, I closed my eyes and lost myself.

The bite was brutal, pain flaring deep before it was gone, leaving behind that floating feeling. Where it was us...just the feel of leather-covered fingers around my wrists, and the feel of his length driving deep over and over again as he suckled at my neck. I opened my eyes, my heart booming, pumping blood into his mouth as it fought to survive.

As my orgasm barreled down on me, I knew what I had to do.

What I'd always needed to do.

It was so clear now.

Clearer even than our love.

I cried out, bucking and rocking my hips against his, as he let out a deep, guttural moan. He pulled away, licking my wounds, and staring into my eyes. His breaths were hard and fast. He started to move, pulling his hands away.

"Don't," I gasped. "Don't let me go...not yet," I pleaded. "Just a second longer."

"Then you're mine, mortal." The savage tone came from the doorway.

Justice stepped inside, his gaze taking in the leather against my skin. "And you can leave the harness on..."

Elithien pulled away, sliding from between my legs. "We aren't perfect, Ruth," he commented. "But we'll always be protective."

"None more than me, woman." Justice strode forward. His leather eyepatch glistened in the light as he stopped at the edge of the bed and, with one powerful slide of his arms underneath me...he pulled me up into his arms.

The room was a blur as he turned and carried me out the door.

But it didn't matter...I only saw him.

That was all I needed...for now.

Chapter Twenty-Seven

You're mine now. Justice's voice invaded my head as he carried me along the hallway toward his room.

I brushed my fingers over the puckered edge of the scar peeking from the leather patch and answered, "Always."

Silver glimmered in his eye as he turned, pressed my body against his chest with one hand, and punched in the code to his room. The steel door slid open with a rush of air, and we were inside, melting into the darkness...leaving the other Vampires behind.

My body hummed with an energy of its own. Synapses fired... nerves tingled, aching and ready for him. The door closed and we were falling onto the bed.

"Mine to protect," he murmured against my neck. The vibration of his growl sent shivers along my spine. "And mine to fuck."

He reached down between us and released the button on his pants. Leather creaked, pulling tight against my thighs, opening my folds. I was hot, swollen, ready for him. One brutal thrust, and he was inside. I closed my eyes and cried out, gripping his powerful shoulders as he rose above me like a god.

He *was* a god in this moment.

A breathtaking, fanged god.

He tilted his hips, driving himself deeper.

"Mine..." he insisted, pushing up on his arms.

His body was a cage around me. His cock rammed home, forcing my thighs wider as he drove me into the mattress.

"Mine. Ruth. *You are mine.*"

I lost myself in him, in the impacts of his hips, in his length driving into my core as he kissed the hollow of my neck. I still felt the marking of Elithien on the other side, the rush of panic, and the pounding of my heart.

"Don't worry," he whispered, the pointed tips of his fangs dragging along my vein. "I won't take much."

He bit, sinking the needle-fine tips through the flesh to puncture my vein. "Fuck me," I cried out, my core convulsing.

He took one draw and pulled back, licking the ache and stealing the pain away. "That's what I'm trying to do," he growled.

His driving hips slowed, settling into that final pace as he slid an arm under my arched back. We were one...just like we were meant to be one. One sixth of a whole...my Vampires...and my Unseelie. One perfect houseful of Immortal lovers. I didn't make love to just one...I made love to them all. I caressed his cheek, my heart aching as he turned his head, nestling into the touch. As he stared into my soul, he curled his lips, baring the bloodied tips of his fangs. Desperation. Devotion as he gave into that surrender and came.

Hard breaths between us, that undeniable connection roaring in his eyes. I drank him down, every raw emotion that raced through his eye, and slowly, his lips slid over his fangs. I lifted my head, straining as I kissed him, relishing the metallic taste of my blood, just as I had tasted my salty desire from Rule.

But there was no letting me go as my powerful Vampire eased his body to the side, dragging me with him. He stayed like that, silent...*raw*. Staring into my soul. This connection we shared was beyond my mortal existence...and his Immortal control.

That's where we lingered, in that space...as the room grew cold around me. Sleep came, forcing my eyes closed. I clung to him, nestled against his massive chest, and let myself go.

JUSTICE WAS quiet when I woke. Still. Sated, and *dead*. Shock raced through my body at the sight. I hadn't seen them like this, not this hollow and lifeless. I pressed my hand to his chest and felt the silence. There was no heartbeat, no spark of life...no movement in his veins. For all intents and purposes, he was gone from me. Tearing through that dark void of emptiness...the one I'd touched for a second and never wanted to feel again.

I pulled my hand away and stared at his face. But he wasn't dead, nor was he gone. He'd come back to me...they'd *all* come back to me—as soon as the sun went back down.

By then, it'd be over and we would've won.

Elithien would be safe...and there'd be no more Caedes to worry about.

Unless it all went to hell.

I tried not to think about that and rose from the bed, then hurried for the shower. But not even the hot water could warm me today. A day of endings and beginnings. I washed, dried, and dressed, then strode from Justice's bedroom to hear the ratchet of a gun slide in the living room. Sunlight glinted from the rows of weapons laid out on the table.

"I woke you?" Russell asked as he turned and met my gaze.

There was a sweep of his focus. One that lingered at the hollow of my neck, then carried along the rest of me. He was looking for an injury, looking for bruising or blood, Looking for a reason to take me away from them. Maybe I was naive to think we'd always get along...but there was still hope. And while I had that, I'd do everything in my power to keep us together.

"No," I answered, and crossed the room toward him.

My bodyguard palmed the Glock and opened his arm, pulling me close to bury his face in my hair. "You okay?" he asked, drawing in my scent.

"More than okay," I murmured, winding my arms around him, taking comfort in his heavily muscled chest and tight abs. "The question is, are you okay?"

He gave a low, gravelly chuckle. But I suspected that his fear was anything but funny. "Not gonna lie." He pulled away enough to stare into my eyes. "Seeing you like that did things to me I never thought were possible."

"Good things...or bad?"

Unseelie darkness slipped through his arctic blue eyes. He kept the gun in one hand and with his other, he gripped my hand and gently eased it to the hardness of his cock. "I've relieved myself three times so far...and I'm still hard as fucking rock."

Excitement surged inside me. He liked it...liked seeing me like that. Liked me in leather...liked me vulnerable—as vulnerable as a person could be. "Maybe after this is over, I'll wear the harness for you?"

His eyes widened, showing me the wholesome, righteous man underneath. "You'd do that?" His voice deepened with desire.

"Russell," I turned, making him my sole focus. "I'll do anything you want. Wear *anything* you want. Just you and me...no one else...*all* night long."

Throat muscles worked as he swallowed.

I flattened my hand over his cock, feeling a twitch underneath his black cargos and murmured, "I'll take care of this...and I'll take care of the Unseelie."

"Jesus, Ruth," he muttered, and lifted a hand, dragging his fingers through his hair.

I'd never felt so powerful as I did in this moment. A smile crept across my lips as I dragged my hand away. "Now, are you going to let me help you?"

His smile grew wider, lips flattening. "Just when I thought you couldn't turn me on any more, I remembered who you are."

"A Mafia Princess," I reminded him with a smile of my own. "Who knows her way around a gun or two."

He chuckled and nodded once more, leaning in to kiss me. "That you are...*and* you do."

I took his kiss, cupping his face, tasting the remnant of coffee on his lips. "Coffee...I need some...actually, I need lots."

"There's a fresh pot," he said, motioning toward the kitchen.

"Refill?"

"Always." He gave me a smile and moved back to the weapons.

I stopped for a moment, watching as he bent and placed the Glock on the table before picking up a semi-automatic...and a cold shiver cut through me. I stood on the precipice here—my toes curled over the edge, and stared into that gaping black void.

He worked methodically, his big hands finding the tiny pin to pull the weapon apart. Laser focused, his strong jaw bulging as he worked, readying for a war...a war that'd never come—if I succeeded.

I caught my breath, spun, and strode to the kitchen, biting down on a sob. Pain stabbed through my chest as I stumbled through the door and hunched over the counter. I couldn't breathe, couldn't function.

I could only see the end...and the path I had to take to get there.

Deceit. Betrayal. It revealed itself in the midst of their love.

And no matter how many times I tried to find a better solution, I realized there wasn't one. Caedes wouldn't stop...he'd never stop. Not until Elithien was dead...and that I would *never* allow, not while there was breath in my body and fight in my soul.

"You hungry?" Russell called. "I made an extra sandwich and put it in the fridge for you earlier. I figured you'd be hungry when you finally woke up."

Finally woke up. I turned my gaze to the sunlight outside. Softer than the midday sun. I still had a few hours left before sunset. A few hours with them.

"Ruth?" Russell called. "You okay?"

My heart hammered as I turned to the doorway.

Don't...you tell him and it's all over.

You tell him and there won't be any stopping this.

You tell him, and Elithien is dead.

Cold clarity filled me, driving me into action. I crossed the kitchen, yanked open the fridge, and grabbed the neat sandwich, tearing through the plastic as fast as I could before I turned. Heavy boots rang out as he headed toward me. I took another bite, filling my mouth, as he stepped into the doorway.

I smiled, cheeks full of the thick ham and cheese. "So hungry," I mumbled around the wad of food before I chewed and swallowed. He looked at the half-demolished sandwich, and beamed with pride. "I can make you another? It's no problem."

I shook my head and swiped my hand across my mouth, dislodging a few crumbs. "This is perfect and so damn good." I crossed the kitchen, wound my arm around his neck, still holding onto the plate, and kissed him. "Thank you for taking care of me." *Please forgive me.*

I pulled away, my happiness bleeding away. Still Russell smiled, then licked the taste of honey mustard on my lips, and grabbed two fresh cups from the counter before pouring the coffee. *Déjà vu* roared back to me...memories of the place in the city came rushing back. We'd come a long way since that moment...

And I was about to ruin it all.

I took the coffee, drank, and finished the sandwich. Russell went back to checking the weapons as movement came from outside. I scowled and stepped closer to the windows to catch one of the mercenaries outside. "Wait...aren't they Vampire?"

"Apparently not just any kind of Vampire. Feralis exercitus...or something. The alive undead...different to the other undead, so Rule said. Bound by some kind of dark magic. They aren't governed by the laws of normal Vampires. Still ugly as fucking sin, if you ask me."

Panic surged inside me. Would they stop me from leaving? My thoughts raced as I turned and glanced at the rows of guns on the table. They would try to stop me...of that I had no doubt. Unless they were busy. "On second thought, I am rather hungry," I murmured.

"You are? Then another sandwich, coming right up. Just like old times, eh?" he joked, then rose from the edge of the sofa and went to the kitchen. I closed my eyes, stopped the tremble, and opened them once more.

You can do this...you have no choice. It's you or Elithien...make your motherfucking move.

I crossed the room, grabbed the Glock, and slid it under the back of my shirt, then moved the others to take up the space. Movement came from the window once more. I hurried, moving to the cupboard, and grabbed Rule's key to the Audi and my phone, checking the time before I slipped it into my pocket. It was almost five. Two hours at most until dark. Two long...agonizing hours.

"Here you go," Russell offered as he headed toward me, one perfect sandwich on the plate.

"Thank you," I smiled, and took it from him.

I wasn't hungry, not really. Still, I grabbed the first half and took a small bite while Russell carried the guns from the room, placing them beside every door and every window. He was planning to hole up here. They all were, until the bullets, the favors, and the money ran out. Which they would eventually... they always did.

I knew that more than anyone.

Phantom and Shrike had broken their loyalty and we were on our own...I carried the half-eaten sandwich back to the kitchen, rewrapped it, and placed it back in the fridge. *Would he find it tomorrow...or the day after? Would he wonder if I'd stood here planning my betrayal...*the thought of that hurt.

I walked to Rule's room, pressed in the code, and opened the door. Silence greeted me as I stepped inside. I made my way over to the bed. My Rule, my provider, always ready to give me what I wanted...and what I needed. I leaned down and kissed his cold lips. "I love you," I whispered, tears shimmering in my eyes.

I had to hurry...my own will wasn't strong enough. And there was no backing out of this, not once I started. I hurried to Hurrow's room and stepped inside.

"You will always be mine," I whispered, leaning over to kiss him.

Tears dripped on his cheek, racing down the hard line of his jaw. I left him behind and hurried to Justice, finding him in the same position I'd left him. "My protector," I murmured, tracing his cheek with my finger before I kissed him and left.

There was only one left...for now.

I pressed in the code, waited for the door to open, and strode into Elithien's bedroom. There was so much of me in here. My clothes in the closet. My lotions on the vanity in the bathroom... and my heart clutched in his hand...my Vampire lover.

My protector.

My provider.

My Alpha.

A sob tore free as I neared the bed. Low, thick, choking. I knelt and grasped his hand. I couldn't kiss him...not yet. Not when there was so much left unsaid between us. "Thank you for saving me."

I pressed my lips to the back of his hand and rose on trembling legs.

Their power hummed inside me. I felt their energy. Their purpose. Night would soon be here, and with it, the end. I headed for the closet, grabbed my leather jacket, and slipped it on. I checked my phone. Five thirty. I had an hour and a half... maybe even less.

Thirty minutes to do what I needed and get to the warehouse.

Then make it to the city as the sun went down.

And then?

The question lingered...fate was a cruel bitch. She took and she gave. Ruthlessly.

I lifted my gaze. Just like I was about to.

Maybe...she was me?

I glanced at the bed, to his still body and checked the time once more. It was now or never.

The end was racing toward me...but it wouldn't be his end.

That I'd never allow.

I crossed the bedroom, leaving a piece of my heart behind as I pressed the combination, waited for the door to open, and walked through. I hurried for the study, slipped inside, stepped around Elithien's desk, and sat in his seat before I hit the keyboard and the monitor came alive.

I wanted more of the Vampire, to swallow down every scent of him, to immerse myself in his world for just a second longer... until the very end. I trailed my fingers along the surface of the desk, then lifted my gaze to the monitor and set to work punching in the web address that'd get me Ace.

Pekingese, Justice's voice filled my head. *Sounds like a damn rodent, but let's do it.*

I smiled at the memory. But as fast as the heady feeling rose, it turned cold. Reality crashed in, giving me the shock I needed. I set my fingers to the task, punching in the details to get into the chat. But instead of typing into the fast-moving current of hidden messages disguised as pet trainers and groomers, I selected the message box instead.

You are the best trainer I could've hoped for.

I'm sorry about the big scary dogs. They are just protective and, well...I love having them around. But the time has come to move on. I want you to find a new client.
Find new dogs.
Don't ever stop living and training.
Find some peace.
Love, R.

I swallowed...and swallowed again, exiting the chat. Trying my best to swallow that lump in my throat until I could breathe without shuddering. I glanced at the time on the monitor. If I was going to do this...then it had to be now.

Footsteps moved around at the front of the house and I rose from the desk. I listened for Russell at the doorway before I reached around my back, slipped out of the doorway, and headed for the back of the house.

My hands trembled...nerves screaming. I swallowed a shuddery breath and opened the back door. The mercenary was there... just like I knew he'd be. I felt these possessed Vampires, felt the darkness that controlled them, felt their inhuman hunger.

"Ruth?" Russell called from the back of the house as I drew the gun from behind my back.

"Ruth, what the fuck are you—"

Bang! I squeezed the trigger pointblank into the mercenary's chest.

"RUTH!" Russell roared, his steps booming like thunder.

I stared at the snarling Vampire and stumbled to the side, lowering the gun along my thigh. The undead solider lowered his gaze to the bullet hole in the center of his chest. The blackened hole was already closing, shrinking in on itself as the mercenary lifted his gaze, fangs bared, and stared at me.

"Ruth, *get down!*" Russell yelled, lunging and slamming into the Vampire as he came for me.

The crash of the blow was sickening. Strength met strength as Russell drove the Vampire outside. But I was already moving, my heart clenching and tearing apart as I raced for the front of the house.

My fingers trembled as I dug into my pocket and yanked open the front door. Rule's midnight blue Audi gleamed, waiting in the driveway. I knew this car...knew the speed, knew the handling. I hit the button and climbed in, throwing my gun and my phone on the passenger's seat...now I had to pray I could drive fast enough.

"Please," I pleaded as I stabbed the button, and the engine came to life with a growl.

I glanced at the house. All I needed was time...time to get where I needed to go...time to drive like a goddamn demon. I shoved the car into reverse and punched the accelerator as I spun the wheel to back into the turnaround area, before braking and slamming it into drive, then lunging forward.

Night was coming. I could already feel it.

Barreling down on me.

"Please God, help me save them...they're all I have left."

Chapter Twenty-Eight

I scanned the rear-view mirror for movement and gripped the wheel, taking the corner faster than I'd ever done before. The engine roared and the tires squealed. My pulse was deafening in my ears, muffling out everything else.

Faster…

That urgency took hold.

He's coming.

I turned my head to the dimming sun. He wasn't the only predator I was racing against. Night hurtled toward me, faster than expected. I lifted my gaze to the mirror as the curve smoothed out, leaving one long straight run, and punched the accelerator. The sports car responded, surging forward, and the speedometer climbed.

What if the Vampire overpowered him? I flinched at the thought, harsh breaths sawing. *What if he was hurt…what if he needed me?*

The car began to slow. *No.* That'd never happen. The moment I started the car, Russell's Unseelie beast would've raged. He'd be coming for me...by four-wheel drive or on foot.

A chill crept along my spine. He'd be coming for me.

I stomped the accelerator as the city glinted in the distance. Something sparkled in the mirror, drawing my gaze. Sunlight glinted off glass...another car raced toward me, taking up both lanes in their fury. I smashed the accelerator, tearing past the first abandoned buildings, barely tapping the brakes into the corner.

My stomach clenched tight, my hands trembled with fear as I jerked the wheel of the Audi and felt the back tires slip before they caught once more.

"Please," I whimpered. "Please, just get me in there."

The Unseelie was my only barrier...my big, beautiful, terrifying barrier. My end and my beginning. I whipped past the Wolves' clubs and that pang in my chest moved deeper. I thought of Arran...and the friendship he'd given me. One that wasn't built on wanting influence or money. But that was all gone now... along with their alliance.

I turned the wheel once more, catching the glint of steel, and prayed whoever manned the cameras and the gate would open it. The brakes squealed and the engine groaned as I pulled up hard and lowered the window.

"What do you want, mortal?"

"I have information," I answered, and stared at the building. "So let me the fuck in, *Unseelie.*"

"Shrike isn't here." Came the snarl.

"I don't care," I cried frantically. "Just open the fucking gate!"

A howl of tires slipped through the air. My heart lunged as I whipped my gaze over my shoulder...*come on...COME ON!*

The buzzer sounded before the gates slowly rolled back. I was already nosing the Audi through before it opened fully. Steel screeched against the paintwork. I winced at the sound and slammed the accelerator, plunging the Audi toward the warehouse's side door as the roar of the Explorer savaged the air.

I was so close now. *So very close...*

I killed the engine, shoved open the door, and scurried out of the car. Gravel slipped under my boots, pitching me forward. I slammed my hand to the ground, the sting on the heel of my palm instant. But I kept going, driving myself toward the corner of the building and the side door.

I gripped the handle and twisted. The lock held. Panicked, I lifted my gaze to the building. "Please." I whispered. "Please, let me in."

Tires on the four-wheel drive howled as the vehicle hurtled toward me. The lock gave a click as its brakes squealed. But I was already yanking open the door and lunging inside.

My legs shook as I stumbled inside the warehouse and raced for the stairs.

"RUTH!" Russell roared outside.

But I ran...like his life depended on it. Because it did. I took the stairs two, and three at a time, twisted the handle and shoved my way inside. Millions of dollars were piled in the sealed vaults underneath me. Stacks and stacks of green just waiting to be collected. But I couldn't have cared less. My life wasn't about money or prestige anymore.

It was about *them*. I leaned against the door behind me for a second as energy crackled through the warehouse.

"Ruth!"

I rushed forward, letting the office door swing shut behind me with a *thud*, and scurried for the hallway. Memories assaulted me as I slammed into the wall and shoved towards that buckled doorway. Sex. Darkness. *Love*. Power...it was all here. Every beautiful, dangerous second. The way he'd touched me. The way he'd *loved* me. I pushed through the open door and raced toward the remaining unbuckled shackle as heavy steps thundered in the hallway.

"Woman..." Russell growled, that inhuman sound finding me as I bent, dragged the thick shackle from the floor, and turned.

Tears shimmered in my eyes as I turned, finding him in the doorway. Thick sobs lumped in the back of my throat.

Dark anger lashed his gaze as he met mine. But in an instant, that anger melted away. "You scared the fuck out of me, Ruth." There was blood on his hands as he stepped inside. "What the fuck happened back there?"

I shook my head, slick tears raced down my cheek. His brow furrowed as he crossed the room in an instant. He didn't even look...not at the room...or what I held behind my body. He just grabbed me, and pulled me to his massive chest. His strong arms wrapped around me and that Unseelie darkness melted away in an instant.

"Don't ever scare me like that again, okay? Don't do that again."

"I won't," I cried as I slid one hand along the bulging muscles in his arm and lifted my gaze to his.

He saw only me in that moment. *Only me.* My love...my *undying* purpose. The shackle bit around his wrist as I snapped it shut. He didn't even register it. Not even when I stepped out of his embrace and backed away.

Links clanked as he lifted his hand. Confusion crowded his gaze as he glanced at the shackle, then to me.

"Thank you," I sobbed, and tried to swallow the lump in my throat. "Thank you for always putting me first. I only wish we'd had more time together."

"Ruth..." he warned through clenched teeth. Pain savaged his eyes. His breaths were hard, filling that beautiful chest.

"I love you," I whispered, and turned to the door.

"Ruth!" he roared.

I could hear only him...*only feel...him.* He was everywhere, consuming this place, as I hurried for the door and rushed down the stairs once more. As I hit the bottom...that *unmerciful* howl of torment tore through the air and shuddered the walls.

I don't know how I made it out.

Shadows clung to the building as I climbed back into the Audi and started the engine. My hand shook so bad, it slipped on the gearshift. I cried out, shoved it into gear, and backed out before I shot forward.

He'd been my only hurdle, my selfless bodyguard. There's no way he would've let me go...and no way I could've gotten around him.

The sky seemed to tremble and darken in the rear-view mirror as I tore out of the warehouse driveway and headed for the east side of the river. Tears slipped down my cheeks. But inside, I was numb. Numb from the emptiness...and numb from the pain. There was only one thing left now.

One conversation that hung like a rock around my neck. I swiped the tears away with my thumb and reached across the seat as I hit the on-ramp to the bridge. My fingers skimmed the gun, then my phone. I grabbed the cell and straightened, glancing at the first faint twinkle of stars in the mirror behind me.

I divided my focus, glancing at the bridge, then the numbers, as I tapped and hit the speaker icon.

"Ruthy?" My uncle's deep drawl came through the phone. "Everything okay, kid?"

I swallowed that lump and lifted my gaze to the rear-view mirror once more. In the distance behind me, a dark sedan moved amongst the traffic.

"Yeah. I'm okay." Silence filled the other end of the phone.

I glanced at the screen and the seconds counting and dug into that gaping void of pain, finding the strength to finish what I had to say. "I just wanted to say thank you for looking out for me at the end. The company isn't important...it was never really important, not after Dad. Love," I forced the word. "That's what's important."

"You're scaring me, kid. What's going on over there?"

I tightened my grip on the wheel, fighting that desperate need to pull over as I exited the off-ramp and head into the city.

"Nothing," I lied, and reached out with a trembling thumb, hovering over the end call icon. "Not anymore. This time, Uncle...don't look for me. Take care of yourself."

I tapped the icon, my thumb slipping before the call went silent.

There was nothing left for me now.

Just pain.

Just an ending.

You will lose him, Ruth. You understand that. Caedes' words rang in my head as I stabbed the button on the armrest, waited for the window to roll down, and tossed the cell from the car. The screen lit up as it left my hand. The name Jerry illuminated for a second before it was gone and the last tie to my life with it. My uncle was persistent...a true Costello. *Unlike me...*

Those words lingered, hardening my resolve as I headed for the alley of Sixth and James. I'd meet Caedes, make the deal with the Vampire Lord to save Elithien's life, and figure out a way to end the sonofabitch...if it was the last thing I did.

Elithien flitted through my mind as the headlights of the Audi flicked on. The sky had darkened to night around me as I headed deeper into the city. I knew the alley where we'd meet... knew it all too well.

It was the same alley where I'd almost died.

And the same alley where I was reborn again.

My blood had been spilled on those bricks. It was still there, hard and dried in the cracks. I was part of the city, just as it was part of me. I lifted my gaze as the traffic picked up heading into the throbbing, beating heart of my world. I prayed that my tie to this place looked after me now as I tapped the brakes and turned the corner.

Bright lights sparkled...mortals...*mortals?* Did I really think like that now? Maybe there'd always been the distinction inside me —me and them. Still, they walked along the streets, some hand in hand and others alone. Dressed in Gucci and Armani, as places like the Jewel demanded. But as I pulled into a parking space further down the street from the Jewel, I saw something I didn't expect. Total darkness.

The place was closed. Yellow police tape strewn across the doors prevented entry. As I leaned forward and killed the engine, I saw the front doors were boarded...as though there'd been an attack. Tension rippled inside me as I reached across the seat, grabbed the gun, and slowly climbed from the car.

Ruth! Elithien's howl tore through me as the door closed with a thud. *WHAT HAVE YOU DONE?*

I stumbled forward, headlights blurring in my gaze. I was back in that void again...that dark emptiness that whispered of the end. "For you," I whispered, my voice thick with choking sobs. "To live."

NO! He screamed.

In a heartbeat, they were all there, crowding my head with their rage and agony. I stumbled across the street and toward the alley. They were all I could hear...all I could feel, like a shotgun blast to my chest.

Don't do this! Elithien raved, his voice deep and desperate. *Tell me where you are right now...*

I stepped up on the curb and lifted my gaze to the alley. My knees shook, my steps stuttered as shadows wailed and whipped against the walls in a fit of rage. The air shuddered with that unmerciful sound of agony. Russell pushed into my head, snarling and savage, unable to speak...but just *be*.

Be breathtakingly dangerous. Be *Unseelie*...Be *unforgiving*. Still I drove myself forward one step at a time, until I gripped the corner of the building, stared into the dark, and walked into the alley.

He was there, standing amongst the overfilled trashcans and the choking stench of wet moss.

I walked to him, each step leaving me numb as I left more of my soul behind, until I stopped in front of the figure. "I'm here."

"Yes." Caedes reached up and pushed the hood from his face. "You are. You made the right choice, Ruth."

"Yeah, well...you didn't leave me much of one, did you?"

His smile was chilling, dark eyes sparkled. "I guess I didn't. You came for answers."

"I *came* because you said you'd spare Elithien's life," I snapped. "You can shove your fucking answers."

That smile grew wider. He took a step toward me and lifted his hand. "You remind me of your mother. So intense. *So alive.*"

I moved instantly, stepping away from him, my hand sliding around to my back and drawing the gun free. "Do not fucking touch me, motherfucker...and don't talk about my mother."

He froze, then gave a nod. The shadows seemed to shift behind him, but I didn't dare take my gaze from the Vampire Lord. "You don't want to talk about your mother...fine. How about we talk about your father? How he betrayed the one person who trusted him...your poor *honorable* Elithien. Do you want to talk about that instead?"

I froze. My heart clenched tight and stared into those cold, lifeless eyes. "What are you saying?"

He smiled then, empty eyes boring into mine. "Who do you think ordered the hit on the Vampire Prince?"

I tried to swallow. "That's a lie."

"Is it? I take it you found the DNA report. Your father held a great many lies."

He paced like a damn lion, my uncle's words repeated in my mind. *Broken-hearted, soul-fucking crushed. But you know us Costellos, we don't stay down for long.*

He went to work.

My father went to work.

"He found out," I whispered. It made sense now, made sense why he'd never told me. "He knew she betrayed him."

"Revenge is always the sweetest when the woman you love breaks your heart. He was a powerful man..."

"But he was the one who made the deal to help him." I shook my head and lowered the gun. "He was the one Elithien trusted."

"The Vampire Prince. What better Vampire to be executed? Your father would've killed us all if he could."

I shook my head, clenched my jaw, and forced the words through gritted teeth. "Why Alliard? Why him?"

"Because he hated...he hated so much his hate became a cancer that riddled his body. And because he couldn't get to the one he wanted to kill most of all...*me.*"

The alley seemed to sway.

Tilted.

Shifted.

I stared at him...and in my head, that video of my mother came roaring back. "It was you? You and my mother?"

Caedes stepped closer. This time I was too stunned to move. Pieces slid into place now. The fake ring, the way he seemed to always know where I was. That sinking feeling I had around him, that *foul* tremor that resonated through the very depths of me. As he came forward, the entire alley seemed to move with him. They came out of the darkness...Vampires...Wolves...and the powerful Unseelie I'd seen before.

"It's over, Ruth," Caedes murmured. I flinched at the sound and jerked my gaze to his. "You belong to *me, my* daughter and my future. Elithien and his coven will be gone after tonight... and you'll rise at my side, untethered...unrestrained, to become the woman you were always meant to be...*Ruthless.*"

"The debt." The words burned as they ripped free. "This was the debt. My life. My mother's betrayal."

"The debt not owed to any coven," he growled. "The debt owed to *me*...and paid for in *blood.*"

But it wasn't *my* blood that would be spilled.

It was theirs.

My Vampires.

I'd thought the debt had been money, an alliance. I'd thought the debt had been *an agreement.*

I'd been wrong...

"No," I whispered as the ground seemed to open up and swallow me whole. Caedes' army strode forward and swallowed us in a rush.

This was why he'd lured me here. I'd betrayed them...I'd sealed their fate. Agony roared through me as I turned to that savage, pitiless storm raging inside my head, the one filled with my Immortals, and I summoned every bit of strength I possessed and screamed, *"NO!"*

Chapter Twenty-Nine

ELITHIEN

"WHERE IS SHE?" JUSTICE ROARED. HIS EYE WIDE, FISTS clenched and bloodied. He stood in the middle of broken furniture and punched-in walls. The living room of our house was utterly destroyed...

This was what had happened when he couldn't find her....

This was what had happened when *none* of us could find her...

We'd been here before...and it was almost too late.

I closed my eyes as desperation swelled inside me. I couldn't get a bead on her...couldn't quite feel where she was. *For you,* she'd whispered in my head. *To live.*

Come on...*please*...come on. I clenched my jaw and felt the sting from my fangs. Somewhere in the house, a phone rang, the chime shattering my hold and she slipped away from me once more.

"She did what?" Hurrow growled.

I opened my eyes and looked at him. Desperation swirled around us like a tornado, destruction and death all around us. The mercenaries were gone when I awoke...and with them, Ruth and the Unseelie. It was the only thing holding me together. The male would protect her...with his life.

"She chained him and left him there?" Hurrow strode forward, his face a mask of savagery. "We're on our goddamn way...tell him to stay the fuck there. *That's a command.*"

We were all moving, tearing through the house, leaving it ruined in our wake, and piled into the Explorer.

"She chained him, E. She lured the Unseelie to the warehouse and chained him with the damn wards."

"Jesus." Justice snarled.

He wasn't with her...the agony was suffocating, *unbearable.* I pressed against that connection we shared as the Explorer roared to life and shot forward.

Why, Ruth? I drove that desperation toward her. *What are you up to?*

The engine of the four-wheel drive howled as it redlined. Still, Hurrow gripped the wheel, down-shifted into the corner and gunned it on the straight. Seconds felt like a lifetime. An eternity without her. Not again, I pleaded, as the past rose like a tsunami.

Still, that bite of her anger drifted through the connection we shared. *I came because you said you'd spare Elithien's life.* Her words were faint, but I clung to them. *You can shove your fucking answers.*

Save my life? "I can hear her," I growled. "She's trying to spare my damn life."

"Caedes," Rule answered through clenched teeth. "It has to be."

She went to him...to protect me? My chest ached, silent and cold. "Hurrow," I urged.

"I got it," he responded as the city lights grew closer. "Just...try to get through to her. *Goddamn, stubborn, fucking addictive woman.*"

She was torture.

A beautiful drug you'd kill to taste once more.

"Ruth, please hear me." I cast my words through the void. "You don't have to save me...if I lose you, I'm dead anyway."

"We all are," Justice added, his voice etched with pain.

Soul pain. The kind you didn't come back from. She still didn't understand...didn't comprehend my need for her. In a blinding moment, I was dragged back there, to the day I'd met with her father to discuss Alliard's plan for Senator. He'd been so cold at first...until that night, when the image of her fell from his desk and landed on the floor.

I'd picked it up, and the world stopped.

She was breathtaking, red hair fanning out like fire. Those damn eyes drawing me in. The ache in my chest pounded like thunder as I stared at her.

Stop looking at her like that, Vampire, he'd warned. *She's out of bounds.*

He snatched the picture from my hand. But it didn't matter. It was burned in my memory. But something happened in the months following. Something changed his mind, and he began talking about her. Telling me how he was damn proud to have a daughter and not a son. He told me she was going to set the world on fire...I just didn't realize it was going to be my world.

That night at the Jewel was to be our first introduction.

I need someone to look out for her, Vampire, to protect her. If you're up to the task. She's not like other people. The kid is special. Special in ways you couldn't understand.

I would've offered him the world just to meet her.

She was all I'd hoped and more.

The woman was breathtaking.

I gripped the dashboard as we took the corner hard and shot past the bright lights of the Wolves' clubs. Oncoming headlights were blinding. Horns blared, but we passed in a blur, braking hard as we turned and charged through the opening gate.

Russell was there, headlights washing over the midnight eyes of the Unseelie.

He was enraged, still wearing the warded shackle like a damn bracelet.

"Jesus." Hurrow braked hard, stopping an inch away from him. The bodyguard looked haunted in ways only this woman could invoke.

He strode toward us as Hurrow lowered the window. "She's gone. Took the damn sports car."

"You mean the Audi?" Rule cut in. Russell glanced at him in the backseat, and nodded.

"I've got a LoJack installed." Rule shoved the door and climbed out, yanking his phone free. "I can track her."

Russell stared at Rule, his eyes widening, before he stumbled backwards and yelled, *"Follow us!"*

Hurrow shoved the Explorer into reverse as the bodyguard and Rule climbed into the second Explorer. Movement came from the corner of the building as we reversed hard and braked, waiting for the others to circle and charge headfirst out the gate.

Shrike stepped out from the shadows to stand under the overhead lights. The Unseelie's gaze bored into mine until I broke the stare and looked away, the wounds of betrayal still too damn raw. But I couldn't think about that now. It was Ruth I focused on...

Only Ruth.

The bodyguard drove like a man possessed, taking up both lanes as he shot past the strip clubs and turned toward the bridge. Helicopters roared overhead, wide spotlights cutting through the traffic as we raced against time.

"She has to be alive, E," Justice pleaded in the back seat. "Whatever we have to do."

I sank into the beast inside myself, knowing exactly what he was saying. Dead or alive, she was coming home...I'd turn her if I had to...make her mine forever. Bonded by blood. To be her Sire...desperation burned through me...would both torment and wake me in ways I could only imagine.

"Whatever it takes," Justice growled.

"Let's just get to her first," I urged as Hurrow raced through the traffic, sweeping between the cars in an effort to gain even a second.

But the bodyguard handled a car better than even my own second. The steel gray Explorer was a hurtling bullet between the cars as we launched off the bridge and headed toward the heart of the city.

*Boom...BOOM...BOOM...*gunshots rang in my head.

ELITHIEN! she screamed for me. *NO!*

"Hurry," I commanded, and turned to my second. *"FOR CHRIST'S SAKE, HURRY!"*

Fangs were bared in a howl of rage as Hurrow's eyes widened and we plunged further into the city. I could feel her grow stronger. Feel her fear...and her rage...

But more than that, I felt *them* all around me. My cell phone rang, making me snarl and bare my teeth. I wrenched it free and barked "Not now!"

"Not now?" The old man snapped on the other end. "It better be right *fucking now, Vampire.* Where the fuck is my niece... and why the hell did she tell me not to look for her?" Jerry Costello roared through the phone.

I flinched at the desperation in the mortal's voice. "I'm going to find her."

"Where?" he demanded.

"We're heading into the city."

Justice's phone beeped in the back seat. "Sixth and James," he read out loud.

"Sixth and James," I repeated.

"The Jewel? What the hell is she doing there?" The sound of a car engine howled in the background.

"Are you driving?"

"*No, I'm not driving*. My goddamn son's tryin' to kill me. The Jewel, idiot," he snapped. "Get us there alive, okay?"

The call ended with a beep...beep...beep. I glanced at the screen and growled. "Looks like the Costellos are joining us," I muttered as we pulled up hard across from the Jewel, stopping behind the gray Explorer. But the bodyguard was already out of the vehicle, head down, charging across the lanes of traffic, heading toward the alley.

I shoved open the passenger door, glanced at the dark blue cop car parked two spaces ahead, and tore across the street, hunting her scent.

The Unseelie stood in the middle of the filthy alley, fists curled at his sides as he just stared into the darkness. "She's not here." He turned away, not bothering to look at me, and strode from the alley.

Justice and Hurrow just stood there, staring into the shadows.

She wasn't here...

I drew in the sweet and foul scent of the alley. Soft green moss protruded from the gaps in the bricks, mingled with the ripe stench of the overflowing trashcans. It was here I'd found her. I thought it was here I'd save her. I was wrong.

The wind picked up...and the scent of blood slammed into me. That stony thing in my chest clenched as it hit me...*it was her blood.* "Hurrow," I hissed. My second snapped to attention, striding toward me. "Do you smell that?"

He tilted his head, drew in the air, and lowered his gaze to the ground. "It's her blood." He took a step to the left, closer to the wall, and bent down over the remnants of a smashed bottle. Her blood coated a shard. It was small...not nearly enough to be life threatening, just a few drops. But it was enough...and there were more. More drops that led deeper into the alley...and toward the side door too the Jewel.

Drops that trailed like breadcrumbs.

She was leading us to her.

That's my woman.

"Hey!" Hurrow called to the others as I charged toward the doorway.

There was a small smear of her blood on the handle. Crimson glistened, the edges of the stain already drying, but some of it was still fresh. Footsteps thundered behind me as I shoved through and stepped into the hallway. The bitter stench of gunpowder stained the air. I dragged in the stench of death...*and Vampire.*

The warning rumbled in the back of my throat and spilled into the air. They were waiting for us. I dragged in their scents—six of them *and the Unseelie.*

Hate raged inside. Dark. Seething. *Eager.*

Justice was beside me in an instant. A powerhouse of pure rage. Fangs shone in the darkness as the six Vamps spilled out into the hallway ahead of us. There was barely a snarl of warning before Justice lunged. I followed, my lips curled, hatred wrenching my fist into the air as I hit the first of the enemy and took him to the floor. Dark eyes flared wide as I slammed him down again. "Where is she?"

His lips curled into a sneer as the dark room slowly brightened with the emerald hue of Unseelie green.

"I said...where is she?"

"You'll never get to her in time," the bastard smirked. "He's been waiting her entire life to become her Sire..."

Her Sire...

Blood-bound to Caedes for eternity.

"She *is* his daughter, after all."

My hold eased as terror crashed inside me. "What did you say?"

"Didn't you know?" he laughed, dark eyes glinting with malice. "Caedes is her father...and will soon be her Lord."

"No!" I snarled. "Nonono, *NO!"*

The back room of the Jewel plunged onto darkness.

Shadows and power clashed with deafening booms as the Unseelies went head to head. The room shuddered, cracks raced along the floor, toppling chairs and tables. But I focused on the smiling piece of shit underneath me and unfurled my fingers, before I punched them into his chest.

His eyes widened for an instant, his mouth gaped as I tore his heart from his body and threw it to the floor. There was nothing left for him now—nothing left for all of them, but a final death.

Justice let out a savage roar as he threw a Vampire clear across the room, then lunged after him, savaging with teeth and fists.

"He's going to turn her." I lifted my gaze to Hurrow as I rose over the dead Vamp. "He's going to become her Sire." *Because he's her father.*

"Like hell he is," He snarled, releasing the dead Vampire in his grasp. The body hit the floor with a *thud*...and that's where it stayed.

But the bodyguard still battled. Sickening blows mingled with unmerciful sounds of fury. Midnight shadows swallowed the green before the emerald power fought back.

"Kill him!" I roared. "Or she is dead! *Do you hear me, bodyguard? KILL HIM OR SHE IS DEAD!"*

The beast that was part Kapre threw his head back and howled with rage.

Chapter Thirty

"*NO!*" I ROARED.

They were all I thought of...all I could feel.

Their faces...*their love.*

My Immortals.

This was nothing more than a setup, luring me away to go after those I love. I punched my desperation into that empty void of rage, lifted the weapon, and took aim.

Boom! The gun kicked in my hand before a blur tore toward me.

I was hit by that blur, lifted from my feet, and hurtled backwards across the alley to slam against the bricks with a *crack.* Blinding agony tore through my head and radiated into my neck as I crumpled to the ground.

Snap...crunch. Glass shattered and pieces flew under my hands. The sting was instant, as a shadow swallowed me.

"Fucking *mortals*," the Vampire spat as he reached down and yanked the gun from my grip.

I tried to breathe, tried to gather myself. I was alive...*alive*. I fought the pulsing pain and lifted my head, focusing on Caedes, now standing behind his men.

Weakass bitch.

I saw him now...saw who he truly was. Revulsion burned in my gut...bitter and foul.

"Enough of this, Ruth. You have no choice here. Get up and come to me."

I have no choice? The words resounded and the faces of my men rushed to me. "No choice?" A chuckle spilled from my lips as I lowered my gaze to the broken glass around me. "I *always* have a fucking choice."

I slid my hand along the ground, leaving blood trails behind on the shards, until I found the thickest, strongest piece, and pushed upwards. "I'm a *fucking Costello*."

The blue eyes of my father haunted me as I stumbled, slammed my hand against the wall, and straightened. My chest hurt...the agony in my head boomed like a heartbeat. But I was ready... ready to go down fighting. I had nothing left to lose.

One jerk of Caedes' head, and the Vampire came for me again. Only this time, the cocky bastard swaggered and grinned. *Fucking mortal,* isn't that what he'd called me? Like it was an insult. I settled on the ugly bastard's gaze. Maybe to him *us* mortals *were* an insult.

He grabbed my arm and yanked me forward. "Move," he commanded.

"Move your fucking self," I seethed, and spun, turning into him before I grabbed him by the shirt and kneed him in the balls.

The pale bastard blanched even more as his eyes widened.

It was nice to know even Immortal guys weren't immune from dick pain.

He coughed and doubled over. I yanked my hand upwards and drove the piece of glass down with all my might, slashing the bastard's face with a howl of revenge. I was wild in that moment, savage and terrifying.

Past the point of all control...*and I didn't care.*

There were no holds now. No feeble mortal life left to give a fuck about. There was nothing left for me but to take down as many as I could. I yanked the bloodied glass free and moved in close, stabbing like it was a shiv, landing whatever blows I could until the bastard shoved me backwards with a roar of desperation.

"Get her the fuck off me!" he howled.

His face was a gaping, bloodied mess...the white of his teeth shone through his flaring cheek. Splatters and smears bled outwards onto his shirt as it soaked up his blood.

"The *bitch* is fucking crazy!" the Vampire barked, stabbing a finger at me.

I bared my teeth and spun, sawing breaths consuming me as I scanned the next one to come, and settled on Caedes—he smiled. The motherfucker smiled, his eyes shining with pride.

"Don't you fucking look at me like that. You fucking *disgust me.*" That savage part of me howled with release....as I unlocked her goddamn chains. "You disgusted my mother, too."

That smile wavered, falling away like shattered glass.

Yeah, that's right, motherfucker. Let's rip the scab off this right now, shall we? Let's dig our fingers into this fucking wound and see what infection we can find. "That's what all this was over, right? You loved her. You loved her and you couldn't stand to see her with a—" I glanced at the bleeding pissant at my feet. "*A fucking mortal.*"

Caedes flinched before cold, cutting rage pushed to the surface.

I pushed deeper...*harder.* "It's no wonder she couldn't love you. Did you compel her? Force her to keep coming back to you? Yeah, that's it...that's what you did."

He grew still...so utterly still.

Like a viper ready to strike.

I lifted my hand and swiped the Vampire blood and sweat from my lips, then settled that hot fury into bitter, subzero rage. I knew all about vipers...lived with them my entire fucking life. It made sense the biggest one would be waiting for me—*and here he was.*

"You compelled her to stay, and even that wasn't enough in the end, was it? You couldn't force her to your side, not with all your *Lordly Vampire* powers. My father was twice the man you could *ever* be, and he lived a fraction of your life."

Caedes stepped from behind his wall of Vampires, eyes blazing, hate raging. "He was a *murderer*. He betrayed the Vampire you sleep with. How does that fit in with your precious *mortal* ideals, I wonder?"

I rocked with the words. Pain plunged deep, tearing me apart... but there was no fucking way I was letting him know that.

"That was my father's choice...not mine. The same way as I make mine now."

He didn't want me dead. I knew that. I was too much like my mother, someone he so desperately wanted to control. "Did she die running away from you?" Terror and agony cut across his gaze for a second before they were gone.

"She was *supposed* to live *forever*," he forced the words. "At *my* side, ruling with *me* for eternity. One bite and she'd forget all about *him*. One goddamn bite, but she couldn't." Hate was an explosion in his soulless eyes as he repeated. "She couldn't."

"That's what drove her away that night, wasn't it?"

He swallowed hard and a surge of desperation filled me. "She was so desperate to get away from the monster she was forced to love and drove straight off the road into the power pole. You didn't kill her, but you may as well have. She died the moment you took instead of allowing her to choose for herself."

"And *you* are a product of that taking," he snapped, striding forward. "You are mine."

I smiled and shook my head. "You know, for someone who's lived as long as you have, you're still fucking clueless where women are concerned, aren't you?"

"Clueless?" he growled. "I prefer *cruel*. I grow tired of your tantrum, *child*." He jerked his head toward me and not one... but five of the savage bastards came. "Now *move*."

I was grabbed, both arms yanked out taut as I kicked and thrashed. Screams burned along my throat as I was hauled toward the fire door of the Jewel. "*Get the fuck off me!*" I twisted and kicked, driving my heel out as far as I could.

But I couldn't reach them. I could do nothing but grip the goddamn shard in my fist and stumble forward. *Blood...*if Elithien had heard me...he'd track my blood. Hope swelled inside my chest as I clenched my grip tighter. That cutting sting moved deeper, slicing into my palm.

Warmth ran down my wrist and along my arm, until it dripped.

I focused on that drip, fighting and thrashing, driving all my focus into bleeding...until I saw the ruined Jewel.

The place was dark, soft lights from the bar the only illumination in the ruin. It was once beautiful. It was once *prestigious.* It was once glittering lights and powerful men. I dragged back to the memory of that night. The night it all started...the laughter, the cigars. *My dad.*

But before the memory could take hold, I was shoved forward. My arms bowed back, tendons screamed in agony and I could do nothing but walk...and leave what was left of the Jewel behind.

We strode across the mess of overturned tables and shattered chairs to the other side of the room. There were bullet holes in the walls...*a lot of them.* A sob tore free as I pushed into the hallway. I shoved to the side, leaving a smear of my blood against the wall, and kept on walking.

A bitter wind picked up, slicing through me as we exited through a service entrance on the other side and out into the open.

"Walk," the Vampire behind me ordered.

My boots scuffed as I stumbled forward, taking as much time as I could, until we passed the rear building and headed toward a brightly lit, open warehouse. The pounding of my heart grew louder, the closer we came. This was it...this was where it was going to end for me.

I had no illusions now. Caedes would take by force, just like he'd always done.

I clung to every thud in my chest...and every life-giving breath.

Still that dark, empty void waited.

A void I knew well...

Death.

I was shoved forward and released. My hands fell to my sides, numb and aching. It took all my strength to lift one hand and rub the pain.

"You're worried it will hurt." Caedes shook his head. "I promise you it won't. I can make it painless. One bite, Ruth, and you'll forget all about Elithien and his coven. You'll be at peace, and have all the answers you've ever wanted. That's what you want, isn't it? Now, put down the glass and come to me."

He held out his hand, summoning me like a dog.

A good dog...a faithful dog.

"You think I care about pain?" I stepped closer, my fist clenched around the glass. The sting was quick, *cutting,* narrowing my world down to this blinding moment of pure, black rage. "You think I give a *fuck* about myself?"

Caedes eyes glittered like black glass. Soulless...cruel. "You are mine," he growled again.

"Like *fuck* she is." Elithien's voice echoed through the space. "The woman belongs to us."

My heart leaped at the sound. Breaths burned through my chest as I turned. They were born from the darkness...shadows fanning out to lash the ceiling and the floor. Elithien, Justice, Hurrow, and Rule...and the darkness coming from one man. I met Russell's frightening midnight gaze. But there was no hate in there for me. He shifted that blast of fury to Caedes. I followed the blinding rage to the glowing green air behind Caedes as the Unseelie enemy appeared.

"Caedes." Elithien stepped to my side, Justice and Russell flanking us. "Come for her and you'll have to go through us."

Guns were drawn by the enemy. The steel glinted in the space.

"Make one fucking move," Justice urged, gripping the biggest fucking sword I'd ever seen with a terrifying smile. "I'll tear you apart."

The first shot rang out, hitting the steel wall behind us before the warehouse erupted in a roar of gunfire.

"Do not shoot her!" Caedes howled. "She is my future!"

But it didn't matter. The moment the first shot rang out, all five of my Immortals lunged, shielding me with their bodies, arms open wide, protecting me with every inch they had. I felt every impact from the bullets...and screamed my rage.

Hurrow tore free in the sickening lull, and charged toward them. His savagery was glorious and terrifying as he hit the first Vampire, wrenched his head backwards and jerked. Blood shot up into the air as Caedes roared. *"Stop shooting, NOW!"*

My ears rang with the sound. I could barely breathe...barely think. All I could do is feel as Rule fell to his knees...his body riddled with bullets. One had shattered his cheek, another had torn through his neck. Blood spilled from the wounds...so much blood! My heart quivered at the sight, my hold on the glass shard gone.

"*Rule!*" I screamed. "*No...no...no!*"

I lifted my gaze and found him...that *thing* that shared my bloodline. "I hate you, you disgusting piece of filth..."

Danger flittered through his gaze. His pale lips curled, revealing his fangs, as he lifted his hand. From behind him in those shifting shadows came more of them...more than we'd ever be able to defeat. Twenty became fifty...and still they were coming.

The thud of multiple footsteps rang out loud in the space. The familiar *clack...clack...clack* of riding boots was unmistakable to me. Elithien turned his head and I followed the sound, and felt my stomach sink. "Uncle Jerry...is that you?"

He shuffled in, flanked on one side by my cousin Judah, and Blane on the other. Behind them were ten of the biggest, beefiest guys I'd ever seen in my life...*and they were armed to the teeth.*

"Kid." Jerry lifted his gaze to mine, those blue eyes shining clearer than I'd ever seen. He shifted his gaze to Caedes and the army of Immortals behind the Vampire Lord and muttered, "So you're the wife-stealing sonofabitch. Ugly fucker, aren't you? She sure got her looks from her *real* father, thank Christ."

Judah gave a nod toward Russell, gripped the pump-action shotgun, and cast it through the air. My bodyguard caught it in an instant, as well as the Sig Blane threw his way.

Tears blurred my uncle's face as he met my gaze and gave me a nod. "For blood," he murmured.

He'd come here to die tonight...they all had. *For me.*

But even with their ten soldiers, we never stood a chance.

Still, they swept around us, mortal...and Immortal. It wasn't lost on me this was what Alliard had wanted. For us to stand side by side together. An alliance...until my father had him killed. I swallowed that painful realization and turned to Caedes.

"Fuck you, Caedes," I growled. "And the *bitches* you rode in on."

The Vampire Lord looked at me, those cruel eyes never wavering, not even when he said, "I made a mistake in coming here. You aren't the daughter I expected you to be."

I smiled at the words and glanced at Elithien. But he showed no emotion...no disgust—no rage. Just pure fucking purpose.

"Damn right she isn't," Jerry muttered, his hand resting on his gun.

"You want me to leave?" Caedes turned and nodded to the others around him. "Then I'll leave..." He moved so fast, grabbing the gun from the Vampire at his side before he turned back. "But I'm taking the bitch with me."

The shot rang out in the warehouse, cracking like a whip. Jerry stumbled backwards, his blue eyes widening as blood bloomed against his white shirt.

"Dad?" Judah called, and lunged to his side. *"Dad!"*

My uncle collapsed as the gun went off once more. Blood spread over his chest, his blue eyes wide. But Judah rose from his father's side with pure, *merciless* calm, lifted his gun...and opened fired on them all with a howl of fury.

Caedes and his army blurred as they lunged toward us. My lovers were there, meeting force with force. Immortal met Immortal in a sickening, swirling haze. I stumbled backwards as a savage roar filled my ears and saw the open jaws of a Wolf leaping toward me.

Justice roared, and flung himself forward, swinging that sword back and forth in front of him. Black mist whipped around me, lashing like the swirling mayhem of a deadly tornado as Russell rushed forward. He lifted the shotgun and that mist became terrifying, punching through a Vampire as the enemy charged.

Boom! The blast tore through the air.

I was lost in the horrific onslaught as both Justice and Russell savaged and killed. They blended together, both men protecting me with fangs, sword, shotgun, and Unseelie rage.

Immortal and human battled in the bloodthirsty onslaught. I stumbled backwards, my gaze finding the silver shine of a gun. I bent, picked it up, and turned.

"Fuck you!" *Boom.* "Come after what's mine!" *Boom.* I aimed and fired, finding the center of a chest...or a head...or *anything* as I scanned the swarm for Caedes.

He stood behind a wall of Vampires, watching as his men were killed one after the other. I turned to Elithien, who traded blows with a Wolf twice his size in an attempt to get to the Vampire Lord. But there was no getting to him...not that way.

My damn hand trembled as I glanced at my uncle, and his open, glazed eyes. Blood trickled from the corner of his mouth. It wouldn't be long now and he'd join my father. *For blood.* His words burned inside me as I swung my gaze to the weakass bitch and stumbled out from behind my powerful protectors and smiled. "You want me, Caedes? Come and get your future, you piece of shit."

I didn't need the power behind my name to be ruthless. I sure as *hell* didn't need a lord's bloodline. I needed those willing to die for me, for family and friends. In that moment I had it all... every bloody, violent end.

We fought savagely and endlessly. I took aim and squeezed the trigger until there was only a *click*. Then I scurried for another, lifting my gaze as Blane hurled himself toward a Wolf that had Judah by the throat.

I turned my head as panic seized me. Hurrow was there, a blinding, unmerciful fury, following my gaze to my cousins. Hate flared for a second as he caught sight of them, before he lunged after them to take down the Wolf instead. A hiss came at my feet. The Vampire, still barely alive, bared his fangs until I lowered the sight of the Sig and shot him point-blank in the head. "Outlive that, you sick fuck."

Caedes' gaze sparkled as he tracked me. He couldn't help himself. He didn't understand devotion...and he sure as hell didn't understand me. All he saw was a woman he thought he could control. One he could claim...just like he'd done to my mother. He pushed between his wall of Immortal soldiers and strode toward me. Elithien watched it all, every step as I readied my stance and dropped my shoulder.

Justice tossed a dead Vampire through the air and rushed forward at the same time. My world slowed in that instant. Three forces were colliding. Silence filled me, that empty void of nothing waited as I reached out, fingers open as the sword sailed through the air toward me.

Caedes howled victoriously, his fangs bared as he reached for me...and I drove that sword with all my strength into his stomach. The blade sliced deep, silver wards flared and glowed as it punctured the powerful Immortal.

"I told you before," Elithien growled, and reached around me, grasping his head. "She belongs to us."

My Vampire gave a brutal twist. The crunch of bones was sickening, something squelched before flesh and bone tore free, and Caedes' headless torso crumbled to the ground.

Boom!

Boom!

Boom!

A howl of agony filled the warehouse. I turned in time to watch Justice stumble backwards, his chest shredded, that sickening green Fae glow coming from pellets in the middle of his body. The sea of the enemy pushed toward us. There was still no way we were getting out of here...

"*E!*" Hurrow roared, drawing my gaze. He was a bloody mess... we all were.

In a corner of the warehouse came that pulsing Unseelie green hue, faint at first, before it grew bolder. Out of that portal came shadows, striding toward us with animal grace and savagery.

Phantom emerged, his long legs eating the distance between us. Sleek, powerful muscles rippled as he moved, his quick eyes scanned the battleground and the blood before he curled his lips and bared thick canines. His long hair was gone, now cut short on both sides, making him look even more dangerous than he was before. He was a towering Immortal. His long, wicked fangs shone under the lights. Arran strode behind the pack, his gaze connected with mine and a charge of adrenaline hit me. He gave me a smile and a wink...even in the midst of this terror, he was here for me. Behind him in that eerie green Unseelie glow was Shrike...and the rest of the Fae clan charged forward behind him.

They were monstrous, towering, brooding. Power rippled through the room to slam into me like a wave.

"Didn't think we'd miss out on all the fun, did you?" Phantom growled, and cracked his knuckles. He looked at Shrike, then back to Elithien, his hard expression softening for an instant. "We were wrong."

Elithien gave a slow nod, pride and determination blazing like an inferno across his face, before he jerked his gaze to the bloody battlefield. "There's plenty left."

Through the open warehouse door came the sound of a midnight black helicopter landing in the middle of the city street.

"*Go!*" Phantom commanded. "Get out of here!"

Elithien turned to me, desperation and determination in his gaze. He lunged forward and grabbed me around the waist as Russell dropped beside Justice. He heaved the bleeding Vampire up from the floor and lifted him over his shoulder.

We were gone in a pounding, erratic heartbeat, charging through the open warehouse doors to the waiting helicopter.

"Rule!" I screamed, seeing him battling on his own.

He turned his gaze toward me, looked back at the carnage, and lunged after us. Helicopter blades whipped through the air overhead as I was bundled inside. Elithien jumped in after me, then Russell carrying Justice. He laid my big Vampire onto the cabin floor. I scooted forward, lifting his head into my lap as Hurrow, and finally Rule, climbed in and pulled the door closed.

The whir of the motor above us was deafening as it picked up speed. We were lifting in an instant, leaving the unmerciful chaos behind. Bloodied faces, shell-shocked gazes, but we were all alive. *We were all alive.* Justice gave a cough, blood flying through the air as I held him.

"You're going to be okay," I crooned, and held him hard against me. "You hear me, Vampire?"

He gave a nod and lifted his gaze to mine. "Wanted to protect you."

"You did." I forced the words around the lump in my throat. "You all did."

And as we lifted high into the air, I caught movement below...as Special Agent Carina Chase stepped through the open doorway, her gun in her hand as she rushed headlong into the bloody, frenzied carnage.

She'd die in there.

Good...

Maybe I was a ruthless bitch, after all.

I leaned back and held onto my Vampire as we soared through the night.

WE LANDED outside the city somewhere, in the expansive backyard of a two-story house. The door opened and the Breed, Vicious, was there. Rule and Hurrow climbed out before Russell glanced at me and gave a gentle nod. Still, I couldn't let go of my protector, not even when Vicious stepped into the cabin of the helicopter and took a look at the shimmering Unseelie glow in the center of Justice's chest.

Vicious turned to Elithien and something unspoken passed between them before Elithien gave a slow nod and turned back to me.

Movement came from all around me. The pilot shoved free, heaving a case with him. I caught a symbol on the top before the case was given to Rule and Russell dragged Justice out.

We limped and stumbled, battle-weary and blood-sickened, toward the bright white lights of that house. A pool sparkled as we passed, glittering with the reflection of shimmering red and white lights as the helicopter took off, leaving us behind.

"Hurrow, you know what to do. Get him downstairs," Elithien growled, and clutched his own side.

In the harsh lights of the house, I saw them...in blinding, bloody clarity.

Russell disappeared with Justice, Hurrow, and Rule, leaving us alone.

Still, I couldn't move.

Frozen with fear.

Tortured with all the terrible things that lay between us.

Until he dragged his hand from his side and opened his arms. "Come here."

I rushed forward, tears bursting inside me like a dam. My knees trembled as I slammed into him, winding my arms tightly around him. "I'm so sorry. So fucking sorry."

"It's okay." He held me, pulling me harder against him.

Mind, and soul. The body could wait.

"Caedes is my biological father," I blubbered.

"I know."

"And Dad was the one who killed Alliard."

He froze, hands pressed against my back, unmoving for a long time before he finally murmured, "It's okay. None of that is your doing. Your father gave me so much more than he ever took."

Tears continued to stream down my face as I pulled away to stare into those unflinching eyes. "I thought I was a repayment for the debt."

"Debt?" Elithien shook his head and brushed a strand of hair from my face.

"The one we owed for not protecting Alliard. How was I to know—"

Sadness crowded his eyes as he shook his head, and loyalty raged. The kind of loyalty I was now starting to understand. Loyalty and love.

"No, Princess." He lowered his head to kiss me. "Not a debt. A promise."

Did Justice survive?

Or did he become more of a beast?
Ruth's story isn't over...it's only just begun.
Dive into this FREE book in the Mafia Monster's world and be
seduced by the seedy Underworld desires found in Arcania.
Click here to grab your free copy today.

Epilogue

WE STAYED IN THAT MANSION OUTSIDE THE CITY, hunkered in the underground lair that took up two floors underneath the house. I stayed at Justice's side, even when they crowded around his bed and opened that case...and drew out the syringes.

Elithien said the drugs were synthetic, said they'd help him heal, said there was no other way he would survive the spelled Unseelie pellets. So I cupped my Vampire's face and stared into his eyes. I took that journey with him as they shoved that *shit* into his veins.

I saw him change...saw him become something else.

Saw a monster lurking in the shadows as he screamed and bared his fangs.

And slowly, I saw him heal. They plucked out the glowing Unseelie pellets from his body, leaving a mass of scars behind.

"You won't love me," Justice's hoarse words were scared and raw.

"Too late for that," I answered. "You're stuck with me, Vampire."

He slept after that, a faint smile on his lips, as though my pledge of love lulled him through the darkness. He slept for days, until they dragged me away, forced me to eat and bathe, forced me back to them. And I did come back, stalking, hunting anything that moved. I ached more than I thought possible, and still that empty void waited inside me. That *death* that wasn't really death.

I knew what it was...even if I couldn't say what it was.

My lovers knew as well.

Sly glances. A careful caress. *It's okay,* their kisses whispered.

But it wasn't...I didn't know if it ever would be. I carried the blood of a dead Vampire Lord in my veins. One bite and it'd be over. That's what Caedes had said...one bite and I'd be his.

But would I be? That was the unknown, wasn't it?

No, you wouldn't that hollow voice inside me answered. *They would still be yours...all of them. Every Vampire. Every seat at their pathetic Inner Circle. Yours for the taking...are you ready... are you ready, Ruthless?*

I ignored that voice and pushed aside that yearning.

Instead, I showered, took time in washing my hair, then dried myself in the bathroom I shared with Elithien. He was asleep on the bed. Dead was a better word, but who gave a fuck about better anything anymore? I didn't. I stepped into the closet and caught the glint of a chain. The bondage harness left nothing to the imagination. I smiled for the first time since the alley as I reached up and pulled it free.

My skin shivered as I stepped into the harness, and adjusted the chain on a choker around my throat, to a V in a ring above my chest. The second part of the harness plunged down, slipping under my breasts to circle around my back. I slipped on black sheer panties and looked at myself in the mirror. "*There* you are," I whispered.

My own reflection stared back. Changed forever, powerful in her own skin. Ready to fuck and fight and defend what was hers. But right now, I had a promise to fulfill. I slipped the satin robe from the hanger and pulled it on, tying the sash around my waist.

I left my Vampire Alpha in the bed, each beat of my heart a second closer to the moment he was awake...and went in search of my Unseelie. My powerful, terrifying Unseelie. My Kapre half-breed. My midnight mist hunter.

I walked out of the bedroom to the elevator that took me to the upper floors. It was a sprawling estate, equipped with a large swimming pool, a nine-car garage, and a state-of-the-art training facility. My thoughts returned to that night...barely a week ago, when we'd climbed from the helicopter. Vicious took one look at Justice and handed him that poison that both saved him and changed him. The elevator doors opened to the blinding midday sun. I blinked, lifted my hand to shield my eyes, and walked out into silence.

I knew where my Unseelie would be...the same place he'd been every second of the day when he wasn't with us—training, fighting. Testing his endurance and leaving busted equipment in his wake. Nothing could withstand his punishment—even himself.

The *clang* of weights ripped through the air as I made my way across the lawn to the expansive gym set off from the main house. The ache in my eyes eased as I stepped through the open door and into the building, finding him curling every mammoth weight the barbell could hold. Still it wasn't enough, he barely raised a sweat. Those midnight eyes lifted to the mirror as I came closer.

"Ruth," he croaked.

Darkness lingered, faint mist lashed out around him. It hadn't gone since the fight in the warehouse. He thought I hadn't noticed. But when it came to them...I noticed *everything*.

"Bodyguard," I greeted.

"Did you need something?" Concern flared as he bent and lowered the barbell to the floor before straightening. "Are you hungry?"

"Ravenous," I answered, and tugged the sash from around my waist. Silk slid against my skin as the robe fell to the floor.

"Fuck me," he muttered, and turned around, the reflection paling against the real thing.

"I intend to, Unseelie," I whispered, my gaze gliding down that massive chest, to the hard, ribbed abs and that delicious V that sat just above the waistband of his shorts. "Many...*many* times over."

"I need to tell you some—"

I moved closer and reached up, pressing my finger against his lips. "Shhhh....no, you don't."

"But—" he mumbled under my finger, and sank to the bench in front of me. His big hands slid around my waist, his thumbs caressing the chains.

God, his lips felt good.

I dragged my finger free and chased the touch with my thumb before I rose over him. "Now...where is that big Unseelie beast?"

Surprise widened his eyes. "You know?"

I lowered my head, kissing him softly, taking my time, relishing the feel of him before I answered against his mouth. "Always..."

A deep, rumble of desire echoed in the back of his throat. Part animal, part human...and all lust. He gripped my waist, lifting me as he heaved all six-foot-three of his powerful frame to stand. I wrapped my legs around his waist, my core settling against the growing hardness of his cock.

He looked down to the sheer panties...and smiled.

And my world plunged into pure Unseelie dark

The Wolves are here...

I carry his bite mark on my shoulder...and the memory of what I'd done in his bed.

Phantom, the Alpha of Crown City Wolves might think he has a handle on me...

He might think this is more than what it was...

He's about to find out he's wrong.

I don't belong to the Wolves of Crown City. I belong to the FBI.

My sole purpose has been hunting scum who sit in their ivory tower and shatter people's lives.

I've hunted the Costello for years now.

They're lower than low...they are liars...they're mobsters.

They're Mafia.

This is more than a case for me.

This was personal.

The last bullet in my father's policing career. Ruined because of them.

Only a war erupted. A war which I'm now part of...a war between
the beasts that roam my city and the powerful Immortals they
answer to.

I replayed that night in slow motion. Fangs. Blood...*and Phantom.*
The Alpha of the Wolves. The one I saved from a rogue Vampire.

And the one who saved me.